"Where's your father?" she asked the girls, who were still working on their projects at the kitchen table. **"I need to talk to him about something important."**

"He said he was going over to the Jones farm," Yolanda said helpfully. "That's the next one down the road. I think he got a call about a sick calf."

"Oh. Okay." Again, Amelia retreated to her bedroom, heart thumping in her chest. She eyed her packed bags sitting neatly on her bed. She'd never been an impulsive person, preferring careful planning over spontaneous action, but right now the panic clawing at her overrode reason.

Yet how could she walk out without talking to Ted face-to-face?

* * *

If you're on Twitter, tell us what you think of Harlequin Romantic Suspense! #harlequinromsuspense

Dear Reader,

I loved creating the fictional community of Getaway, Texas, and adored writing about the people who make this west Texas town their home. *Texas Rancher's Hidden Danger* is the second book set there, after *Texas Sheriff's Deadly Mission*, and some of those same people make appearances in both books.

This book is the story of rancher Ted Sanders, a man who is quietly raising twin teenage daughters and trying to keep his ranch going, and Amelia Ferguson, a once-successful therapist on the run from a dangerous serial killer who is a former client. I met Ted first in *Texas Sheriff's Deadly Mission* and just knew he had his own story to tell, but until I sat down to plan this book, I had no idea who would be the woman he could love.

A small town, good folks and a serial killer make for an interesting combination. Throw in the fierce attraction between a man who guards his heart and a woman trying to guard her life and add in disappearing teenagers, and it all becomes fascinating! It's a story of starting over, new beginnings, danger and, most importantly, love. The kind of love that lasts forever, if both people can survive the outside threat.

I hope you enjoy this story and this town as much as I do. And look for a third story set in Getaway, Texas, coming out later this year.

Karen Whiddon

TEXAS RANCHER'S HIDDEN DANGER

Karen Whiddon

HARLEQUIN
ROMANTIC
SUSPENSE

HARLEQUIN®
ROMANTIC SUSPENSE™

Recycling programs
for this product may
not exist in your area.

ISBN-13: 978-1-335-75955-9

Texas Rancher's Hidden Danger

Copyright © 2021 by Karen Whiddon

For questions and comments about the quality of this book, please contact us at CustomerService@Harlequin.com.

Harlequin Enterprises ULC
22 Adelaide St. West, 40th Floor
Toronto, Ontario M5H 4E3, Canada
www.Harlequin.com

Printed in U.S.A.

Karen Whiddon started weaving fanciful tales for her younger brothers at the age of eleven. Amid the gorgeous Catskill Mountains, then the majestic Rocky Mountains, she fueled her imagination with the natural beauty surrounding her. Karen now lives in north Texas, writes full-time and volunteers for a boxer dog rescue. She shares her life with her hero of a husband and four to five dogs, depending on if she is fostering. You can email Karen at kwhiddon1@aol.com. Fans can also check out her website, karenwhiddon.com.

Books by Karen Whiddon

Harlequin Romantic Suspense

Colton 911: Chicago

Colton 911: Soldier's Return

The CEO's Secret Baby
The Cop's Missing Child
The Millionaire Cowboy's Secret
Texas Secrets, Lovers' Lies
The Rancher's Return
The Texan's Return
Wyoming Undercover
The Texas Soldier's Son
Texas Ranch Justice
Snowbound Targets
The Widow's Bodyguard
Texas Sheriff's Deadly Mission
Texas Rancher's Hidden Danger

Visit the Author Profile page at Harlequin.com for more titles.

As always, to my family and friends.

Chapter 1

They say blondes have more fun, but Amelia Ferguson now knew that to be untrue. After all, she'd been blonde her entire life and she couldn't even remember the last time she'd had fun. Maybe once or twice as an undergraduate.

Sure, she'd had a job that satisfied her, an upscale condo she'd loved and an education of which she felt justifiably proud. But now, with her hair colored a vibrant red that gleamed like copper in the sunlight, and nothing but the few items of clothing she'd been able to grab when she went on the run, she'd laughed more in two weeks than she had in months. Maybe even years. Totally changing one's life tended to give one a fresh perspective.

Funny, that. She'd always counseled her clients that they couldn't run away from their problems. Turned out she could, at least so far. Though in her case, she had to, if she wanted to stay alive. Sometimes she missed her condo and her patients, but most days she just absorbed her new existence.

She'd landed in the small west Texas town of Getaway on purpose, though she'd been careful not to do any research on her personal computers or phone, just in case someone might be monitoring her. Getaway was a tiny dot on the map of a huge state. No one would think to look for her here. She now worked as a salesclerk for a colorful woman named Serenity Rune, who claimed to be the town psychic and certainly dressed the part. Her store, appropriately named Serenity, appeared to be a combination flower shop, bookstore and metaphysical store. This wild combination was the sort of place Amelia would never have spared a second glance before. Now the utter weirdness of it felt freeing. As if she could let go of the somber seriousness of the world and embrace the nonsensical for once in her life. She'd never realized how badly she'd needed to metaphorically let her hair down until she'd been forced to.

There was, she knew, a lot that needed psychoanalyzing in that. But for now, she refused to think too long or too hard about anything other than the fact that she was alive and safe. Hopefully she could keep it that way.

The cheery little bell over the door announced the arrival of a customer. This was the part Amelia enjoyed the most, because she'd met all kinds of bona fide characters since landing this part-time job.

Hurrying to the front of the store, she eyed the newest customer and froze. She'd never had a thing for cowboys, but if ever a man could make her change her mind, this one could. Tall, lanky, though with broad shoulders and muscular arms, he wore his cowboy hat pulled down low, though not low enough to hide his dark eyes.

He stopped short when he saw her. "Where's Serenity?" Like everyone else around here, he spoke with a Texas twang.

Luckily, she found her voice. "She's not here I'm Amelia I work here now how can I help you?" One long run-on sentence without taking a breath. She could feel her face heat, which was so unlike her, she wondered if she might be coming down with something.

Clearly thinking her unhinged, the handsome cowboy took a step toward the door. "That's all right, Amelia. I'll just come back when she's here. Any idea when that might be?"

She could do better than this. She had to, especially if she wanted to keep her job. She took a deep breath, straightened her shoulders and took a step forward. "I can help you, I promise." She made her tone soothing, using her best therapist voice that had never failed to calm anxious clients. "I work for Serenity. Why don't you tell me what you're looking for and let me find it?"

Looking down, he shifted his weight from one boot to the other, clearly uncomfortable. "I'll wait for Serenity, thanks." And he beat a hasty retreat out the door.

It wasn't until he was gone that it hit her. He must have come for a psychic reading or something, though she could have sworn Serenity said she only did those by appointment.

Two hours later, after Amelia had helped one other person find a book on the healing powers of stones, Serenity arrived. Wearing one of her trademark flowing caftan-style dresses, long dangling earrings, fringed high-heeled boots and an armful of bracelets, she breezed into the store. Rushing up to Amelia, she gave her a big, full-body hug, a practice that had at first startled the hell out of Amelia, though now she'd gotten used to it.

"How has it been going?" Serenity asked, staring hard at Amelia. "I sense something went wrong."

"Not wrong, exactly. A man came by earlier today, but wouldn't let me help him," she said. "He didn't give me his name, but he was wanting you."

"A tall drink of water with a cowboy hat?" Serenity's eyes sparkled when Amelia nodded. "That was Ted Sanders. He comes by sometimes just to talk. That poor man is raising twin teenage daughters and trying to run his cattle ranch all by himself. He's got his hands full—that's for sure."

"Twins?" Amelia asked, shaking her head. "He doesn't look old enough to have teenagers."

This comment made Serenity laugh. "He became a father young. I think he's close to forty."

"Really?" Amelia smiled.

"Yes. And as you no doubt noticed, he's easy on the eyes. He's also Getaway's most eligible bachelor," Serenity warned. "Every single lady within fifty miles of here has been chasing after him. He barely even notices. So, if you're thinking you'd like to try, be aware that you'll have plenty of competition."

"Oh, I wasn't," Amelia immediately responded. "I don't have the energy to date anyone right now." This was true. Being on the run and rebuilding a new life from the ground up didn't leave much room for anything else.

Her reply made Serenity laugh out loud. "That's what Ted says too whenever I press him about at least going on a date. How funny. I think you two might have a lot more in common than you'd realize."

"Matchmaking? Please don't." Amelia felt comfortable enough with her boss to speak up. Running away from her previous life hadn't changed her personality, after all, and she'd never been the quiet, timid sort.

Shaking her head, which sent her earrings swaying, Serenity moved away. "I never matchmake," she called back over her shoulder. "I believe in letting fate take care of itself."

Not sure how to even respond to that, Amelia got busy rearranging a display of pretty crystals. The irony of this job wasn't lost on her. She didn't believe in luck or fate or destiny. Or that crystals or rocks had powers. Animal totems, mystical insights or mediums. Yet here she was, working in a store that specialized in the metaphysical. Even stranger, she didn't have to suppress the urge to offer counseling to any of the customers who came in here clearly looking for answers. Previously, this had been a bad habit of hers that she'd often wished away.

Now, in letting go of her previous life, she'd also let go of that. The thought made her smile.

Her shift ended, a good thing since her stomach had started growling. After telling Serenity goodbye, Amelia drove past all the fast-food places on Main Street, even though she really wanted to stop and pick something up. But she only treated herself once a week. Operating on a fixed amount of cash made her super careful. She definitely couldn't support herself on the money she made working part-time at Serenity's store, which meant she had to dip into her savings more than she liked. She'd need to find either a second part-time job or a better-paying full-time one. Since she couldn't hang out her own shingle—to do so would invite too much scrutiny and likely reveal her location—she had to find other kinds of work.

She'd waited tables in college, even done a stint of bartending while in graduate school. Surely she could find something similar in Getaway.

As soon as she had enough money coming in, she needed to rent an apartment and get out of this motel. Though she paid a weekly rate, the cost was much more than rent would be. But this was a small town and jobs were scarce. Every weekend, she purchased the Sunday newspaper and read both the help-wanted ads and the for-rent ones too. Apparently, employers in this tiny town didn't use the internet as a source to recruit employees. At least not that she'd been able to tell. Most of the available jobs required skills she didn't have. Truck driver. Cattle wrangler. Pilot to fly a crop duster plane. Nothing she could or would be able to do.

Amelia had discussed all this with Serenity, not wanting the one person who'd taken a chance on her to be blindsided if she found a full-time, better-paying job. Unsurprisingly, Serenity had responded kindly, promising to keep an eye out for both work and lodgings. Amelia appreciated that the older woman asked no questions, though then again, she claimed to be psychic, so maybe she already knew everything.

Shaking her head at her nonsensical thoughts, she put down the newspaper, no longer able to ignore her hunger pangs. Taking a look inside her minifridge, she considered again what she might have for dinner. Since the little motel room had a kitchenette as well, she'd cook something fast and simple.

She settled on fixing a box of macaroni and cheese,

adding in cut-up hot dogs for the protein. Not exactly gourmet or healthy, but she needed comfort food today.

Once she'd eaten, she did her usual scan of the internet, looking for any news on the Coffee Shop Killer. Nothing. No news should be good news, but in this case, she only wanted to read that he'd been apprehended and taken back to the prison from which he'd escaped. The fact that he hadn't even been mentioned worried her, as this meant he was lying low, being careful not to do anything that might give away his location.

Though she tried not to, she kept replaying that moment, that awful moment during his trial when she'd stepped up to testify. Simon Barron, aka the Coffee Shop Killer, had locked gazes with her and mouthed a threat and a promise. Then, just in case she hadn't understood, he'd called out to her. Loudly and unflinchingly, he'd vowed to finish what he'd started. *You're a dead woman, Amelia Ferguson.*

Shuddering, she pushed the memory away. The woman she'd been—Dr. Amelia Ferguson, a highly educated, respected therapist—was gone, just like her sleek blond hair and her trendy condo with a view. She'd even claimed a new last name, though not legally. She'd had to change everything the instant she'd learned Simon had escaped while being transported to the federal prison that was supposed to be his home for the rest of his life.

With Simon free, Amelia knew he was coming for her. He'd sworn she'd pay. If she'd stayed, her life would have been forfeit. Acting quickly and decisively, as she always did, she'd gone on the run.

Taking deep, calming breaths, she reminded herself that he'd have no reason to look here, so far from Westchester County, New York. She'd picked the tiny west

Texas town of Getaway purely on impulse, after having read a story about them having their very own serial killer. Since they'd caught him and, statistically, the chances of them ever having another were slim to nothing, she figured her chances of safety were excellent. She'd told no one where she was going and she'd destroyed her credit cards and cell phone before leaving New York. Having emptied her bank account, she operated on a strict cash-only basis, which made her spending untraceable. She hadn't made contact with any of her former friends, employees or clients, severing all ties to her previous life.

For all intents and purposes, Amelia Ferguson had vanished. Here, she went by Amelia Smith, which, while not creative, did the job. The instant Amelia had seen the help-wanted ad for a part-time clerk at a store called Serenity in downtown Getaway, Amelia had applied. Serenity had interviewed her and hired her on the spot, remarking that she could tell Amelia would be someone she could count on. When Amelia asked, Serenity had been agreeable to paying her in cash, which meant Amelia hadn't had to give her Social Security number. There was no way she could use her real one, so she would have had to make one up. However, she knew if she wanted to rent an apartment, they'd run a credit check, which she absolutely could not allow. Somehow, when that time came, she'd have to figure out a way around that. She wouldn't put it past Simon to have someone monitoring her credit profile.

Luckily, she'd managed to sock quite a bit of cash away in a savings account. She'd withdrawn it all. It wouldn't last forever, though, no matter how carefully she spent it. She had no idea how long it would be until the authorities recaptured Simon, so she had to be prepared to survive as long as it took.

Once again struggling to quash the panic blossoming in her chest, she changed into her workout clothes. The one luxury she'd splurged on had been a gym membership, though maybe *splurged* wasn't the right word since it was only ten dollars a month. With only one gym in town, she would have thought the place would be packed, but it wasn't, at least not at the times Amelia went. She'd even made a tentative sort of friend there. Rayna Coombs, the sheriff, had become Amelia's occasional workout partner.

At first, the idea of hanging out with someone in law enforcement had made her nervous. But then she'd reminded herself that she'd done nothing wrong, committed no crime, and could only benefit from having a small-town sheriff on her side if things went south. Which hopefully they would not. Surely they'd catch Simon soon so she could breathe again.

A good, pulse-pounding, sweaty workout would do wonders for improving her state of mind.

Rayna wasn't there when Amelia arrived, so she did a quick warm-up on the treadmill before hitting the free weights section. When she'd first starting lifting, she'd felt intimidated to be one of the only women using the dumbbells, but she'd soon gotten over that.

While she worked out, she watched the large television that had been mounted on one wall.

A headline scrolled across the screen. Coffee Shop Killer Releases Video on Social Media.

Amelia froze. Slowly and deliberately, she set down the pair of fifteen-pound dumbbells she'd been using and took a step closer to the TV.

She swallowed hard as Simon's face filled the screen. He laughed, the same high-pitched, manic sound that had set off alarm bells when she first started seeing him as a patient.

"I'm coming for you," he crooned. "You can run, but you can't hide. I will find you and you will pay. Your death will not come quickly, but it will be exquisite, I promise you."

Transfixed, heart in her throat, she shuddered.

"That guy is so full of himself," a voice said.

Amelia jumped and spun. "Rayna! You startled me."

"I see that." Rayna grinned. "You were intent on watching the breaking news."

Heart pounding, Amelia tried to act casual. As a cop, Rayna might recognize her despite the hair color change if they showed her on TV. "I don't like serial killers. Who do you suppose he's talking to?"

"Only one of his victims got away and she testified against him," Rayna replied. "In fact, I think she was his therapist. He vowed to make her pay. Now that he's escaped, I bet the FBI put her in WITSEC."

They'd wanted to. Amelia had promised to give them an answer, but she knew the witness protection program could be hacked by anyone skilled or determined enough and Simon was both. She'd taken matters into her own hands instead.

"Probably so," Amelia agreed, picking up her dumbbells and resuming her workout. "I'm doing upper body today. How about you?"

Rayna checked her smartwatch. "I only have time for some cardio. I'm meeting Parker for drinks in thirty minutes." She grinned.

Newlyweds, Rayna and Parker were the cutest couple. Amelia had met the rugged biker a couple of times and really liked him. "Have fun," she said, meaning it.

"You're welcome to join us," Rayna offered. "It'd do you good to go out once in a while."

"Thanks, but not tonight." The declination came easily. Not only did Amelia not want to intrude on her friend's date night, but she didn't want to waste money on drinks. "I'm going to finish my workout and watch my favorite shows."

"Suit yourself." Rayna appeared unsurprised. As she turned to head over to one of the treadmills, Amelia couldn't resist glancing back at the TV. But the news had moved on to another story, so she went back to her workout. Unsettled, she knew Simon's piercing stare would haunt her dreams that night.

It had been a long time since a woman had affected Ted Sanders the way that woman in Serenity's store had. Amelia with her flaming red hair and bright blue eyes. She'd been short and curvy and far too serious for the kind of people Serenity usually employed. The instant flash of attraction he'd felt the moment they'd locked eyes had startled him. Worried him too. He spent way more time than he liked dodging the Baptist Women's Singles Group members. He didn't know for sure, but he believed they might have a competition going among them to see which one of them could get him to date her first. He'd lost count of how many home-baked apple, peach and coconut cream pies had been dropped off at the ranch house.

Since he more than had his hands full with his twin daughters, Yolanda and Yvonne, plus trying to keep his small cattle ranch out of the red, he took great care to do nothing that would give anyone the slightest shred of belief that he wanted to date them. He hadn't been on a date since he'd dated his wife, and once she'd died, he'd been too busy grieving, raising the twins and running the ranch to have time to try.

Months had become years and some things never changed. These days, at nearly forty, he figured he might be too old to get a second chance at love. He really didn't mind, since he still didn't have the time or the energy for that anyway.

In fact, he had no idea why he was even thinking of this now. Amelia. Serenity's new clerk. How could meeting one woman for less than a minute completely disrupt his life and make him want things he'd long been fine without? Shaking his head at himself, he continued driving home to the ranch.

Still, there had been something familiar about her. The instant flash of recognition that had gone through him when he'd locked eyes on her had been strong and decisive. But he knew beyond a shadow of a doubt that he'd never met her before. He'd definitely remember meeting a woman like her.

He'd come to the shop to ask Serenity's advice, as he was prone to do lately now that both his daughters were freshmen in high school. Their capacity for drama constantly astounded and terrified him, though he had to be careful not to show it. Never let a teenage girl sniff the faintest scent of weakness, Serenity often said. Ted believed her. He'd picked them up at school, dropped them off at the house with orders to do their homework before they did anything else and headed into town.

Which was why when he walked in his front door and instantly realized the house was full of smoke, he tried like hell not to panic. Even as he ran for the kitchen, detouring toward the laundry room and snatching up the fire extinguisher on the way, he worked hard to keep his face expressionless. He hollered for the twins, several times, but received no response. He prayed they were all right. They had to be.

In the smoky kitchen, a small pot sat on top of the stove, the gas burner on medium. Whatever had been in the pot had long since been cooked away to nothing and now the bottom of the pot had scorched and begun to smoke. Five more minutes, and there likely would have been an all-out fire. Luckily, he'd arrived home in time to avert it.

Meanwhile, neither of the girls were anywhere to be seen.

Ted set the fire extinguisher down, turned off the stove and carried the smoking pot outside to the back porch. He opened all the windows, left the back door open and turned on the stove vent fan, as well as the ceiling fan in the den.

Hopefully this would clear the smoke out of the house.

The reality of what could have happened hit him. If he hadn't come home when he had...

"Yolanda! Yvonne!" he hollered again. "Get in here now!"

No response, only silence. Not unusual, these days, but still infuriating.

Storming down the hallway toward the room they shared, he found the door closed, like always. He knocked sharply, three times, and then pushed it open without waiting for an answer.

Each girl, headphones firmly in place, laptops open, sat on her separate bed, completely oblivious to anything and everything but whatever music or video game was playing.

Glaring at them, Ted flicked the light switch. Off. On. Off. On.

Finally, this got their attention.

"Daaaad." Yolanda removed her headphones. "What are you doing?"

Yvonne didn't respond at all, choosing to simply ignore his presence.

"Let me text her," Yolanda said, thumbs flying over her phone screen.

Yvonne's phone chimed. She glanced at the screen, heaved a loud sigh and reluctantly removed her headphones. "What?"

"Who left the pot on the stove?" Ted asked.

Yolanda shrugged. "Not me."

They both looked at Yvonne. Face impassive, she stared right back. "So?"

Counting to three for patience, Ted took a deep breath. "When I got home, the entire house was full of smoke. I'm guessing you didn't notice because your bedroom door was closed. If I'd been a few minutes later, that pot would have burst into flames, likely catching our entire house on fire." And with them oblivious, they'd have been trapped in their room until it was too late. "You could have died," he said.

Yvonne rolled her eyes. "You're so dramatic, Dad. I'm sorry I forgot, okay?"

"No, it's not okay." He crossed his arms. "I need you to be more careful. I want your promise that you won't do something like this ever again."

His cell phone rang. Though sorely tempted to ignore

it, he checked and saw it was the high school. Great, just great.

He kept his gaze locked on his girls while he answered.

Expressionless, he listened while Mrs. Eisner, the assistant principal, outlined Yvonne's behavior during the school day, culminating with her storming out of class and marching herself down to the nurse's office, claiming she had severe PMS.

By the time Ted ended the call, he had a headache. Since he didn't dare leave the twins home alone after what had happened earlier, he got himself a beer and started preparing dinner. He'd tried to get the girls to take turns cooking and that hadn't worked out. He wasn't sure if they'd ruined food on purpose or if they truly had no cooking skills whatsoever, but he'd learned if the family was going to eat, he'd have to make the meals.

Tonight, he'd made spaghetti with meat sauce and a side salad. Garlic toast too. He sent a text to both of them, letting them know dinner was ready. Almost instantly, they both appeared, cell phones in hand despite his no-electronics-at-the-table rule.

"Put them on the desk, please," he said, his curt tone leaving no room for arguing.

Heaving dramatically loud sighs, they did as he asked. He supposed he should consider himself lucky that they'd recently abandoned their heavy eyeliner and purple lipstick, going for a more natural look.

They ate in relative silence, which Ted hated, but in order to get his own daughters to talk, he had to pepper them with questions. Sometimes they'd answer in more than monosyllables; sometimes they wouldn't. He never knew which, but he wasn't up to making any effort tonight.

If Yolanda or Yvonne noticed his disquiet, they didn't comment. Each girl ate with single-minded determination, Yolanda expertly twirling her pasta on her fork while Yvonne cut everything up. Neither of them touched the salad, until Ted finally had to order them to get their greens on.

As expected, they rolled their eyes in unison at his lame attempt at humor, but they each filled their small bowls with lettuce, topping their salads off with a huge mound of ranch-style dressing.

As usual, once they'd finished eating, the twins grabbed their phones and attempted to beat a hasty retreat to their rooms. "Wait," Ted ordered, stopping them in their tracks. "Is your homework done?"

Yolanda nodded. Yvonne said nothing, staring sullenly at her phone. "Yolanda, you can go. Yvonne, take a seat."

Once her sister had disappeared, Yvonne dropped into her chair, still clutching her phone.

"The school called," Ted said. "Mind explaining to me what the hell you were thinking when you stormed out of a class?"

Instead of answering, Yvonne burst into tears. His heart sank. Was someone bullying her?

It took time, but he finally got a story out of her involving two of her former friends and some boy whom they all liked. He'd stopped to talk to Yvonne and now her two girlfriends were mad at her and had snubbed her. Ted ended up hugging her, smoothing her hair away from her face and trying to console her, though he had no idea if he said the right thing. Times like this were when he really missed having a woman his daughters could turn to for advice.

Finally, after extracting a promise from her that she would do all her homework immediately, he allowed her to join her sister in their shared room. He spent the rest of the evening planted in front of the television, trying hard not to think.

The next morning passed in a blur of activity, as they all did these days. Up long before sunrise, Ted hit the floor running, aware he not only had to get the livestock fed but the girls ready for school. He'd made their lunches the night before, knowing if he'd asked them to do it, they'd eat candy and an apple or something.

Unfortunately, he didn't have time to cook them a hot breakfast, so they had to choose between cold cereal or instant oatmeal. After slugging back his first cup of coffee, he headed out to the barn, where he threw several bales of hay in the back of his pickup truck and drove out to his cattle in the pastures.

Back at the house, he checked to make sure both girls were up and had showered before taking his own five-minute one. When he hit the kitchen, hair still damp, he made sure they'd eaten something, handed them their lunches—ignoring their protests—and hurried them into the pickup to drive them to school. They refused to take the bus, deeming it for losers, even though if they would, he'd shave a good thirty minutes off his morning rush.

Pulling up to the high school, he admonished them both to behave, managing to avoid staring directly at Yvonne when he spoke. They mumbled something in response and jumped out of the truck as if shot from a cannon. He watched them slow their roll once they hit the sidewalk, sauntering toward the front doors as if they hadn't a care in the world.

Deep breath. Shaking his head, he put the shifter in Drive and headed back to the ranch.

His one ranch hand, an older man named Floyd, had arrived and gotten busy repairing a section of fence that a recent storm had damaged. Ted stopped and shot the breeze for a few moments, then headed into the barn to check on a sick cow he'd been treating.

The morning passed so quickly he didn't realize he'd missed lunch until his stomach started protesting. He glanced at his watch, surprised to see he only had ninety minutes before he had to pick up the girls from school. Impulsively, he washed off, jumped into the pickup and headed to town. After grabbing a double cheeseburger from the drive-through, he headed toward Serenity's. Pretty soon, he felt quite sure she might start charging him for therapy, but he'd lose it if he didn't have someone to talk to. Part of him suspected she knew this as well and took pity on him.

Either way, he tried to show his gratitude by occasionally bringing her small gifts. Today, he'd gotten her an individual apple pie, one of her favorites. He found a parking spot right in front of her store, for the first time wondering if the redhead from yesterday would be there. At the thought, he felt a flash of what might have been anticipation, though he couldn't be entirely sure. Regardless, he didn't like it.

Squaring his shoulders, he grabbed the paper bag and got out of the truck. As usual, a bell tinkled when he walked through the door.

"Ted, there you are," Serenity sang. "Come meet my new employee, Amelia."

Ted raised his head, looking everywhere but directly at the curvy redhead, who appeared to be wishing she could hide behind one of the displays. He could definitely relate.

"We've met," he said, trying for bland and polite, as if his damn heart hadn't already started racing.

At Serenity's pointed look, Amelia moved forward, smiling. "We have, though I didn't quite catch your name."

"Ted," he replied, wondering if he should remove his hat and deciding against it. "Ted Sanders."

Still smiling, Amelia held out her hand. Stunned, he took it, trying not to marvel at her soft skin. She smelled nice too, like peaches and vanilla. He nearly shook his head, realizing it had been a long time since he'd let a woman get under his skin. And this woman wasn't even trying.

"Pleased to meet you," she said, smiling faintly. Again, that hint of an accent, the exact location he couldn't place, though definitely not Texas. Maybe not even the South.

She slowly pulled her hand free, making him realize he'd been hanging on to her fingers like a fool.

Serenity watched quietly, her too-wise eyes missing nothing.

"Can we talk privately?" Ted asked Serenity, trying to sound nonchalant so neither woman would realize how close he was to being at his wit's end. "It won't take long, I promise."

Serenity nodded. "Amelia, will you watch the store while I take a walk with Mr. Sanders?"

"Of course," Amelia responded, keeping her attention on rearranging a floral display case. Again, Ted fought the urge to let his gaze linger, which ticked him off to no end. Again, he felt that feeling of familiarity.

"Come on," Serenity said, watching him with a knowing expression in her eyes. "Let's walk."

Once they hit the sidewalk, Serenity crossed to the other side of the street so they could stay in the shade. Ted went with her, waving a quick hello to Old Man Malone, already out with his metal detector, hunting for treasure.

"What's wrong?" Serenity finally asked. "Your aura is troubled."

Like always, Ted ignored the metaphysical stuff. If he had an aura, he certainly couldn't see it.

"I don't know what to do," Ted began, trying unsuccessfully to keep any hint of desperation out of his voice. He outlined everything that had been going on with the twins. "I can't afford to hire more than one hand to help out around the ranch. Which means I need to devote a lot of hours to keeping it running or I could lose everything. But if I do that, I won't be able to spend as much time taking care of the girls. They need me to supervise them, make their meals, help with their homework and—" he grimaced ruefully "—keep them alive."

"Can't you hire someone to cook, clean and help with the homework?" Serenity asked. "That would take a huge load off of you, plus give the twins female companionship and guidance."

"I would love that, but I can't afford to pay a competitive wage. Even for part-time."

Serenity's eyes narrowed. "What if you offered room and board in there, along with meals? That would cut the salary requirements way down."

"It would," he agreed. "But I really don't have anywhere for someone to stay."

"Yes, you do. What about that spare bedroom that you use as an office? The one the twins have been begging for so they could have separate rooms? Convert that into a guest bedroom and you're all set."

He thought for a moment. "The girls would be furious," he mused. "But they'd get over it." Hope, until now an unfamiliar emotion, began to bloom in his chest. "Then it would just be a matter of finding someone. It couldn't be any of those women from the Baptist singles club, though." He shuddered at the thought. "I need someone who could focus on the job."

"I just might have someone in mind," Serenity said, smiling. "It so happens Amelia not only needs a better job, but she's looking for a place to stay."

Amelia. "I'm not sure that would be a good idea," he said slowly.

"Why not? Granted, she's new in town, but I can vouch for her character. And she's living out at the Landshark Motel, so she could really use someplace else to stay."

When he didn't reply, Serenity shrugged. "Just think about it, okay?"

Searching her face, Ted finally nodded. "I will." He planned to talk to the sheriff too. He trusted Rayna, and with her law enforcement background, she was an excellent judge of character. If he even planned to think about letting Amelia around his girls, he needed to make sure her background checked out okay.

Chapter 2

"You want to hire me to do what?" Staring at the handsome cowboy, Amelia tried to understand.

"I have a small cattle ranch outside of town," Ted explained. "Two teenage twin girls who are freshmen in high school. I need someone to cook, clean and help look after my daughters. I can offer room and board, meals and a small salary." Hat in his hands, he swallowed, painfully earnest and impossibly handsome.

Touched despite herself, Amelia looked past him to her boss. Serenity smiled encouragingly. "I recommended you."

"But I wouldn't be able to work here anymore," Amelia replied, still trying to wrap her mind around the idea.

"And that's fine." Still smiling, Serenity placed her hand on Amelia's shoulder. "It's been kind of slow anyway."

That was when Amelia realized Serenity had most

likely hired her only out of the goodness of her heart, not because she'd needed the help. But then again, she had run an ad looking for a part-time store clerk.

"I should let you know that I spoke to Rayna," Ted added. "I asked her to run a background check."

Amelia's heart skipped a beat. Luckily, no one knew her real name, date of birth or any personal information necessary to run even a basic background check. "What did she say?" she asked.

"She wouldn't do it," he responded. "Said it was unethical to do without your permission. But she did tell me that she considers you a friend."

Touched, Amelia nodded. "I'd like to think about this," she told Ted. "Can I give you an answer tomorrow?"

"Of course." Ted Sanders nodded, holding her gaze. And then he smiled.

Damn. If a man could be called beautiful, Ted Sanders with that smile that crinkled the corners of his eyes came damn close. She sucked in her breath, shaken.

"Serenity has my number," he said, clearly unaware of his effect on her. "Give me a call once you decide."

Cramming his hat back onto his head, he turned to go. Halfway to the door, he turned and glanced back at her. "I really do need the help, but only agree if you're serious. I need someone trustworthy and solid, someone who will stay awhile. Teenagers are a handful, but they're also easily hurt. My girls are my entire world, and I'll do anything to keep them safe and happy."

With that, he left.

The therapist in her felt intrigued. The frightened and lonely woman on the run longed for what he offered—

steadiness, stability, a chance to be part of a family, even if only temporarily.

"It might be good for both of you," Serenity chimed in, as if she read Amelia's mind.

Amelia heaved a shaky sigh. "Please tell me you're not trying to get inside my head."

"What?" Serenity cocked her head. "I thought you didn't believe in my psychic abilities."

"I don't."

With a sniff, Serenity waved that comment away. "You don't have to be a mind reader to see how badly you two need each other."

"You said you never tried to make matches. That sort of seems what you're doing right now."

Serenity frowned, appearing shocked. "Seriously, I'm not. I wasn't meaning romantically when I mentioned you two need each other. That poor man has been through a lot. The last thing he needs is his heart broken."

Though she wanted to ask Serenity why she felt Amelia would do such a thing, Amelia didn't. She really didn't need to know. She had an important decision to make, and she wanted to do it with her mind clear and not clouded by emotions. Luckily, in her years as a therapist, she'd grown quite skilled at compartmentalizing.

"You might as well finish up your shift and take off," Serenity suggested. Today she wore multiple rings, as many as two or three on each finger, and they flashed as she waved her hands. "Take a walk, get outside in nature. It will help you think. If you decide against it, you still will have a job working here."

Touched, Amelia swallowed hard. She managed to

choke out a thank-you before she grabbed her purse and left.

In her previous life, before she'd been abducted by her own patient and kept prisoner for several days, Amelia Ferguson, aka Smith, had been a decisive person. She'd rarely hesitated, used to quickly weigh all the pros and cons ahead of making her choice. She'd been known to decide something, and when that turned out to be wrong, she'd had the ability and confidence to pivot on a dime and go the other way, cleaning up her mess as she went.

Now she hardly recognized herself. The one thing Simon Barron had taught her, and taught her well, was exactly how damn vulnerable she truly was. True, she'd managed to escape with her life, and her testimony had helped put a serial killer away, but her inner landscape had been forever altered.

No more could she stride confidently down a deserted street or go for a jog alone in the early-morning hours as the sun rose. Now she constantly looked over her shoulder, startling at every little sound. She couldn't say she liked the person she'd managed to become, but she couldn't see any way she could go back either.

Suddenly, she knew what she would do. She'd accept rancher Ted's offer, move into his home and become a modern-day governess. He'd never know he'd be getting domestic help from a woman who'd gotten her doctorate and opened her own successful practice in White Plains, New York. She'd make sure he never knew this. The only stipulation he'd made that worried her had been the way he'd asked her to make sure she could stick around awhile. If Simon Barron located her, that would not be an option. Other than that, she'd be fine with staying.

Serving others had always been good for her, she

thought. Who knew? Maybe she could use her hard-won therapist skills to help Ted and his daughters. And since she wouldn't have to pay for lodging or food, she could really build up her savings. Since she didn't know how long it would be until the authorities managed to recapture Simon Barron, living on a remote ranch would definitely help her stay hidden.

In fact, even though she didn't believe in luck or serendipity, the way this had fallen into her lap certainly felt like fate. She'd be a fool to pass this up.

Though she'd barely made it to the end of the block, she turned on her heel and marched right back to Serenity's.

"You've decided," Serenity said, her voice serene as if there'd never been any doubt.

"I have." Amelia allowed herself an uncertain smile. "If you truly vouch for him, I'm going to accept his offer."

Serenity hugged her. "I think that's a good decision. Let me know if there's anything I can do to help."

Hugging the older woman back, Amelia exhaled. "You've already done more than enough. If I ever can repay you…"

With a tsking sound, Serenity shook her head and moved away. "His number is written on the pad by the register."

Amelia took out her phone and went and added the number to her contact list. Then, before she chickened out, she called to let Ted know her decision.

When he answered, he sounded harried. And surprised once she told him she'd like to come and work for him. "How soon can you start?" he asked. "I need to clean some stuff out of the room you'll be using."

"Tomorrow?"

"Sounds good, though it will have to be after I take

the girls to school. Say, eight? Get my address from Serenity." He paused for a moment. "Do you need help moving your belongings?"

Her belongings all fit in a couple of suitcases. "No, thank you. I'm good."

"Okay then. I'll see you tomorrow at eight." He ended the call.

Early the next morning, Amelia loaded everything she possessed into her car and turned the room key card in at the office. Then she drove into town and treated herself to a hot breakfast of pancakes and eggs at the Tumbleweed Café. The locals had begun getting used to seeing her around town and quite a few greeted her by name. This warmed her heart and she was smiling by the time the waitress brought her food. She'd plugged Ted Sanders's address into the GPS on her phone and knew the drive would take approximately ten to fifteen minutes, so she knew she had no reason to rush.

She tried to eat slowly, to remain calm, but her nerves got the better of her. Though the food tasted delicious, she couldn't even finish her pancakes. After settling up her check, she got a coffee to go and went back out to her car. If she drove out there now, she'd be too early, though not by too much. Driving slowly should take care of that problem and, since she despised sitting around waiting for something to happen, she headed out toward Ted Sanders's ranch.

After leaving downtown, the paved roads gave way to gravel. The flat west Texas landscape shimmered in the sun and the cloudless blue sky appeared to go on forever. She didn't know what it was about this place, but the sheer openness of the area made her feel free. At night, the inky sky glittered with stars. Sunrises and sunsets sent tendrils of pinks and oranges, reds and purples into the horizon, a different kind of beauty than she'd seen back East.

Learning her way around downtown Getaway had been a different experience. And now a ranch. Which meant cattle and horses, maybe even a dog or two. Teenage girls—twins—a family. Another new experience. Even though she'd been hired to cook and clean and help out with the girls, she had zero experience in that area. She'd been frank with Ted about that, though he'd told her he didn't mind and she'd catch on quickly. She guessed he was probably right, but that didn't help her nerves.

Despite driving slowly, taking in the scenery, she still ended up arriving ten minutes too early. As she turned off the gravel road onto the long driveway, she took in the long, ranch-style brick house. The structure appeared to have been built in the sixties or early seventies, but it looked well cared for. A circular gravel drive curved around the front of the house. There were no flowers and the few landscaping shrubs had sparse vegetation.

Beyond the house, she saw a large red barn in need of a fresh coat of paint, though otherwise in excellent shape, and what appeared to be miles and miles of nicely kept fences. A herd of cattle grazed in one pasture, while several horses huddled underneath some shade trees in another.

There were no vehicles in the driveway. Since it was 7:50 a.m., she guessed Ted would be on his way back from taking his daughters to school. Sure enough, a few minutes later, a cloud of dust from the dirt road announced his arrival. She got out of her car and watched as a pickup truck pulled up and parked near the garage.

Feeling awkward—she didn't know what to do with her hands—she waited for Ted to get out of the cab and greet her.

As he sauntered toward her with a rolling gait, she eyed him, aware the sight of him had kicked her heart rate into overdrive. Though she'd met him exactly two times before, today she realized he was really tall. Much taller than she remembered. He still wore the same white cowboy hat pulled down low enough to hide his eyes, a Western-style shirt with snap buttons and Wrangler jeans over his boots.

"Good morning," she managed.

"Welcome," he replied. He held out his large hand almost as an afterthought.

Again, her heart jumped into her throat the instant her fingers connected with his. His hands were calloused, the rough hands of a working man. Though his grip was firm, he took care not to hold on too tightly, which she appreciated. They shook, each releasing the other quickly.

"Follow me," he said, the deep rumble of his voice pleasing. "I'll show you to your room. Do you need help getting your stuff out of your car?"

"No, thanks. I've got it." She reached into the back seat and grabbed her suitcases, setting them on the ground one at a time.

Hands hooked in his belt buckle, he looked from her to the luggage and then back again. "That's it?"

"Yes." She lifted her chin and met his gaze. "All my worldly possessions. I believe in traveling light."

"Okay." He turned again. "The room that will be yours was formerly my office. I've moved most of my stuff out of there, and we had an old daybed that I moved in. It's got clean sheets on it." He glanced sideways at her as if to see how she was taking all this. "There's a closet, but the dresser is an old one from when the girls were little. It's kind of beat-up, but it will work."

He sounded so apologetic that she wanted to reassure him. "It's all good. I don't need much." She hefted one bag, hoping that might help prove her point.

"This way."

She followed him through the front door.

Inside the house, the scent of leather mingled with a faint burnt odor. In the middle of the living room, a Western saddle sat on top of a wooden saddle tree, which, along with the furniture, explained the leather smell.

"New saddle," he explained. "It's Yolanda's and she's been cleaning it. I asked her to put it back in the tack room inside the barn, but she clearly hasn't gotten around to doing that yet."

Amelia nodded as if she understood. Who knew? Maybe it seemed perfectly normal to have a saddle in the house if you lived on a ranch.

But the burnt smell… She glanced at the kitchen as they passed it, wondering if someone had burned their breakfast. He must have noticed her sniffing because he stopped and grimaced.

"One of them left a pot of something on the stove and forgot about it," he explained. "I came home to a house full of smoke. I opened the windows and doors and tried to air it out, but you can still smell it."

"Wow."

"I know. Lucky I came home when I did. Here we are." Turning left into a short hallway off the main living area, he led her into a small room with a single window. A white metal daybed, made up with sheets and a faded but clean comforter, sat against one wall. An old dresser, once white but now yellowing and adorned with stickers—hearts, balloons, bears and unicorns, just to name a few—was across from the bed. The room had no mirror, no pictures on the walls, and though blinds covered the single window, there were no curtains. It might have been the room of a monk. Looking around once more, she slowly nodded. He hadn't been kidding. It wasn't much. But it would do just fine.

"This is perfect," she said, meaning it. "Thank you."

"I'm glad you think so." He scratched the back of his head. "I should warn you that the twins are likely going to be upset. They share a room and have been bugging me for quite a while to clear out this room so they could each have their own."

"Ouch." She winced. "What did they say when you told them about me?"

He looked away, a muscle working in his jaw. "I haven't yet."

"Double ouch. Does that mean you're planning for them to come home from school today and find out at the same time they meet me?" As a therapist, she found this intriguing, to say the least. Talk about throwing her right into the middle of things.

"Basically, yes. I'm sorry." He didn't sound sorry. If anything, he appeared resigned. "It's been a little hectic here, and honestly, I didn't have time to deal with more drama. I'll tell them when I pick them up from school. That will give them the drive home to get used to the idea."

"Do you really think that's long enough?" The instant she spoke, she inwardly winced. That came from the therapist in her. She needed to be more careful with what she said. It wasn't her place to question or make judgments.

In response to her question, he shrugged. "It's not like I actually have a choice. Come on. Let me show you the rest of the house before I have to get back to work out there." He jerked his thumb toward the outdoors.

He showed her the laundry room, the kitchen and the large freezer he kept in the garage. Though he'd already outlined her duties verbally, he'd also taken the time to type them up and print them out for her, which, oddly enough, she appreciated.

"You're in charge of the menu," he explained. "And you can choose when and how often to do laundry. I'd appreciate if you'd clean at least once a week. Whatever rules you make, once you communicate them to the girls, I expect you to keep to them." His gaze searched her face. "Will that work for you?"

Structure and stability. "That makes sense." She smiled, feeling more at ease by the moment. "I'm assuming you will be present for all the meals, right?"

"Breakfast and dinner," he replied. "If you could just make me a sandwich for lunch, that would be really helpful."

"Will do."

Nodding once, he looked around. "Well, I've got work to do. I'll check back in here around noon."

"Okay." She smiled. "I'll make sure your lunch is ready."

"Thanks." And he went out the back door.

She watched him through the window, unable to keep from admiring his denim-clad backside.

Once he'd disappeared from view, she set about familiarizing herself with the house, starting with the kitchen. She checked out the contents of the surprisingly well-stocked pantry, along with the fridge and freezer. Finally, she took a look inside the large stand-alone freezer in the garage, which had a lot of frozen meat.

First up, she needed to figure out what to make for dinner tonight. She wanted it to be something plain and homey, a meal teenage girls would like but filling enough for a hardworking cowboy.

Since all the meat was frozen, she'd have to use the microwave to defrost something, plus take out whatever she planned to make tomorrow.

Thrilled at all the choices, she decided to make a nice pot of chili. She had a favorite healthy recipe and luckily Ted appeared to have all the ingredients. For tomorrow, she decided oven-baked fried chicken, so she put a package of chicken breasts in the refrigerator to thaw.

She used the microwave to defrost the beef, and once it was no longer frozen, she browned and drained it before adding it to the slow cooker she'd located.

She spent the next half hour peeling sweet potatoes—her secret ingredient—and chopping them into cubes, and adding onion, bell pepper, canned pinto beans and diced tomatoes, plus all the seasonings she knew from memory.

Next, she made one of her favorite spice cakes for dessert. While that baked, she cleaned up the kitchen.

Now that she had dinner cooking, she needed to see if anything needed cleaning. She also wanted to set up some kind of schedule, since she'd prefer to do laundry once per week.

It took her a couple of hours of dusting and vacuuming, toilet scrubbing and countertop cleaning, but she finally felt as if she had the house sparkling clean. A quick glance at the clock told her she had time to take a break before making lunch.

She made herself a cup of coffee and carried it out to the back porch. Oddly enough, all the physical labor had invigorated her. Maybe this job might actually work out after all.

Ted wasn't sure how he felt about leaving a stranger inside his house. It felt weird, for one thing. But he really needed the help, and the idea of someone else doing all the cooking and cleaning felt like a weight had been lifted from his shoulders.

Soon, he got busy with work and managed to stop worrying about it.

Shortly before noon, Floyd stopped by the barn to let him know he was heading to town for lunch and asked him if he wanted anything. "I'm going to eat up at the house," Ted replied, as he always did. "But I appreciate you asking."

Once Floyd had driven off, Ted walked back to his house, a strange combination of anticipation and curiosity filling him. He'd asked for a sandwich and had a decent selection of cold cuts, so it shouldn't be a problem. He wondered if Amelia would eat with him. It had been a long time since he'd had company at lunch. He kind of thought he might enjoy it.

Walking into the house, he smelled something so delicious, his mouth started watering. Chili. Damn, he hoped he had a bag of corn chips. He loved them in his chili, along with shredded cheddar cheese and sour cream.

"Hey," Amelia said, looking up as he entered the

kitchen. She brushed back a lock of her wavy hair from her face. "Have a seat. Lunch is coming right up."

"Just a sec." He washed up at the kitchen sink, overly conscious of her presence. "What are you making?"

His question made her grin. "Chili. It's one of my favorites. I hope the girls like it."

"They do. And since we haven't had it in a while, I'm sure they'll be thrilled." Once they got past the shock of having Amelia here, that was.

He took a seat, relieved when she carried two plates to the table.

"I hope you like chicken salad," she said. "If not, I can make you something else."

She looked so sweet and earnest with her frizzy red hair and bright blue eyes, so unusual in a redhead. A rush of attraction hit him, so strong it momentarily rendered him at a loss for words. How could he have forgotten that his life had once been like this, sharing a meal and a conversation with a pretty woman? Except that he'd loved his wife and Amelia was a stranger.

"I'll make something else for you," Amelia said, clearly taking his silence for disapproval.

"Wait." Finding his voice, he waved her back to the table. "Chicken salad is fine. I'm sorry. I was just thinking about something else."

Though she eyed him as if she wasn't sure whether or not to believe him, she brought the two sandwiches back to the table. Her hand shook slightly as she set his plate in front of him, making him realize she might be as nervous as he was.

"Sit. Please." He waited until she'd pulled out the chair across from him and dropped into it. "We'll get used to each other once some time has passed," he offered, just as much for himself as for her.

Looking from her plate to him, she slowly nodded. "I'm sure we will." When she flashed a quick smile, he realized she had a cute little dimple in one cheek. His mouth went dry. To cover this, he reached for his sandwich and took a bite.

Still watching him, she did the same.

The chicken salad was good. Pleased, he took another bite, chewed slowly and swallowed. "It's been a long time since I had chicken salad."

"Do you like it?" she asked, still looking slightly anxious.

"I do. I can guess most of the ingredients," he said. "Chicken, mayo, hard-boiled egg, celery, onion, maybe a bit of mustard and something else. Am I right?"

Since she'd just taken a bite, she held up one finger while she finished chewing. When she swallowed, he couldn't help but watch the slender lines of her throat.

"You're right on all counts. The other ingredient is chopped apple." Her eyes sparkled. "I've always liked to cook, but it seemed a waste to do much just for myself. I'm looking forward to cooking for you and your family."

Again, that unwelcome rush of attraction. Instead of looking at her, he focused on finishing his meal. She'd also filled a bowl with corn chips, so he helped himself to a handful of those too.

The silence felt slightly uncomfortable, but he liked how she didn't try to rush to fill it with a bunch of empty chatter.

"Do you mind if we turn on the midday news?" she asked quietly. "I like to keep up with what's going on in the world."

Seizing on that idea, he got up and grabbed the remote and clicked it on. They could see the large TV in the den clearly from the kitchen table.

The meteorologist had just begun detailing the weather report for the next week. As Ted listened, he continued to eat, feeling himself relax. The normalcy of listening to the local news in his own kitchen made him realize how absurd and unwarranted his nervousness had been.

The silence between them now felt companionable instead of awkward.

They finished eating about the same time. He checked his watch, surprised to see only twenty minutes had passed.

On the news program, they'd switched to national news. Apparently, some serial killer who'd escaped a while back was still on the run, and authorities were worried he'd captured the chief witness against him, a Dr. Amelia Ferguson, who'd disappeared without a trace. The camera panned to a photo of a stern-looking woman with sleek blond hair and glasses, wearing a well-cut business suit and sensible shoes. She'd been, the female anchor explained, the only one of the Coffee Shop Killer's victims who'd gotten away.

The instant that news segment concluded, Amelia got up and began gathering the dishes from the table. She seemed to have gone all stiff and uncomfortable again, though Ted told himself it was probably just his imagination.

"I enjoyed lunch," he said, also pushing to his feet. "I've got to get back to work. I'll be picking the girls up at three thirty, so be prepared to meet them a little before four."

"Sounds good," she called, without turning around.

When she started rinsing the plates off in the sink and then stacking them in the dishwasher, he realized he'd been dismissed.

Amused, he let himself out and went back to work.

The rest of the afternoon passed quickly, and when his watch alarm went off to remind him to head into town, he felt satisfied with all he'd gotten done. Usually, this time of the day, he'd be frantically trying to figure out what he could feed everyone for dinner, while driving slightly over the speed limit since he always seemed to be running late.

Not today. Knowing someone else would be in charge of dinner felt like a weight had been lifted off his shoulders. The only unpleasant task he'd have to deal with would be filling the twins in on the new situation up at the house.

Though Ted wasn't sure how the girls would take the news of a live-in female worker, he suspected it might not be good. He rehearsed what he wanted to say several times on the drive to pick them up from school.

In the end, he figured the direct approach would be best.

Chapter 3

Ted arrived at the high school early and scored a prime pickup parking spot close to the front door. He waited, watching the crowd of teenagers spill from the doors a few seconds after the bell rang.

He spotted his two a minute or so later. They always came out together, and today was no exception. As usual, they eyed his pickup with identical bored expressions before strolling over and climbing up into the cab. Sometimes they took turns, one riding shotgun and the other in the back seat, but today they both went into the back.

"How was your day?" he asked, deliberately cheerful.

"Fine," Yolanda answered. Today she wore her straight dark brown hair up in a jaunty ponytail. Her sister, hair hanging in a curtain hiding her face, didn't bother to respond.

Well then. Might as well get right to it. "We've got company at the house," he said, his tone conversational.

This, naturally, got both of their immediate attention.

"Company who?" Yvonne demanded.

"I've hired someone to cook and clean and help out around the house. Her name is Amelia."

He watched them in the rearview mirror while they digested this news.

"Are you moving in your girlfriend?" Yolanda wanted to know. "But pretending it's something else?"

This made him laugh. "When would I have time to date anyone?" he pointed out. "I don't have a girlfriend. But I do need help around the house. This is the perfect solution."

"How are we affording this?" Yvonne this time. "Our budget is tight as it is, or so you're always telling me."

Now came the tricky part. "Because I'm offering room and board, including meals, I'm not having to pay a large salary."

"Room and board?"

"Yep." He'd known that part would catch their attention. "Amelia will be living in my office."

Two audible gasps from the back seat.

"But that was going to be my room!" Yolanda protested.

"I never agreed to that."

"I was still working on convincing you," she replied.

"I'm sorry. But for now, it will be Amelia's bedroom."

They'd made it to the gravel road that led to the ranch.

"What's this Amelia person like?" Yvonne asked, her voice suspicious. "I'm picturing a round little white-haired lady who will bake cookies and cakes for us."

"I like that idea," Yolanda agreed. "Is that what she's like, Dad?"

He laughed. "You'll find out in about five minutes, now, won't you?"

When they pulled up to the house and parked, both girls were slow exiting the truck. Normally, they dashed into the house, not once looking back. Not this time. They hung back so much that he passed them and ended up leading the way.

As he opened the door, the smell of freshly baked chocolate chip cookies wafted out.

"Oh wow," Yvonne gasped. "That smells soooo fab!"

Yolanda elbowed her. "Maybe this might be a good thing," she muttered.

Just then, Amelia came out of the kitchen carrying a plate of still-warm cookies. "Hi, girls," she said, smiling. "I'm Amelia."

At the sight of her, flame-colored hair swirling around her shoulders, a pair of soft, faded blue jeans showing off her lush figure, the twins' gleeful looks changed to identical expressions of suspicion.

"*You're* Amelia?" Yolanda asked, exchanging a glance with her sister. They both turned to eye Ted, as if they thought he'd been lying to them.

"Yes, I'm Amelia." She held out the plate. "Would you like a cookie?"

Never one to resist a sweet, Yolanda helped herself to two. A second later, Yvonne followed suit. After shooting another baleful glance at their father, they carried off their cookies to eat in their room.

Right before disappearing around the corner, Yolanda looked back over her shoulder. "Thank you," she said. A moment later, the door closed firmly.

"That went well." Amelia grimaced, her shoulders sagging. "Do you think I tried too hard?"

"You did just fine," he reassured her, reaching out and touching one arm lightly before letting go. "That's just normal teenage behavior, unfortunately. They're still a little ticked off about me giving you the room they'd been badgering me to give them. They'll get over it, I promise."

"I sure hope so. What time would you prefer to eat dinner?"

"Five or five thirty," he replied. "That chili smells amazing."

To his surprise, she blushed at the compliment. "Thanks. I make it fairly often. I serve it over corn chips with shredded cheddar cheese on top. We even have sour cream in case anyone wants to add that."

That made him laugh. "You've just named exactly how I prefer to eat chili."

She laughed along with him. "I think that's probably how most people like to eat it."

Something about her laughter... Eyeing her thoughtfully, though he'd earlier told himself not to get too personal, he decided to ask anyway. "Where are you from? I can't quite place the accent, though I can tell it's somewhere up north."

She froze, staring at him, wide-eyed. "Do I really have an accent?"

"You do." He didn't bother to hide his smile. "That's why I'm asking where you're from."

"Oh." Clearly not wanting to answer, she swallowed. "Originally, I'm from New Jersey."

"That explains your accent, then." He scratched the

back of his head. "I'm going to go get cleaned up. I'll let the girls know to show up in the kitchen at five."

She nodded and he took off. It still felt weird, though maybe in a good way, to have a woman staying with him and the kids in the house. He guessed it would just take some time for them all to get used to it.

Only once Ted had left her alone again did Amelia exhale. She'd been feeling unsettled since learning from the news story at lunch that the authorities believed Simon had already captured her. The thought alone gave her a creepy feeling. Déjà vu maybe? Or perhaps she should simply be glad that she'd managed to disappear so completely.

Still, the feeling of unease had lurked around her all afternoon. Though she'd been slightly nervous about meeting the twins, she was also glad for the distraction. Of course, the second she'd heard them pull up in the driveway, she'd gone tense, rushing for her tray of carefully prepared baked bribes.

The cookies had been a peace offering of sorts, and she'd made several different varieties. If they hadn't liked chocolate chip, she'd planned to offer oatmeal raisin or peanut butter or, finally, the basic vanilla butter cookie. She'd baked enough to feed a small army.

They were taller than she'd expected, and beautiful. While she could see Ted in them, with their dark hair and deep brown eyes, she thought their mother must have been beautiful. Briefly, she wondered what had happened to her, and then decided it was none of her business.

Now she just had to kill time until dinner.

Checking on the chili, still simmering in the slow

cooker, she set the table before heading back to her room for a moment or two. Once there, she turned on her laptop and realized she'd need to get the Wi-Fi password from Ted.

Since she still had forty-five minutes to kill, she wandered back into the den—still deserted—and clicked on the news. Watching, she remained ever hopeful that the next news update she'd see would say the Coffee Shop Killer had been recaptured. It was bound to happen eventually, though she thought the sooner, the better. Since he'd sworn to finish what he'd started, she wouldn't feel safe again until Simon had been locked behind bars once more.

The local news made no further mention of her nemesis and the national news would be coming on while they were eating dinner, so she turned the TV off and went back to wait for everyone else to show up for dinner.

The twins appeared in the kitchen at exactly five o'clock, per their father's instructions. Ted arrived a minute later, his hair still damp, clearly having showered and changed. The sight of him sent her heart hammering in her chest. There was something so intimate about the way he looked and she found it hard to breathe. Luckily, one of the girls made a snide comment to the other, starting a mini-argument that necessitated Ted intervening, and Amelia shook off the weird feeling.

"I'm going to let everyone serve themselves from the slow cooker," she said. "Corn chips, shredded cheddar and sour cream are over here too."

Clearly curious, the twins rushed over, jostling each other for the chance to be first.

"Settle down," Ted ordered. "There's plenty for everyone. Don't make poor Amelia think I've raised a couple of unmannered hellions."

They giggled at this, shooting sideways glances at Amelia, who smiled back. Both of them got a heaping bowl of chili, walking carefully back to the table.

"Go ahead," Ted said, gesturing for Amelia to precede him. "Ladies first."

Once they were all seated, everyone dug in.

"This is good," Yolanda said, her tone surprised.

"I know, right?" Yvonne kept spooning chili into her mouth. "Really tasty."

Ted had finished his own bowl and got up to go back for seconds. When he returned to the table, he smiled at Amelia, making her heart skip a beat. "You're a good cook," he said.

She could feel her face heat. "Thank you."

The twins watched this exchange with interest.

"Where do you two know each other from?" Yvonne asked.

"Serenity's," Amelia answered. "I was working for her part-time. She recommended me for the job."

"Oh." The girls exchanged a meaningful glance. "So that means you two aren't dating?"

"Definitely not!" Both Amelia and Ted answered in unison, in the same shocked tone.

Again, the two teenagers looked at each other, as if silently communicating. Finally, Yolanda shrugged. "Whatever."

"I made dessert," Amelia offered, hoping a change of subject would help. "Spice cake with cream cheese frosting."

"Yum!" Yolanda cheered. "That sounds amazing."

Yvonne shook her head, her expression full of disgust. "I can't eat that," she groused. "I've already had a couple of cookies. If I have cake too, I'll totally blow my diet."

"Diet?" Yolanda snorted. "Yeah, right."

"Girls." Ted's warning came sharp. "That's enough."

Not sure what to do now, Amelia looked at Ted.

"I'd like some cake," he said. "Thank you so much for taking the time to make it."

"Me too," Yolanda chimed in, shooting a gleeful look at her sister.

Yvonne muttered something that sounded suspiciously like a curse word, pushed back her chair and slammed her way out of the room.

They all sat for a moment in stunned silence. Ted finally shook his head and then dragged his hand through his short hair. "Well. That went well."

Yolanda laughed. Amelia, not sure how to react, got up and retrieved the cake. It was a pretty thing. She'd made it in a Bundt pan, and after frosting it, she'd caramelized some pecans and dusted the top with them.

"That looks amazing," Ted said quietly.

"Thanks." Though she'd lost her taste for a sweet dessert, Amelia cut them each a slice of cake. Oddly enough, she really wanted to go find Yvonne and see if she wanted to talk about what was wrong.

But Amelia was a stranger there. She wasn't sure how such an action would be perceived, and even if the teen would welcome her intrusion. So she did nothing, eating her cake in silence. She waited until the others had finished before getting up and carrying the plates to the sink. For some reason, she felt on the verge of tears, which honestly made no sense.

"Are you all right?" Ted's deep voice came from right behind her.

She started, just a tiny bit. "Sure." She tried to summon up a smile to match her easy answer. "I'm just not used to teenagers."

"It'll get better," he said. "Maybe. Their mood changes so fast it can make your head spin. They can be angry and indignant, and kind and generous and sweet, often all at the same time."

"Hey, Dad, I'm right here," Yolanda protested. "Can you not talk about me when I can hear you, please?"

Ted rolled his eyes, but he chuckled. "See what I mean?" he asked, nudging Amelia with his elbow. A laugh escaped her, despite herself, making him grin.

Heaven help her, but this man had a beautiful smile. She especially liked the way his brown eyes crinkled at the corners.

Shake it off, she told herself. Taking a deep breath, she rinsed the dessert plates and put them in the dishwasher before turning back to face the others.

"Do you need any help with homework?" she asked Yolanda, remembering what Ted had listed as her duties.

Yolanda's dark eyes, so like her father's, narrowed. "What are you good at?" she asked. "How are your essay writing skills?"

"Pretty good, but I'm not doing your work for you," she pointed out, gently but firmly. "I'll be happy to help with research or whatever else you might need."

"I'm good," Yolanda declared, sliding out from behind the table. Her phone pinged and she dug it from her pocket. "Gotta run."

Amelia looked at Ted once she'd gone. "I have to say,

it's admirable the two of them didn't stare at the phones or tablets all through the meal."

He shrugged. "It's against the rules. No electronics at meals."

Impressed, Amelia nodded. "If there's not anything else I'm supposed to do, I think I'll go for a walk."

Expression steady, he eyed her. "Would you mind if I went with you? Or would you rather be alone?"

"You can come. Actually, I'd really like it if you could show me around the ranch." One thing she always did, no matter where she found herself, was to figure out an escape route in case things went south. Having Ted accompany her would definitely help with that.

Again, that flash of a brilliant smile. "Deal. Do you have a pair of boots?"

She looked down at her sneakers. "No."

"What size shoe do you wear? Maybe you can borrow a pair of the girls'."

"Won't these work?" she asked.

"They might get dirty," he warned. "There's a lot of dirt and…manure on a cattle ranch."

"Oh." What he said made sense. "I wear a size seven."

"Come with me. We'll go look in the mudroom and see what they've left there."

There were at least a dozen pair of boots, some dirty, others clean. A few pairs clearly belonged to Ted, but the rest were women's. Ted went through them, checking the insides for sizes. "You're in luck," he told her. "They're all sevens or seven and a halfs, which should work also."

She wasn't sure if she felt super awkward wearing someone else's boots without asking, but she went ahead and picked the plainest pair and put them on, leaving her sneakers in their place.

"Come on," he said. "We've got a little bit before it's dark."

Outside, she saw the sun had already begun to set. October in west Texas didn't show many of the signs of autumn, though it did get dark earlier. Plus, the temperature felt much more comfortable.

"Let's go this way," he said, walking easily at her side. He led her toward the big barn on a slight hill that she'd spotted her first day.

The gravel path led directly to the double barn doors. "Do you keep livestock in here?" she asked, wondering if she was about to get up close and personal with some cows or horses.

"Sometimes. If one is sick and needs doctoring. When a horse is about to foal. Other than that, it's mostly hay storage. And there's a tack room, plus a stall where we can wash off the horses."

She nodded. Flat terrain, not a lot of places to shelter or hide. Not a good thing. Even though she knew it was highly unlikely Simon would ever find her here, if there was one thing she'd learned after he'd taken her captive, it was to be prepared for worst-case scenarios.

"What's up that way?" She pointed up the hill. At least there were a few trees. Not large ones, but the twisted stumpy ones so typical of this part of Texas. They wouldn't provide much cover at all, though they'd do in a pinch.

"A couple of storage buildings and some shelter for the animals. Every pasture has something so the horses or cattle can get out of the weather. They're usually three-sided sheds, but they work."

"I'd like to see," she replied immediately. Though

running uphill wasn't the best option, maybe what was on top would make the trip worthwhile.

"Okay." He glanced at her sideways, no doubt wondering about her sudden interest in pastures and sheds. "This way."

As they walked through the pasture, she finally understood the need for boots. Not only were there piles of manure, but rocks and insects. At one point, she swore she saw a large, hairy tarantula scuttling through the dry grass. The thought of that crawling over her foot made her shudder.

"Watch out for the fire ant mound," Ted said, pointing. "I try to get rid of them before they get too big, but I must have missed that one. I'll get out here tomorrow and take care of it, but you'll want to avoid it for now."

The reddish pile of dirt seemed about as high as her knee. Fascinated despite herself, she walked over for a closer look, her feet skidding on pebbles and dirt. "I don't see any ants," she said.

"They're inside," Ted replied. He picked up a stick and poked one side of the mound. Hordes of small red ants swarmed out from where he'd made an opening.

"Wow," she murmured. "They look…aggressive."

"Oh, they are." Tossing the stick, Ted stepped back from the mound. "Fire ant bites itch like the dickens."

Like the dickens. The phrase made her smile. People here talked differently than she'd been used to. Kind of folksy, an unabashed sort of down-home country that often hit perfectly on point. She'd found it grew on her and now she quite liked it.

"Come on." Ted turned and continued up the hill. "I take it you're not afraid of livestock, right?"

"Why?" she asked. "Am I about to come face-to-face with a huge bull or something?"

The wickedness of his grin sent a bolt of heat through her.

"Not quite," he replied. "Come up and see."

Deciding not to be too worried—he wouldn't put his brand-new housekeeper in harm's way—she hurried up the slope right behind him.

A herd of horses, their coats gleaming with health, swung their heads around to eye them as they approached.

"Whatever you do, don't run," he warned, one corner of his mouth kicking up as if he was trying very hard not to smile.

She froze. "Why? Will they chase me?"

"No." He finally laughed. "I'm just messing with you. I take it you haven't spent much time around livestock."

"I haven't." Not sure what to make of this relaxed, convivial version of her new boss, she finally shrugged, shoving her hair away from her face with one hand. "While I'd never heard of horses chasing after any-one before, a lot of things are different out here in west Texas."

When she looked up at him, she was surprised to see something hungry in his gaze. Or maybe she imagined it, because the next second, it was gone.

"Are you ready to go back?" he asked.

Glancing around, she pointed toward two large metal buildings. "What are those?"

"Equipment storage, mostly. I also keep more hay there for the winter."

Possible hiding places. "Do you mind showing them to me?"

"Why?" Definitely suspicious.

"I don't know." *Keep it casual*, she reminded herself. "I guess I'm just really curious about all the ranch operations. But if you'd rather not show them to me, that's fine. We can head back."

"I think that's wise," he said as he checked his watch. "The sun is setting and it will be dark soon. If you really want to see them, we can check them out another time."

Startled, she realized he was right. The light had begun to fade, darkening the sky. Though the sun hadn't completely set, it would be there in a matter of minutes.

"Lead the way," she said. "Especially away from that ant hill."

To her surprise, he laughed again. "Come on. We can make it if we hurry."

He held out his hand. After a second's hesitation, she took it. "Ready?" he asked, his eyes sparkling, the wind ruffling his hair under his hat.

Before she could answer, he gave her a tug and they were off, running down the hill, slipping and sliding in spots, but still moving fast. His wide-open grin told her how much he was enjoying himself. With a start, she realized she actually *liked* this man. Not in a romantic, he-could-be-the-one way, but in a maybe-they-could-be-friends scenario. Since she knew it actually made any job better if you got along with your boss, she felt this would be a good thing.

"Here we are," he called out, his voice triumphant as they skidded to a stop in a small slurry of gravel and dirt. As soon as she'd found her footing, he released her hand.

Which made her feel oddly bereft. To cover, she hurried into the house, taking refuge in the kitchen by getting busy making a cup of hot tea.

"Did you want me to fix you anything?" she asked, without looking back over her shoulder at him.

"No, thanks," he replied. "I'm just going to grab a beer and watch a little TV. You're welcome to join me."

"Maybe later." Though she doubted it. "Thanks for showing me around your ranch."

"You're welcome." He opened the refrigerator, got his beer, and a moment later, she heard the pop-click as he opened it. He disappeared into the den. A few seconds later, the television came on.

Tempting as it might be to go sit and watch some mindless television show, she'd already had way too much togetherness for one day. She couldn't afford to let down her guard too much. Simon hadn't been caught yet. Until he was, she shouldn't relax. She had to be ready to take off at a moment's notice if necessary.

Chapter 4

Kicking back in his soft leather recliner, cold beer in hand, Ted tried to relax while a thirty-minute sitcom played on the TV. It had been a pleasant evening, starting with a delicious dinner and a clean house.

But the best part of the day had been showing Amelia the ranch. He honestly couldn't remember the last time he'd laughed so much. He wasn't sure if that was good or bad, but either way, it felt nice to be with a woman knowing she wanted nothing more from him than a paycheck. No ulterior motives, not competition with other ladies in her singles church group, just hanging out. No pressure. He also had to admit that it didn't hurt that she was easy on the eyes. It would be nice if they could become friends. Especially if she could provide a positive feminine influence on his daughters. That was what really mattered.

The first day had gone well, he thought. He felt pretty sure the twins would get used to Amelia, and after years of being subjected to his barely edible cooking, they'd probably even come to appreciate her. He already did. Not having to figure out what to feed the girls for dinner and then actually make time to cook it had removed a huge load from his shoulders.

So much needed to be done around the ranch, from repairs to new construction, and with only one hired hand to help, it often seemed a never-ending cycle of trying to catch up. He hoped now that he'd hired someone to take over all of the household chores, he could make a serious dent in it.

The sitcom ended and he realized he hadn't watched a single minute of it. He'd been too lost in thought.

"Dad?" Yolanda bounced into the room and perched on the edge of the couch. "Can we talk?"

The seriousness of her tone guaranteed he'd pay attention. He grabbed the remote and paused the television show. "Sure," he replied, giving her his full attention. "What's up?"

Twirling a strand of her thick dark hair around her finger, she glanced toward the kitchen. Reflexively, he did too.

"She's gone?" Yolanda asked in a stage whisper.

"Most likely to her room," he answered, also keeping his voice low. "I'm guessing you want to talk about her?"

She nodded.

Bracing himself since he'd been expecting one or both of the twins to raise Cain about him turning his office into a room for Amelia, he waited.

"You and Amelia went for a walk," Yolanda muttered. "Yvonne said you were probably making out in the barn and that you lied to us about her being your girlfriend. Is that true?"

Torn between wanting to be appalled and amusement, he shook his head. "No, it is not. Amelia wanted to see the ranch, so I showed her. We're not dating, have never been dating and won't ever be dating. She's here to work, which will be a huge help for me."

"But why'd you let her live here?" Yolanda asked. "I mean, you moved this strange woman in without even asking us."

He carefully considered what he had to say next. "Because I need someone to stay here to do all the work I've asked her to do. She'll be cleaning and cooking and doing laundry, as well as helping you girls with homework or anything else you might need. Plus, she was working at Serenity's and living at the old Landshark Motel. By being able to offer her room and board, plus food, I could save on the salary I have to pay her. I wouldn't have been able to afford her otherwise."

"Oh." Expression solemn, Yolanda considered his explanation. "So you're saying she's not here with expectations of becoming the next Mrs. Ted Sanders."

"Not at all." He shook his head. "This is going to be a good thing—you'll see."

"I hope so." Springing up from the couch, his daughter headed for the kitchen. "I wonder if there are any cookies left."

"I'm sure there are. Bring a couple to your sister too, please."

Once Yolanda had gotten her treats and disappeared back inside her room, Ted settled back into his chair and tried to focus on the TV. He went to sleep that night feeling more at peace than he had in a long time.

The next several days settled into a comfortable rhythm. He liked getting up to find a fresh pot of coffee made, coming into the kitchen after his shower to find a hot breakfast waiting, the girls digging into scrambled eggs and bacon with smiles on their faces.

For lunch, she always made him a hearty sandwich or a bowl of homemade soup. She'd taken to making extra for Floyd, who soon joined them at the house.

Though he still drove the girls to school, Amelia offered to go and pick them up so he didn't have to stop whatever he was doing, try to get reasonably clean and drive to town and back before trying to finish the chore. After a moment of consideration, he accepted her offer, and when he told the twins, they didn't even protest.

Dinnertime, though, had become his new favorite time of the day. They say the way to a man's heart is through his stomach, and if he'd been in the market for a romance, he would have agreed that was true. Amelia made simple but hearty food. Tasty, reasonably healthy more often than not, but occasionally offering them a treat like homemade pizzas. Yolanda and Yvonne had helped out with those.

All in all, Ted felt very pleased with his decision to hire her. The next time he went to town to pick up supplies at the feed store, he stopped in to visit with Serenity and let her know.

"Oh, that makes me so happy," Serenity said, clapping her hands together and sending her armful of bracelets jingling. "I just knew you two would be good for each other!"

Her choice of words gave him pause. "In an employer-employee situation, you mean?"

"Of course, of course." She patted his arm. "How is

everything else going? Have things calmed down with your girls?"

"For now, yes," he said. "Who knows how long that will last. But it's all been such a relief. And that Amelia is a mighty fine cook."

Serenity smiled her enigmatic smile. "I'm so glad to hear that."

Because she'd done so much to help him, Ted impulsively decided to buy his daughters flowers. "I need two small bouquets," he said. "Exactly the same. If I buy different ones, they'll find a way to argue over who gets what."

"I understand," Serenity said. Once again, he wondered if she had children. She never talked about her personal life and he didn't want to pry. All he knew was what he'd heard—she'd shown up in Getaway one day, purchased a vacant storefront downtown and hung up her shingle. Back when Ted had been young, she'd done tarot readings and told fortunes, all the while running her florist shop. Gradually, she'd expanded into a bookstore and paranormal artifacts shop and somehow managed to thrive through two recessions in a straitlaced, mostly Southern Baptist, town. These days, she had become simply a quirky and much-loved part of Getaway. A local. In these parts, there was no higher compliment.

While he waited, Serenity put together two autumn floral arrangements, using daisies and mums and even a single yellow rose in each. She gave him a total that he felt was way too reasonable, so he added a few dollars to it. When she tried to make change, he told her to consider it a tip and leave it at that.

As he went to gather up the flowers, he suddenly wondered if he should get something for Amelia. He turned to Serenity to ask her thoughts. "Will it be weird if I bring home flowers for my girls and nothing for her?"

Serenity studied him. "That's up to you. Do you think she will mind?"

He shrugged. "No idea. That's why I'm asking you." In the refrigerated case, he spied a small arrangement already made up. Unlike the colorful flowers Serenity had made for the girls, this one was white and pink. While he recognized mums, carnations and a white rose or two, he wasn't sure of the others. "Is that one there really expensive?" he asked. "That looks like something Amelia might like."

Though Serenity's brows rose at his comment, she went to the case and brought the arrangement over. "It's on the house," she said.

"No. You know I don't take charity." He reached into his pocket and pulled out his wallet. "I'd rather pay."

"You don't understand," Serenity said. "Once a week, someone who wishes to remain anonymous purchases a floral arrangement. They tell me which one to make up and have me put it in my case. When someone expresses interest in it, I'm to give it to them. I just finished that one ten minutes before you came in. Now it's yours." She placed it on the counter next to his other two. "Now take it and skedaddle."

"Only if you let me buy one for the next person," he replied. "That way I can pay it forward."

Serenity gave a startled laugh. "Fine. What would you like me to make?"

"You choose." He placed two twenties near the register and went to gather up his purchases. "Thank you," he said. "For everything."

A grin blossomed over her face, lighting up her eyes.

"Let me get you a box for these. That way you can carry them all out to your truck."

Once the floral arrangements had been carefully stowed in their cardboard box on his front seat floorboard, he thanked her again and climbed into his truck. As he drove home, he had to wonder if the twins were going to make a big deal out of the fact that he'd brought Amelia flowers too. Then he realized he didn't really care. After all, he had good reason. Amelia had proved to be invaluable this past week and a half. Flowers were a simple way of showing his appreciation, nothing more.

When he walked into the house, carrying the flowers, he heard laughter coming out of the kitchen. He kept right on walking past, hoping they wouldn't notice him. He'd prefer to put the flowers in their rooms for them to find later.

But Yvonne caught a glimpse of him from the corner of her eye and squealed. "Flowers!"

Her sister spun around so fast it made his head spin. "Dad!"

Immediately, he changed directions. Placing the box full of flowers on the table, he sniffed the air appreciatively. "What is that amazing smell?"

Neither of the twins responded. Both their gazes were riveted on the brightly colored blooms.

"Chicken cacciatore," Amelia responded, smiling as she watched the girls.

"I got y'all a little something," he said, carefully removing the two identical arrangements. "One for Yolanda and one for Yvonne."

"Wow. They're beautiful," Yolanda gushed.

Always quieter, Yvonne thanked him.

And then, as he'd suspected they would, they both

returned their attention to the last group of flowers. He pretended not to notice. "This one is for you, Amelia. In appreciation for all the hard work you do around here."

Eyes wide as saucers, the twins watched silently while he handed Amelia her arrangement.

"You didn't need to do this," Amelia said and then leaned in to smell the blooms. "But what a sweet and thoughtful gesture. Thank you."

She placed them carefully on the counter next to the stove. He couldn't help but notice that she seemed a little flushed and maybe flustered. Suddenly, he felt unsure, as if maybe he'd erred and shouldn't have gotten her flowers.

"Well," he said, uncomfortably aware of the silence, "I'm going to go get cleaned up and change. I'm looking forward to dinner."

Once he made his escape, he stopped at the door to his room, listening, hoping that the earlier sounds of laughter and chatter would resume.

Instead, a moment later, he heard his daughters close the door to their shared bedroom with a decisive click.

He showered, just as he always did, and changed into the comfortable and clean clothes he would wear around the house. He'd debated whether or not to address the apparent issue of the flowers and ultimately decided not to. Everyone would just have to get over it. If it turned out to be a mistake, it was one he definitely would not make again.

The girls seemed subdued at dinner, though they ate with the same enthusiasm they'd displayed ever since Amelia had begun cooking. The chicken cacciatore tasted delicious, and the angel-hair pasta she'd made to go with it really hit the spot. Ted had never felt the need to make idle chatter, so he was content to eat his meal in the relatively unusual peace and quiet.

Amelia, on the other hand, kept shooting glances between Ted and the twins, almost as if she wanted to say something but had no idea what.

The flowers he'd brought had disappeared. He assumed that meant everyone had taken them to their rooms. Now he wished he'd simply not given in to the impulse and tried to do something nice. Live and learn, he told himself. Live and learn.

Amelia knew the twins were upset that their father had given her flowers. For her part, she completely understood his logic—he'd bought some for the girls and hadn't wanted her to feel left out. It was a sweet and kind gesture, and she wanted to figure out a way to thank him while helping his daughters understand.

Unfortunately, she discarded every idea she had. Without doing a long and boring lecture that would reek of "the lady doth protest too much," everything else she thought of came off as too flippant.

So she said nothing, serving up one of her favorite dinner recipes, heart aching as everyone consumed their meal in silence.

When she brought out the store-bought tiramisu she'd gotten for dessert, everyone said they were too full. Ted escaped to the living room and turned on the TV, and Yvonne disappeared into her room. Only Yolanda lingered, trying really hard not to look at the cake.

"I'm going to have a small slice anyway," Amelia announced, smiling. "Would you like me to cut you a teeny sliver too?"

Worrying her bottom lip with her teeth, Yolanda finally nodded. "Sure."

"Good," Amelia replied. "Dessert always tastes much better when you can eat it with someone else."

The teenager flashed her a tiny smile and watched quietly while Amelia cut them both a slice of the rich cake. "Here you go, sweetie." She slid a plate in front of Yolanda before taking a seat next to her. "I'm glad I decided to go ahead and buy this at the bakery. I found a recipe but it seemed a little too labor-intensive."

Mouth full of cake, Yolanda nodded. When she'd swallowed, she eyed Amelia. "You really like to cook, don't you?"

"I do." Amelia smiled. "I wanted to go to culinary school after I graduated high school, but my mother didn't approve, so I went to a regular college instead." It had been years since she'd thought about that. She'd actually become a therapist because that was what her mom had wanted. She'd been surprised to learn she was actually good at it. As for cooking, she'd relegated that skill to the occasional dinner party.

Now her mom had passed. For the first time, Amelia realized she might have a second chance. Once all this mess with Simon had been cleared up, she might still take a shot at making her long-ago dream come true.

"You would make an excellent chef," Yolanda said, taking another bite of her tiramisu. "Everything you've made us for dinner has been delicious."

Touched, Amelia thanked her.

Once she'd finished, Yolanda carried her plate to the sink and rinsed it off. She returned to the table and sat again, her expression serious. "I want to talk to you about the flowers," she finally said.

Amelia nodded, hiding her surprise.

"I just want to make sure you understand that Dad only bought them for you because he didn't want you to feel left out. He probably bought ours first and then decided it would be a nice gesture to get you some too."

"That's exactly how I pictured it too," Amelia exclaimed. "I was so worried that you and your sister thought there was some other reason."

"I don't know about Yvonne," Yolanda replied. "But I'm glad we're all on the same page."

"Except for one thing. I think your father feels pretty awful. It's a shame to make a man feel bad for doing something nice, you know?"

After considering her words, Yolanda nodded. "We thanked him. But yeah, we made him—and you—uncomfortable. That was wrong."

Amelia liked how Yolanda didn't blame her twin. She wanted to ask Yolanda how she was going to fix it, but didn't want to push.

"I need to talk to him," Yolanda finally said. She slid out of her seat and nodded at Amelia. "Thank you."

Once Yolanda had headed off into the den to talk to Ted, Amelia finished straightening up the kitchen. She planned to make biscuits and sausage gravy for breakfast in the morning and had everything ready.

Then she headed off to her room. She'd purchased a smallish television that afternoon and wanted to get it hooked up. She'd even bought a set of rabbit ears, not wanting to ask Ted to hook her up to his cable or satellite or whatever he used.

It took her a little bit, but she eventually had it up and running. Satisfied and feeling accomplished, she picked a local channel and left it on there while she opened her laptop and checked the internet for any news of Simon.

As usual, she found the same old stories, most of them a day or two old. With no sightings, no activity, media interest had faded. She wasn't sure if that was a good thing or bad, and she knew better than to let herself get too comfortable.

After her search, she closed the laptop and went down the hall to brush her teeth and wash up for bed. Then she changed into her pajamas and climbed into her bed to watch TV with her pillow propped up behind her back.

The next morning, Amelia got up at five, put on her workout clothes and headed to the gym. She and Rayna had decided they'd get their fitness in before starting the day, an idea she'd embraced wholeheartedly.

They'd both signed up for an online workout program, planning to do it together. Today would be day one.

When Amelia arrived at the gym, she saw Rayna already inside, warming up on the treadmill. There were only two other people at the gym this early, both men, one of them using free weights, the other on a machine.

Amelia hurried inside, jumping on the treadmill next to her friend. "Good morning."

"Mornin'," Rayna replied. "Funny how getting up this early sounds like a great idea until you actually do it."

"I don't mind." Amelia increased her speed to a slow jog. "I've always been a morning person anyway. I put on some Crock-Pot oatmeal last night, so it will be ready for everyone to eat this morning."

"Oh look." Rayna watched the television mounted on the wall above them. "The morning news has devoted an entire segment to the Coffee Shop Killer."

Inwardly, Amelia cringed. She wanted to ask her

friend to change the channel but knew that might make Rayna suspicious. Instead, she tried to take a more casual approach. "I hate hearing about serial killers," she said. "It creeps me out."

"Really." Rayna looked at her with surprise. "I find them fascinating. Especially since I took part in capturing one right here in town."

Maybe if she could keep Rayna talking about that, she might divert her attention from the news story. If anyone would be able to see through Amelia's disguise and recognize her as the woman Simon hunted, it would be Rayna the sheriff.

Rayna launched into her story, which Amelia had heard before, though not directly from her. Apparently, Rayna's husband had shown up in town demanding a renewed search for his friend's missing sister. "That's how we met," Rayna said, smiling at the memory. "I couldn't tear my eyes away from him, but I tried to play it cool. It turned out, there was more than one victim."

"I read about that," Amelia admitted, trying not to look at the TV screen. "His friend's sister was still alive, right?"

"Yes. And he made a mistake. One of the high school girls he tried to grab escaped, which proved to be his undoing. In the end, we caught the serial killer and got engaged."

The news anchor was recapping the Coffee Shop Killer story, showing clips from the courtroom where Amelia had testified. Any minute now, they'd be showing her face.

"How about we start those workouts?" Amelia asked, hitting the stop button on the treadmill. "I think we have to do some warm-up exercises first."

"Okay." Rayna jumped off too, following Amelia to the free weights section, which now was vacant. Rayna pulled out her tablet and logged in to the gym's Wi-Fi. "Have you had a chance to check out the video?"

"I did last night," Amelia said, relief flooding her, though she knew she couldn't show it. "Today we're working lower body. It seems pretty straightforward. Squats and dead lifts, calf raises, stationary lunges and hip raises, I think."

"Good memory." Rayna gave her a considering look. "You sound familiar with the exercises. I take it you've done this sort of thing before?"

"I have." Amelia couldn't tell her friend that after escaping Simon, she'd been determined to get as strong as possible, practicing moves she'd gotten from a book about women's strength training. She also incorporated High Intensity Interval Training, or HIIT.

While Rayna pulled up the video on her phone, Amelia opened her notebook. She liked to keep a workout log, writing down the exercise, the repetitions and the weights. That way she had something she could improve on next time.

Mirroring each other, they began the workout. Meanwhile, the news story continued to play overhead. Amelia hoped they'd hurry up and move on to something else. But Rayna appeared riveted, watching it the entire time she went through the circuit.

"Round one complete," Amelia said, punching the timer on her smartwatch. "Now we rest for one minute before we do it again."

"Look," Rayna ordered, pointing at the TV. "That woman. Amelia, that's you."

Amelia's heart sank. On the screen, the camera had

zoomed in on her face. Despite the different hair color and style, despite the glasses she'd worn then, the likeness was unmistakable. Even worse, they flashed her name up on the screen—her real name. Amelia Ferguson. Now she wished she'd made more of an effort to change it.

Rayna took a step closer, her expression concerned. "Are you on the run, Amelia?"

Since there was nothing else to do but come clean, Amelia nodded. "Please don't tell anyone. I've been so careful and there's absolutely nothing to trace me here. Until Simon is apprehended and put back behind bars, I'm not safe. He's actively hunting me."

"I get it and I won't." Rayna reached out and pulled Amelia in for a quick hug. "Still, it's probably a good thing that I at least know, being sheriff and all. At least if the Coffee Shop Killer somehow tracks you here, I'll know to protect you."

"True." Amelia looked down at her hands. "Though, honestly, if he gets wind of my location and shows up, if I find out about it ahead of time, I'm gone. Not only do I not want to take any chances of endangering any innocents like Ted Sanders and his family, but staying hidden is the only way I feel safe." Meeting her friend's gaze, she took a deep breath. "I hate running, but I'll do it as long as I have to."

"Which means until he's caught." Rayna gave the TV a thoughtful look. "And from what I've been hearing, there hasn't been a single sighting. Most likely that means he's got someone helping him. Any idea who?"

"No. I was his therapist before he abducted me." *Calm, steady voice*, she told herself. "He claimed to have no family or friends. In fact, one of the things we were working on in therapy was for him to try to make new friends."

"I guess he did." Rayna set down her dumbbell and frowned. "I'm going to do some quiet investigating into this."

Horrified, Amelia grabbed her friend's arm. "No. Please don't. Just in case he's got someone on the inside watching. I can't take that chance."

"I don't think…" Rayna began.

"Promise me," Amelia insisted. "Promise me you'll pretend this entire conversation never happened. To you, I'm still Amelia Smith. No one of any consequence."

Rayna eyed her for a moment, not saying anything. Finally, she shook her head. "Fine. I won't investigate or poke around. But, honey, know this. You'll *always* be someone of consequence. You're part of our town now and my friend. That right there makes you important. Don't you ever forget it."

Some of the heavy tension that had settled into her chest eased up a bit. "I won't," Amelia replied. "And thank you for agreeing to keep quiet about all this."

"You know, as much publicity as this case is getting, sooner or later someone else is going to notice the resemblance," Rayna said. "What are you going to do then?"

"I don't know. Deny, deny, deny?" Even Amelia realized her attempt at lightheartedness fell flat. "I'll deal with it when it happens. *If* it happens."

Rayna nodded. "All righty, then. Let's finish this workout." She lightly punched Amelia's shoulder. "Just remember, you're not alone. I'm always going to have your back."

Chapter 5

Ted listened with half an ear to the soft murmur of Yolanda's and Amelia's voices, and a sense of peace settled over him. Things were going to work out, all because he'd listened to Serenity once again. While he wasn't sure he believed in psychics or mediums or any of the things Serenity claimed to be, she always gave him great advice. He owed her, because it seemed like Amelia might just be the feminine influence his daughters had needed. He figured Yvonne would come around eventually. Of the two of them, he worried about her the most.

Yolanda appeared, shifting her weight from one foot to the other.

"What's wrong, honey?" he asked softly, wishing he'd decided to sit on the couch instead of his recliner so he could pat the sofa cushion next to him for her.

"I'm sorry, Dad." Twisting her hands in front of her, she met his gaze and held it. "I really loved that you cared enough to bring me flowers and I know Yvonne does too."

Touched, he pushed to his feet and gathered her to him in a big hug. "Thank you. You also understand that me buying Amelia flowers doesn't—"

"Mean anything," she finished. "I know. I talked to Amelia about it too. She gets that you didn't want her to feel left out. I'll make sure Yvonne understands. But I wanted to tell you thank you again."

"You're amazing, you know that?" He kissed her cheek.

She squirmed and giggled. "Daaaad." Bouncing up, she grinned at him before taking off for her room, leaving him alone in the den with the TV.

With a sigh, he went to the kitchen to get a second beer. He couldn't help but hope Amelia would come out and sit with him for a little bit. Funny that, he thought as he got settled back in his chair. He'd never been lonely before. He sure as hell shouldn't be lonely now.

As if on cue, his cell phone rang. When he saw Camille Winters's name come up on the caller ID, he nearly groaned out loud. Camille worked as the Getaway librarian and was a member of the Baptist Women's Singles Group. She had been doggedly pursuing him for years, ever since he'd made the mistake of meeting her for drinks two years ago.

Maybe because he'd been feeling sorry for himself, though more likely because he knew from experience that she'd keep calling until he picked up, he went ahead and pressed the accept-call button. "Hello?"

"Hey, Ted. It's Camille," she drawled, all syrupy sweet. "How are you doing?"

"Fine." He struggled to be polite, but he also knew she'd seize on the smallest thing as an indication to believe he secretly liked her. He might as well cut to the chase, even if doing so bordered on being curt. "What's up, Camille?"

Silence. Then she sighed. "You're not in the mood to chat, I see. Well then. There's a rumor going around and I figured I'd go straight to you and settle it." She took a deep, shaky breath. "Ted, some of the ladies are saying you've shacked up with some woman from up north. A redhead." She said the last with the kind of disdain reserved for vermin.

Shacked up. Interesting choice of phrase.

"Oh, you mean Amelia? Yes, she is staying with me," he said, trying to decide whether or not to elaborate. In the end, he decided to stick to the facts, though he wouldn't offer up more than the basics unless she directly asked.

Camille let out a wail, loud enough to make him wince. "Is that all you needed?" he asked, hoping against hope that he might get out of this awkward conversation easily.

"I want to meet her," she said, her tone silky smooth. "She must be something, to have captured the heart of the elusive Ted Sanders. I'll get together with some of the Bible study ladies and invite her to one of our potlucks."

Time to come clean. The last thing he wanted to do was throw Amelia in the middle of those women. "Camille, Amelia isn't my girlfriend," he said. "She's my housekeeper."

Silence again. Then Camille laughed. And laughed

some more. "That makes sense," she finally sputtered. "It didn't before, but now it does. You have a great day, Ted. 'Bye." She ended the call.

Shaking his head, Ted once again felt like he'd dodged a bullet. Camille had always been pushy, but she'd always backed off the instant he asked her to. At least now she and her friends wouldn't be targeting Amelia.

Changing the channel, he caught the tail end of yet another program talking about the Coffee Shop Killer. It seemed the authorities were getting really worried about some woman who'd been the only victim to escape. He shook his head and turned the television off. It hadn't been that long since Getaway had their own serial killer. He remembered his own terror when one of the girls who went to school with his daughters had disappeared, and how he and some of the other fathers had gathered together in the motel parking lot, ready to confront the man everyone had suspected as being the murderer.

They'd been wrong. Very, very wrong. He'd been ashamed of his participation in what he now thought of as a near mob scene against the man who'd become Rayna's husband. Looking back on that time, he understood he'd allowed fear and suspicion to propel him into acting in a way that he never would have if he'd taken the time to think about it.

He got to his feet and clicked the remote off.

"Not in the mood for television?" Amelia's soft voice startled him. She leaned against the doorjamb, wearing buffalo-plaid flannel pajamas and fuzzy slippers. She looked cute and so unbelievably sexy that his mouth went dry.

Realizing she was eyeing him, waiting for a response, he managed to get himself together enough to reply.

"Just tired of hearing about serial killers," he said. "But if you're coming out here to watch a show, I'll be happy to turn it back on."

"No, that's okay. I bought a TV for my room, as you might have noticed last night. That way I don't have to intrude."

Regarding her steadily, he shook his head. "Actually, I enjoy the company."

Was it his imagination, or did she blush?

"Where are the girls?" she asked.

"In their room. They'd rather do anything else besides hang out with their old dad."

This made her smile. "I'm sure you remember how it was when you were their age."

"I do." He heaved a sigh, eyeing the couch, and came to a quick decision. "Come on. Sit with me. I'll let you choose the show."

It was a big couch, one he'd bought when the girls were younger and used to invite all their friends over. He sat at one end, and after a moment's hesitation, Amelia took a spot halfway between him and the other end.

He handed her the remote. "Anything but the serial killer thing," he said.

"Agreed." She shivered a little.

Now he wished he'd lit a fire in the fireplace. "Are you cold?" He pointed to a fuzzy throw the girls kept on the couch. "You can use that blanket if you want."

"I'm all right." Though she held on to the remote, she made no move to turn on the TV. "Do you mind if we talk instead?"

"Sure." He studied her face, wondering how it was

possible that she didn't appear to realize how her beauty affected him. He'd known several attractive women and they'd all seemed well aware of the power of their looks.

"I don't want to be too intrusive," she said softly. "But do you mind if I ask what happened to the girls' mother?"

"She decided she didn't want to do this." He waved his hand in the general direction of his daughters' room. "Marriage, motherhood, any of it. So she took off. The girls were six months old."

The shock he saw in her expression reminded him of how he'd felt that day, coming back to the house for lunch and finding the two infants crying in their cribs. Their diapers were wet and they were hungry. Their mother was nowhere in sight.

She'd left him a note. This wasn't her, it said. She'd never expected it to be so hard. She didn't love him or them or herself, so she was going before she hurt someone.

He'd heard of postpartum depression. He figured that was what had made Lorelei do this. He vowed to find her and get her help.

But first he had to take care of the babies. Once that was done, he'd called Serenity, the only woman he felt comfortable with asking for help. She came immediately, and he took off to find his wife and bring her home.

As he relayed all this to Amelia, something in her face told him she already suspected what he was going to say next.

"I was too late," he said, hoping she'd let him leave it at that. Finding his wife's lifeless body had nearly done him in. Only the knowledge that he had two tiny girls who needed him had kept him going.

"That's hard," she said, sliding over and placing her hand on his arm. "I'm sorry."

With the ease of long practice, he shrugged off the melancholy. "It's been a long time," he said. "I've moved on. The girls don't even remember her."

"Do they know?" she asked, the sympathy in her gaze touching something deep inside him.

"Only that their mother died when they were infants. I haven't decided whether or not to tell them someday. I might not. I'm not sure knowing is in their best interests."

"I'm sure you'll do what's best," she said. "But I always try to err on the side of the truth."

"Unless the truth rips their hearts out and sets them on fire," he pointed out.

A ghost of a smile tugged at her lips. "Point taken."

For one heart-stopping second, he thought she might kiss him. Suddenly, he wanted her to, *craved* the feeling of her mouth on his.

Instead, she held up the remote and turned the television on. He pushed down his disappointment, chiding himself for his own foolishness, and tried to relax while she studied the on-screen guide, looking for a show.

She settled on a crime drama just coming on, one of those fast-paced shows that took place in a hospital somewhere up north. She quickly became enthralled in the story, gaze locked on the screen, while he couldn't seem to tear his eyes away from her. If she noticed, she gave no sign.

It should have worried him, this sudden torrent of attraction, which felt more than merely physical. As if he were somehow magically young again, experiencing the dizzying rush of emotions he hadn't believed he'd ever feel again. He'd been dead inside for so long that he'd begun to think when Lorelei died she'd taken his capacity for love with her.

Love. Not what this was, he knew. After all, he barely knew Amelia, though he swore there was something familiar about her, even if he wasn't sure what. The way he had begun to feel had to be because for the first time since his wife had left, he'd allowed a woman into his home and his life.

Which meant he needed to start making himself see her as an employee. He didn't want to screw this up. For the first time in a long time, his life actually seemed to be going in the right direction. He could see light at the end of what had previously been a long, dark tunnel. She took meticulous care of their house and their meals, letting him know they mattered to her. His girls had started to react to her, opening up. The sound of their laughter relieved bands of tension he hadn't even been aware he carried.

Nope, no matter what he might think he wanted, he couldn't afford to act on it. Ever.

Amelia enjoyed the easy routine of her days at Ted's ranch. The girls were beginning to get used to her and actually sought out her company occasionally. Ted treated her with a quiet courtesy and respect. They all seemed to enjoy and appreciate her cooking and her efforts around the house. She felt…needed. Something she hadn't even been aware of missing in her life.

She figured she might as well enjoy it while it lasted. Because eventually, due to the unrelenting media coverage, her identity was going to be revealed. Rayna had already figured it out and she'd bet others wouldn't be too far behind. She'd managed to get Ted to change the channel earlier as a precaution, though she'd noticed he kept staring at her. No doubt trying to figure out where he'd seen her before.

If she'd had time and unlimited funds, she might have made more of an attempt to change her appearance. Plastic surgery perhaps, rather than a simple change of hair color and switching from eyeglasses to contacts. But everything had happened so fast, and once she'd learned of Simon's escape, she'd barely had enough time to gather her belongings and empty her bank account. She'd known beyond a shadow of a doubt that the first thing he'd do as a free man would be to carry out the threatening promise he'd made to her in the courtroom. He'd make her pay.

She'd had no choice but to run.

And now, all these weeks later, Simon still hadn't been recaptured. With Amelia watching and waiting and hoping, she knew time marched on regardless. It wasn't easy, trying to lose herself in her new life, her new persona, but she did the best she could, hoping she'd chosen well by picking Getaway as the best small town to disappear in.

Once he knew, she figured Ted wouldn't want her around his daughters. For whatever reason, back home in White Plains, a lot of people had treated her as if being captured and tortured by a serial killer had somehow tainted her. While she doubted Ted would be like that, any reasonable man might worry that her presence would put his daughters in danger if Simon discovered her location.

Personally, she had to agree. Of course, if she ever got even the faintest tip that he'd been sniffing around west Texas, she'd be in the wind so fast no one would even notice her leaving.

She honestly hoped it wouldn't come to that. She liked it here. Best-case scenario—Simon was located, recaptured, and she could finally exhale in relief. She knew she couldn't ever go back to her previous life, and surprisingly, she didn't want to. Until she'd put all this behind her, she knew better than to even think about making any big decisions.

All this... So much, encompassed in two little words.

Though she tried not to think about what she'd gone through, it wasn't easy or healthy to suppress so much. As a therapist, she knew this but saw no other option. Mostly, she managed to succeed during the day, keeping herself busy to keep the thoughts at bay. Nighttime was a different story. Despite her best efforts, she couldn't control her dreams. And she dreamed about Simon a lot. Sometimes, just the sessions when she'd believed him to be just another client. A lonely, depressed man with low-self-esteem issues who needed professional help to work through them. She hadn't seen the monster lurking under his self-effacing veneer, not even once. He'd given her no clue, no psychological signs, nothing. Even when she'd come to and found him bending over her and realized her hands and feet were bound, she hadn't believed the evidence of her own eyes. "This must be some mistake," she'd told him, her bewilderment showing in her voice. "Help me get free, Simon. Please."

He'd met her gaze then, his expression cold, his eyes full of loathing. "You're despicable," he'd spit. "You think you're so much better than me, just like all the others."

Those words, that tone, had been when her first warning bell had sounded. "I don't understand," she said, mind still muddled from whatever drug he'd given her.

"I talked to you, week after week, hoping you would see past the surface BS to the real me, but you never did. I wanted to connect," he continued, the former belligerent tone sliding into something silkier and much more dangerous.

A shiver snaked up her spine as she began to realize exactly how much trouble she might be in.

Later, she'd learned that he usually killed his captives within the first two days. But for whatever reason, he kept Amelia longer. Days turned into a week, then two. Though he did unspeakable things to her, showing her how her pain brought him pleasure, she worked hard to gain his trust. When he confided in her, describing his numerous kills as the Coffee Shop Killer, she pretended to find him fascinating. She wanted to live, by whatever means possible, all the while watching for the slightest opportunity to escape.

Gasping for breath, she jerked herself awake and up, pushing out of the bed as if it were some sort of medieval torture device. While she hadn't yet gotten to the point of dreading and avoiding sleep altogether, she could foresee that happening in the future if these nightmares continued. As a trained therapist, she'd counseled numerous patients who'd suffered from similar night terrors, and though she tried to heal herself, she'd begun to realize that she might not be able to do so alone.

Too restless to attempt to go back to sleep, she decided to go rummage in the kitchen for a late-night snack and bring it back to her room to watch whatever she could find on at 2:00 a.m.

Turning on her bedroom light, she crept out into the

dark and silent house, praying she didn't wake anyone. She made her way to the kitchen, glad Ted left the small light in the vent hood over the stove on at night. She debated for a moment, then flicked on the kitchen light, which shouldn't be enough to wake anyone. Then she rummaged in the refrigerator, emerging with bread and cold cuts, cheese and mayo.

Such a small thing made her happy. Humming quietly to herself, she began assembling her sandwich. Once she'd finished, she turned to put everything back in the fridge.

"Are you all right?" Ted's voice, raspy with sleep.

She froze. "I thought I was being so quiet. Did I wake you?"

"I don't think so." He dragged his hand through his already tousled hair. He wore flannel pajama bottoms and apparently had grabbed a T-shirt to wear also. "I'm not sure what did."

Still holding the bread and sandwich fixings, she asked him if he wanted her to make him one too. This made him chuckle, a deep and sexy sound that woke up every nerve ending in her body.

"Sure. Why not?" He took a seat at the kitchen table while she busied herself making a second sandwich. She swore she could feel the heat of his gaze, even though she kept her back to him. Suddenly overly self-conscious that she wore nothing underneath her pajamas, she felt her breasts tighten. Hell, her entire body felt tight, tingling in places she knew damn well it shouldn't.

Forcing herself to focus on the food, she finished assembling his sandwich. Once she had everything put together, she returned the food to the fridge and carried both plates over to the table.

Though she'd intended to eat hers in her room, she pulled out the chair across from him and sat. "Dig in," she said, smiling.

He did. They ate together in silence, the house quiet, the rest of the world asleep. It felt strangely intimate, but she wasn't uncomfortable. Instead, she kept sneaking glances at him, watching him as he ate, stopping herself in time before reaching out to brush a bit of mayo off his upper lip.

How someone could look so damn sexy eating a sandwich, she didn't know. And she shouldn't be having these thoughts at all.

Abruptly she jumped to her feet. "Let me get this cleaned up so we both can go back to bed."

Though that hadn't come out right, having something to do with her hands helped. She rinsed the dishes and stacked them in the dishwasher. When she turned around, he'd gotten to his feet too. Big and sleepy and too damn cute for her peace of mind. She dragged her gaze away, trying to catch her breath.

"Thanks for the sandwich," he said quietly. "I hope you manage to get back to sleep."

She nodded. "You too."

As she passed him, he reached for the light switch. "Are you good on finding your way in the dark?"

"Sure," she said, sidling past him.

He turned the light off. Blinking, she kept one hand on the wall, waiting until her eyes adjusted to the darkness before moving slowly forward. She sensed, rather than felt, Ted behind her.

At the doorway to her room, she turned, meaning to tell him good-night. Instead, the unexpected movement just as he was sidling past her made him stumble.

He reached out to steady himself, managing to grab her shoulder and nearly dragging her down with him.

Somehow, they managed to cling to each other and remain on their feet. "Sorry," he mumbled, letting go.

In that instant, acting on impulse, driven by need and a visceral, raw desire, she grabbed him and pulled him close again. She could barely see his face, only hollows and shadows. Despite that or maybe because of it, she reached up and pulled him down for a kiss.

The instant her lips touched his, heat sizzled between them. He deepened the kiss, shifting his body so that she was nestled in close to him. Dazed, she let herself get lost in the taste and feel of him, marveling that it was everything she could have imagined and more.

Just as she realized she could be in danger of seriously losing all self-control, the hall light flicked on.

Quickly, they broke apart. Yvonne stood at the end of the hallway, fully dressed, shoes in hand, clearly just now sneaking back into the house.

"What the…?" Ted and his daughter said at the same time.

Amelia looked from one to the other and slowly backed into her room. She quickly closed the door, aware she could most likely still hear everything, though she wasn't sure she wanted to.

"Where have you been?" Ted demanded, pitching his voice low, though anger still clearly simmered under his attempted calm tone.

"Out. Why were you kissing Amelia in a pitch-dark hallway?" Yvonne wanted to know. "Are you two sleeping together?"

From the other side of her door, Amelia winced.

"Not that it's any of your business, but we are not," Ted responded.

"Yet," Yvonne muttered. "I knew you lied to us."

"First up, I did not. Secondly, changing the subject will not get you off the hook. Where have you been and why are you sneaking in the house after 2:00 a.m. on a school night?"

Silence.

"I'm waiting, young lady."

"I went out with some friends," Yvonne finally answered.

"What friends?"

"This isn't about them," Yvonne protested.

"Maybe their parents have no idea they were out this late, just like I didn't." Ted's tight voice relayed his anger. "I'm thinking I need to call them and find out. I want all of their names. Right now."

Silence again. From inside her small room, Amelia waited anxiously to hear what Yvonne would say.

"No." The quiet defiance in Yvonne's single-word answer made Amelia catch her breath. Depending on how Ted responded, this could go one of two ways. It could blow up, wake up Yolanda and keep them all up for whatever remained of the darkness. Or not.

She wasn't surprised when Ted responded with an order to go to her room. "We'll talk about this in the morning," he promised. "Now go try and get some sleep."

After that, she heard only the normal quiet of the house.

Abandoning her earlier idea of watching television, she crawled beneath her covers and shut off the light. She couldn't avoid sleep forever.

When her alarm went off a scant three and a half hours later, she crawled from her bed, her entire body aching. She'd slept, though, and that was something. If she'd dreamed, she couldn't remember. Another good thing. Maybe this day might turn out all right after all.

A quick shower and she made her way to the kitchen, just as she always did. Started the coffee brewing and assembled the ingredients to make blueberry pancakes. She set the table, glad Ted was big on them having breakfast as a family, despite the hectic rush to get to school. She'd learned to time breakfast perfectly, catching them all mid–mad rush. Pouring out their usual glasses of orange juice, she preheated the griddle. Humming, she began measuring and mixing, stirring and pouring.

As everyone arrived in the kitchen, she'd just transferred the first batch of pancakes to a platter and placed them in the middle of the table, along with syrup and butter.

Both girls wouldn't look at her as they took their seats. Instead of echoing their father's cheery good-morning, they stared down at their plates before helping themselves to pancakes.

Ted's jaw tightened as he met Amelia's gaze, but he didn't comment. Amelia decided she wouldn't either, so she went back to the griddle to get the second batch started.

By the time they were done, both girls had gulped their juice down and declared they were full. "Can you take us to school early?" Yolanda asked Ted while her sister went to get their backpacks.

He looked up, midbite. "I'm not finished. And Amelia hasn't even sat down to eat yet."

"But we need to be there early," Yolanda insisted.

"Mrs. Pierce is assigning the special social studies projects today. Whoever gets to her first with their topic is assigned it. All the good topics go early."

"It's true, Dad," Yvonne chimed in, her expression stony. "And I've got the best topic picked out already. I want to make sure I get it."

"What period do you have social studies?" Ted asked. "I know that's not your first class."

"It's not. But Mrs. Pierce lets everyone come to her room before classes start and give her their choices. That's why we want to go early."

"Makes sense." Ted blotted his mouth with his napkin, drained his coffee cup and stood. "Yvonne, we haven't discussed last night yet. Don't think I've forgotten, because I haven't. We'll talk about it after school. I'll be picking you up today instead of Amelia."

"Good," Yolanda muttered, shooting a glance full of disgust Amelia's way. "And by the way, I had nothing to do with Yvonne sneaking out. I didn't even know she'd left. I was sound asleep."

Yvonne stuck her tongue out at her sister, reminding Amelia of just how young they were.

"Let's go," Ted said, herding them out the door without a backward glance. Amelia listened as he started his truck. She heard the sound of tires on gravel as he drove away. Then she sat down and ate her pancakes alone.

While she knew there was no benefit to be had by beating herself up, she couldn't help but berate herself for kissing Ted. She should have simply continued to ignore the sexual tension simmering between them.

Would apologizing make things worse? Or should she simply pretend nothing had happened, since as time went on, she knew the drama of all this would fade?

That was what she would do. Unless the girls or Ted brought it up, wanting to talk about it, she'd go back to her everyday routine and play it by ear. Which carried a certain kind of irony. The Amelia Ferguson she'd been had done nothing impulsively and left nothing to chance. Every hour, every minute of her day had been meticulously planned. Now it seemed all she did was wing it.

Chapter 6

As Ted drove the girls to school, he surreptitiously watched them in the rearview mirror. As always, Yolanda had settled down immediately, intent on scrolling something on her phone, while Yvonne appeared fidgety. Her constant bouts of nervous energy had him worrying about drugs. Though this seemed impossible to him, he knew he couldn't afford to relax his guard. But she was only fourteen. This raising teenagers had barely just begun and he already wondered how he would survive it. And he still had to deal with her breaking every rule he'd set, not realizing how she might have endangered herself with her act of willful defiance.

He took a deep breath. Now was as good a time as any.

"Yvonne, why were you sneaking out last night?" he asked her, barely three minutes into the drive.

Pursing her lips, she met his gaze in the rearview

and glared at him. "I already told you. I was meeting up with friends."

"*Friends* as in plural? Or just one person?"

She rolled her eyes, as if she couldn't believe anyone could be that dim. "Why would I meet one person?"

"You would if it was Chad Carpenter," Yolanda pointed out.

Yvonne blushed. "Well, yeah, but it wasn't. I just met up with a bunch of friends."

"Who?" he asked.

"Nobody you know," she answered, returning her attention to her notebook, clearly dismissing him.

Alarm bells went off inside his head. In the past, the twins had shared the same set of friends. "*New* friends?" he pressed, trying to sound casual.

She didn't respond.

"Yvonne, I'm speaking to you. I asked you a question. These people you met up with last night, are they new friends?"

"Maybe." Yvonne's defensive tone had even Yolanda looking askance at her.

"They aren't *my* friends," Yolanda pointed out helpfully, earning herself a baleful glance from her sister. "I've seen her hanging around with them at school, but none of them would bother talking to me. I guess I'm not cool enough."

More alarm bells. What made someone cool these days? He knew when he'd been a teenager, the cool kids were either the jocks or athletes or the cheerleaders. There was also a group of kids who were stoners or smokers. They'd viewed themselves as the cool ones. The rest of them had been squarely in the middle, aka obscurity. Which had suited Ted just fine.

As far as he could tell, though, Yvonne didn't seem to fit into either category. Of course, he clearly had no idea what she kept hidden from him.

They were only about one more mile away from the school. Ted thought about pulling over so they could finish this discussion, but knew the girls wanted to be there early. Still, he couldn't simply let it go. There was too much at stake.

"Just tell me this," he began. "Were drugs involved?"

"Dad!" Both girls gasped in unison. "You know better than that."

"Just answer the question, Yvonne. You've been acting really…different lately. I need to know if you've started experimenting with anything."

"No. That's gross." Her voice caught and he realized she was almost in tears. They pulled up in front of the high school and he'd barely coasted to a stop before Yvonne opened the door and shot out of the car. Both Ted and Yolanda watched her go, moving at a brisk walk.

Turning in his seat, Ted eyed his other daughter. "Is she okay?"

"I don't know." Yolanda shrugged, trying for nonchalance but unable to hide the hurt in her voice. "She tries to pretend like she doesn't even know me at school. She ditched all of our old friends and started hanging around with a new group of people. A few of them are popular, so there's that." She swallowed hard. "I think Yvonne is embarrassed to be my sister. When she's with her new friends, it's like she's a totally different person. I tried to talk to her about it and she said she needed a change. That's all I know."

His heart ached. "Thank you, sweetheart. And I'm sorry you're going through all that."

"Don't worry about me," Yolanda snapped. "Yvonne's the one with issues." Before he could respond to that or ask anything else, Yolanda got out of the car and headed into school, slamming the truck door shut behind her.

Watching her go, Ted shook his head. No matter how he tried, he hadn't gotten used to the ever-present ache of worry in his chest that had started when the girls turned thirteen. He dreaded how he'd feel once they were old enough to drive.

Someone tapped on their car horn behind him, reminding him he needed to leave. Pulling away, he drove back toward home. He'd try to have a more in-depth conversation with Yvonne after school. Right now, he needed to figure out what to say to Amelia. He still had to address the other elephant in the room.

She'd kissed him. More than that, that kiss had been... electric. He'd gone to bed aroused and had tossed and turned for hours, tormented by sensual images of her. Finally, he'd had to take matters into his own hands so he could get some relief.

He still had no idea what had made Amelia decide to kiss him. Especially since, until that very moment, neither of them had so much as flirted with the other.

Since nothing could or would happen between them, the solution should have been simple. Pretend like nothing had happened. Instead, since his already troubled daughter had managed to witness the hot kiss while sneaking in from doing who knew what, the simple kiss had now become *a thing*.

He'd need to talk to Amelia so he could make sure they were on the same page. They were both adults, he reasoned. If they addressed the issue head-on, surely they could settle it with a minimum amount of fuss.

After all, Amelia wasn't Camille. She'd shown no interest in pursuing anything more than a job.

Pulling up and parking, he took a deep breath before walking into the house. As soon as he entered the kitchen, Amelia turned to face him, wiping her hands down the front of her jeans. "I was up all night worrying. I want you to know that I'm so sorry," she said, words spilling from her in a rush. "That kiss never should have happened and I promise you it won't happen again."

"Whew." Removing his hat, he dragged one hand through his hair. "I agree. It was a mistake. We were both half-asleep, it was dark, who knows. Can we just pretend it never happened?"

"We can." She frowned. "You and I, that is. But Yvonne saw it and blew it up into a much bigger deal than it is. By now, I'm sure she has Yolanda thinking along the same lines. I'd prefer to talk this out with them. If the girls ask me about it, I'm going to be honest with them. I acted on impulse, I was half-asleep, or whatever other excuses I can come up with."

Not sure what to say, he nodded instead and went for another cup of coffee. Part of him wanted to ask her why, but the sane, rational side of him was afraid to hear the answer.

"In fact, I really feel we should both talk to them about it. Present a united front. That way we can cut off any speculation before it gets out of hand."

Speculation. He supposed that was her way of saying prevent the twins from thinking he and Amelia were sleeping together. His body stirred at the thought.

Time to change the subject.

"I'm worried about Yvonne," he said, tentative. The only other person he ever discussed his children with had always been Serenity. However, Amelia had been there when Yvonne tried sneaking back in.

"I think you should be," she replied, carrying her own mug over to the table. "Clearly, something is going on with her. It might be normal teenage rebellion or it could be something more. Have you been having issues with her at school?"

"Yep." He grimaced. "She's insisting on separation from her sister and all of the friends they shared. She now runs with a completely new circle and I'm not sure they're a good influence. Yolanda claims she doesn't know any of them. And she's skipping school and storming out of classes. While I'm guessing part of this is her trying to grow into her own identity, I'm really worried. I don't know what to do."

Her gaze steady, she started to reach out to him but apparently thought better of it and dropped her hand. "I suggest making an appointment with her school's guidance counselor. Once you discuss your concerns with him or her, you can have Yvonne brought in and hopefully the three of you can talk about what's going on."

He sat upright. "That's a great idea," he said slowly. "I've spoken to the assistant principal and a couple of the teachers, but no one ever suggested the counselor."

Amelia shrugged. "It's a great place to start. She might even benefit from some outside therapy."

Though he nodded, he didn't have the heart to tell her that outside therapy was most likely too far out of his budget. Instead, he finished his coffee, thanked her and headed down to the barn to begin his workday.

* * *

For a few minutes after Ted left, Amelia remained at the table sipping her coffee. Somehow, she'd ended up exactly where she was supposed to be. This family needed her, with her therapist skills. Ted tried so hard to be a good father. The love and fear he had for his girls made her heart ache.

Today she planned to go into town for groceries. Ted had given her two hundred dollars in cash and told her to stock the house up, though he cautioned her that she needed to try to stretch that money as far as she could. Since making lists was already her thing, she created a menu for the next two weeks, then began her grocery list.

In the middle of this, her cell rang. When she saw Rayna's name on the caller ID, she smiled. Though today wasn't their usual workout day, maybe Rayna had decided she wanted to see if Amelia had time to meet her at the gym.

"I've got news," Rayna said instead. "There's been a sighting of the Coffee Shop Killer."

Instantly, Amelia froze. "Where?"

"Florida. A woman claims he tried to grab her outside of a supermarket, but she fought free. There wasn't anything on security cameras to back up her claim. She says she got a good look at his face and she's positive it was him."

"That's not his MO," Amelia responded, disappointment replacing her initial alarm. "He doesn't just grab his victims off the street. He's more likely to meet them in a bar and charm them into leaving with him. The FBI knows this."

"Then I'm sure this woman is just trying for her fifteen minutes of fame."

"Unfortunately." Amelia dropped into a chair. "I really wish there'd be a genuine sighting of him. With him simply disappearing like this, I have no way of knowing where he might turn up." Like here. The thought made her shudder.

"From what I remember reading about serial killers like him," Rayna said, "they can only go so long without craving anther kill. Eventually, this guy won't be able to help himself. I imagine that's what the FBI is watching and waiting for."

Though Amelia knew Rayna was right, the thought of Simon torturing and killing another woman made her feel physically ill. "I just want him recaptured," she said. "And locked up behind bars, where he belongs."

"I hear you," Rayna agreed. "I'll let you know if I hear anything else."

"Thank you." Amelia hesitated. "Rayna, you're not doing any digging around, are you? I don't want you to do anything that might garner his attention."

"I'm not and I won't. I just happened to see the story on the morning news."

They chatted for a few moments about other things. Since Halloween was approaching, Rayna was working on making her daughter Lauren's costume. "She wants to be an astronaut," Rayna said proudly. "However, I may have to give in and buy the costume. Everything I've tried to put together doesn't look right."

"Text me a picture of it once you're done," Amelia said. "Ted just pulled up, so I need to let you go."

When Ted walked in with the girls, he hustled them into the kitchen and made them sit. He flashed Amelia an apologetic smile. "I've decided you were right. We need to talk this out."

Yvonne stared down at her hands, clasped together tightly on the table. Yolanda, on the other hand, watched Amelia closely, as if curious to see how she would react.

Though she'd been caught unprepared, Amelia already knew exactly what she wanted to say. The truth.

"First, I want to apologize to you girls," she began. Yvonne, who clearly hadn't been expecting this, stiffened, while Yolanda continued to eye Amelia with a certain curious intensity. "It was late, I was tired and, to be honest, feeling a bit sorry for myself. I kissed your dad. I shouldn't have, but I did. I've promised him and now I'm promising you that it won't happen again."

"Why?" Yvonne finally raised her head. "Why did you kiss him if you two don't have a thing going on?"

Deliberately keeping things light, Amelia shrugged. "Impulse, I guess. Stupid, I know. But I'm sure you've done something on the spur of the moment and regretted it later."

"I have," Yvonne mumbled. "Can I go now?"

"Not yet," Ted interjected. "Amelia has taken all the blame and I can't allow that. I'm just as much at fault as she is. We bumped into each other and kissed. That's all. And she's right—it will not happen again. But to me, that's not the issue here. Yvonne, I want to know what you were doing out so late. Where did you go? What could you possibly be doing until two o'clock in the morning?"

Her jaw tightened. "I already told you. I was hanging out with my friends. We just drive around and listen to music and talk."

Harmless, if she was telling the truth. But still, she was only fourteen. It had been a school night. And she'd been unapologetic about breaking the rules.

"I'm going to have to ground you." Ted's firm, inflexible tone had her blinking in shock. "Two weeks. No phone, no tablet, no going out other than to school and back. You have rules, Yvonne. No going out on school nights, for one. The second, even your weekend curfew is midnight, and that's for events that I actually know about and approve."

"That's not fair!" Yvonne protested. "You can't do this to me."

"You're fourteen years old. I can." He held out his hand. "Now please hand over your phone."

For one moment, Amelia thought the teenager was going to refuse. But then Yvonne shoved her phone across the table with a savage gesture and pushed back her chair so hard it crashed to the floor. "I hate you," she muttered, running from the room.

Ted stared after her in shock. "I can't believe she just said that."

"Well, she's really upset. That really wasn't cool," Yolanda pointed out. "It's one thing to ground her. But to take her phone? For two weeks? We get a lot of our school assignments on our phones. And if we have group assignments, that's how we work on things."

Stomach tied up in knots, Ted heaved a huge sigh. "Maybe I'll rethink this. Thank you, Yolanda."

Yolanda nodded and took off after her sister.

"Well, that didn't go the way I wanted," he said, shaking his head. "I really don't know what to do now. Taking her phone away was the worst punishment I could come up with."

Debating whether or not to get involved, Amelia decided to offer some suggestions. "It does sound like she needs her phone, maybe for schoolwork, but mostly because she's going to feel even more cut off from the world without it. Maybe you can come up with something else. Like having her do community service, maybe some kind of charity work. That will keep her busy and out of trouble. Plus, she might get a chance to realize her own life isn't really all that bad."

Ted studied her, his tight expression relaxing a little. "Another good idea," he said. "Thank you. I'm going to go get cleaned up. Holler when dinner is ready. I assume it will be the usual time?"

She'd made two large pans of chicken enchiladas. All she needed to do was pop them into the oven and heat up the Spanish rice and black beans. "Yes," she replied. "We'll eat at the usual time."

By the time they all filed back into the kitchen for the evening meal, the house smelled amazing. That, Amelia thought, was one of the things she loved about cooking—the scents.

"Mexican food?" Yolanda exclaimed, practically jumping up and down with glee. "That's my absolute favorite!"

Even Yvonne appeared interested, looking around the kitchen for a hint as to what exactly Amelia had made.

"Chicken-and-cheese-sour-cream enchiladas, along with rice and beans," Amelia told them. "They're about to come out of the oven and then I can dish them up."

Judging by the way everyone devoured the meal, her enchiladas were a success. Heart light, she began gathering some of the plates to start cleaning up. To her surprise, Yolanda jumped up and began to help. Working together, they made short work of loading the dishwasher. Yvonne remained at the table, staring at her phone, while Ted went over the day's mail.

"How'd things go at school today?" Ted asked, looking up, once Yolanda and Amelia had come back to the table.

"We got our first choices for the big project!" Yolanda announced gleefully. "I'm so excited."

Even Yvonne, who usually made it a practice to stare sullenly at her plate while shoveling food into her mouth, looked up and flashed a quick smile and nod.

"That means me taking you to school early paid off, huh?" Ted teased. "You're welcome."

"Seriously, thank you, Dad." Yolanda took a bite of her chicken enchilada and chewed slowly and carefully. "This is really good, Amelia."

"Thanks." Amelia smiled at her, trying to include Yvonne, even though she'd already returned her attention to her plate. "What topic did you choose?" she asked.

"I picked women who run successful farms," Yolanda replied. "It's the perfect subject for me to research, since I plan to become one someday."

Glancing at Ted to see his reaction to this statement, Amelia noted how he appeared to glow with pride.

"What about you, Yvonne?" Amelia asked. "What will your project be about?"

For a second, she thought Yvonne wasn't going to deign to answer. But then she raised her head and met Amelia's gaze, a half smile hovering on her lips.

"Serial killers," she said. "I plan to mostly focus on the recent ones, like the Coffee Shop Killer."

Horrified, Amelia froze, struggling to mask her expression. "Why?" she asked, before she could help herself. "Those men are horrible, evil people. What could you find interesting about them?"

But Yvonne had apparently said all she wanted to say. Head down, she dug back into her enchiladas.

"Everyone wanted that topic," Yolanda put in helpfully. "Ever since Getaway had our own serial killer, everyone has been fascinated with that subject. And you have to admit, that Coffee Shop Killer is pretty interesting. No one has been able to locate him in the eight weeks since he escaped."

"Nine weeks," Amelia corrected automatically. "He might be good at staying hidden, but he did awful, unspeakable things to women. I wouldn't think anyone would want to focus on someone like him." She shuddered, not bothering to hide it.

Both Yolanda and Ted eyed her, no doubt curious about her passionate response. Yvonne continued eating, ignoring the conversation.

"I can't help but imagine what it must have been like to have been one of those poor women he tortured and killed." Amelia knew she needed to close her mouth now, before she managed to give herself away. Still, she found it unbearable to think that a freshman high school student would not only be doing a lengthy report on Simon, but seemed to actually *admire* him.

Yvonne raised her head again, the gleam in her eyes making Amelia wonder if she somehow *knew*. "That's what's so interesting about it," she said. "I'm not only studying his methodology but hoping to delve into the psychological aspects of what drove him."

Psychological. Again, Amelia shuddered. She'd been his therapist and had never seen it coming. Whatever demons compelled Simon to torture, maim, rape and kill, he'd managed to keep them hidden from her. Until it was too late.

"Well, good luck with that." Amelia deliberately kept her tone light. "I'm not sure that particular serial killer ever told anyone his motives."

"He might not have," Yvonne retorted. "But some of the others did. I'm thinking I can find enough similarities to draw my own conclusions."

One brow raised, Ted nodded. "Well, you certainly seem invested in this project," he said. "I haven't seen you this interested in something for a long, long time."

Yvonne smiled again. "Thanks. I scored the best topic. Someone else would have gotten it if I hadn't been the first one there."

Amelia stared. Why Ted didn't appear to find this entire thing alarming, she had no idea. Of course, maybe she was the one overreacting. After all, no one else in this room actually had any idea what it was like to have been captured by a psychopathic serial killer.

She took a deep breath and pasted a smile on her face. "Does anyone want seconds?" she asked. "There's plenty."

Later, after the girls had gone to their room, Ted helped Amelia clear the table. "Are you okay?" he asked. "You seemed kind of upset about Yvonne's subject matter for her project."

"Aren't you?" she asked, tensing up again. "I hate when people glorify evil."

"She didn't say she looks up to him or finds him admirable in any way," he pointed out. "She's just trying to find out what drives people like him to do the things he does."

Put like that, it didn't seem so bad. Still, the irony of the situation wasn't lost on her.

"And if you're really worried about it," he continued,

"maybe you can help her research the project. That way you can gently steer her in the right direction."

Careful not to show her absolute horror, Amelia nodded. "Maybe so," she said, busying herself with stacking the dishes in the dishwasher. "If she's even speaking to me, that is."

Ted lightly squeezed her shoulder. "Don't worry. She'll come around. Just continue doing what you're doing and let her be the one to approach you."

Glancing up at him, she managed again to summon up a smile. "Sounds like you speak from experience."

"Oh, I am. Believe me, I am."

Chapter 7

The next morning, after dropping the girls off at school, Ted decided to stop by the Tumbleweed Café for a cup of coffee and to catch up on what was going on around town. He'd been kind of reclusive ever since hiring Amelia, which he didn't like. Ranching itself was by nature a solitary endeavor, so he'd always made sure to keep in at least weekly contact with his neighbors. Other than holiday festivals, the Tumbleweed was by far the best place to do that, except for maybe the Rattlesnake Pub. But since everyone ate and not everyone drank, he tried to stop by the café more often than not.

As usual, the restaurant was packed with the usual breakfast crowd. Almost all of the tables were full, though he spotted a few empty stools at the breakfast bar. To his surprise, he spotted the sheriff sitting by herself at the counter. He liked Rayna, and these days, unless she was on duty, he rarely saw her without her new husband, Parker. The big biker clearly adored her and vice versa. Parker's best friend's baby sister had been the only other of their local serial killer's victims to make it out alive. A teenager who went to school with Yolanda and Yvonne had been the other.

"Mornin'," Ted greeted her, sliding onto the empty stool next to her. "Where's Parker?"

"Oh, he had to go out to Tech," she replied, smiling. "His best friend, who passed away a few months ago, set up a scholarship there, and Parker is the one representing him in the ceremony. I would have liked to go too, but we're shorthanded this week, so I couldn't."

The waitress came over. Ted ordered coffee, still full from the large breakfast Amelia had prepared.

"You're not eating?" Rayna asked, looking askance at him.

"I already ate," he replied, nodding as the waitress filled his cup. "Amelia is a really good cook."

Rayna grinned. "I'm glad to hear that's working out. I really like Amelia."

"I do too," he said, knowing she wouldn't interpret his statement the wrong way. "She's good people." Around these parts, calling someone good people was one of the highest compliments one could give.

"She is," Rayna agreed.

The morning news played on a television on the wall. Rayna held up her hand, attention fixed on the screen. Curious, Ted looked up. A segment on the Coffee Shop Killer had just come on. Ted glanced around, noting the sudden hush. It seemed almost everyone had quieted to watch the segment.

"No news yet," Rayna commented. "Makes me almost wonder if the guy is dead. It seems impossible that he just vanished like that. Even if he had someone helping him, which apparently he did, there should have at least been a sighting by now."

Drinking his coffee, Ted grimaced. "I don't get why everyone is so fascinated with that guy."

"What do you mean?" Rayna eyed him.

He shrugged. "Look around. Just about every single person in here stopped what they were doing to watch the news story. Heck, Yvonne is doing a big report on him for school. She claims several other kids wanted that for a topic, but she beat them out."

"Wow." Rayna's brows rose. "How'd Amelia take that? She's not big on serial killers."

For a second, he wondered what she meant, but then remembered she and Amelia sometimes worked out together at the gym. "She wasn't happy," he replied. "Said she couldn't understand why anyone would want to focus on someone so evil."

Was it his imagination, or did Rayna appear to relax a bit?

"Amelia has a point," Rayna said. "People tend to become so interested in the abstract facts, like the methodology, that they forget the victims were real people, with hopes and dreams. Men like this guy don't feel remorse. In fact, they often gloat over how much pain they caused. I hope your daughter is able to see that when she researches her report."

Impressed, Ted nodded. "I'll make sure and point that out to her if she doesn't." He sat up straight as an idea occurred to him. "Would you mind if I asked her to interview you, to get a law enforcement person's point of view?"

"Not at all." Rayna's breakfast arrived and she smiled at him before digging into her omelet.

She'd barely taken a couple of bites before her radio crackled. "Sheriff?"

With a huge sigh, she pressed the button to respond. "What's up?"

One of her deputy's voices crackled loudly. "We have a situation."

Rayna glanced around the crowded restaurant. Several patrons were unabashedly listening in, while several others were clearly trying to appear not to. "Let me call you on the phone," Rayna said. Glancing at Ted, she grimaced. "No sense in starting a bunch of gossip about whatever it is."

She took a couple more bites and a sip of coffee before picking up her phone. "What's going on?"

After listening for a moment, she sighed again. "I'll be there in ten," she said. After ending the call, she went back to eating her breakfast.

Ted wasn't sure if he should ask. Finally, he figured if Rayna didn't want to tell him, she'd simply say so. "Is everything all right?"

"I'm not sure. Either way, there's no emergency." She leaned close, clearly not wanting to be overheard. "Donella's acting out again."

Last year, Donella Abernathy had been one of the victims who'd escaped Getaway's serial killer. She'd been instrumental in helping Rayna catch him. Ever since then, Donella had become very popular, both among her own age group and with adults. She'd been elected homecoming queen, had her own float in the Independence Day parade and enjoyed a level of celebrity unseen ever before by a teenage girl in Getaway.

Unfortunately, she also had night terrors and PTSD.

Her parents, claiming they didn't have the time or money to take her to an actual therapist, got her counseling with their church pastor, a well-meaning but untrained—and fanatical—man who'd decided she'd been possessed and had organized a ceremony to cast out her "demons." Donella had refused and, despite her parents' numerous efforts to force her, had become sort of a wild child after that. No one seemed to know how to help her.

"I feel sorry for her," Ted said. "She'd been over to the house a few times to play with the girls when they were all younger. I really wish her folks would get her the help she needs."

"Me too." Rayna cleaned up the last of her food and pushed the plate away. "If she keeps on going this path, she's going to end up in jail."

She stood and grabbed her ticket. "Take care," she told Ted, before heading to the register to pay.

A few minutes later, Ted settled up as well. He still had to go by the feed store. After that, he hoped to stop by and visit Serenity. Floyd was working on the back forty today repairing fence, so Ted had taken advantage of the free morning to catch up on errands in town.

Once his pickup truck had been loaded with all the supplies he'd ordered, he drove on over to Serenity's. She still hadn't hired anyone to replace Amelia. Privately, he didn't think she really needed the help. Her floral shop did the largest amount of business and she had a part-time driver to make deliveries. Sometimes, if she wanted to take some time off, she'd hire someone on a temporary basis.

Other than that, Serenity ran the shop by herself.

"Ted!" Serenity's lined face lit up when she saw him. "How are you? How are the girls and how's Amelia?"

"Fine." He couldn't help but notice how she lumped everyone together as if they were one big family. At the thought, his heart ached, making him realize he needed to be even more careful than he'd realized. "Well, maybe not so great," he amended. Then he told her all about what had happened the other night, finishing up with Yvonne doing a report on the Coffee Shop Killer.

Serenity listened intently, saying nothing even once he'd finished.

"I can tell you're really worried about her," she finally said, surprising him. He would have bet she'd have commented about the kiss first. But then, on second thought, that was one of the things he liked about Serenity. She always cut through all the small talk directly to what was really important.

"I am," he admitted. "She's only fourteen. Even though they're identical twins, she seems determined to do the opposite of her sister."

"That's to be expected." Serenity patted him on the shoulder. "She's trying to figure out her identity."

"I get that." And in a way, he did. "I'm just trying to keep her out of trouble."

"How is she getting along with Amelia?"

Surprised, he took a moment to consider how to answer the question. "Well, since she was the one who walked in when Amelia and I were kissing, Yvonne is very unhappy with her. I think maybe she just needs a little time. Both Amelia and I were up-front with the girls and explained it was just an impulsive, half-asleep mistake and that it won't happen again. I'm not sure they believed me."

Gaze steady, Serenity nodded. "Do you believe you?"

That made him frown. "I'm not sure I follow."

"I think you need to be honest with yourself, Ted. There are quite a few ladies in this town who'd love to lock lips with you. Yet you haven't told me any stories about stealing nighttime kisses with them. There's a reason for that. So I'm asking you if you're one hundred percent certain you won't be kissing Amelia again."

He dragged his hand through his hair, agitated. "I don't know," he finally said. "I won't lie. I'm attracted to her. But right now, I need a housekeeper more than I need a girlfriend. She's an employee, Serenity. It wouldn't be right."

"That's what I like about you." Serenity clapped him on the back. "You're a man of honor and principle."

"Thanks." From somewhere, he dredged up a smile. "I don't understand why I constantly seem to make things harder on myself."

"You'll be fine," she said. "As long as you follow your heart."

All the way home, that phrase kept rattling around inside his head, like one of those catchy songs you can't shake loose. What did that mean, follow his heart? His daughters were his heart, and as long as he lived, he'd devote his life to keeping them safe and making sure they knew how much they were loved.

But what about his needs, his wants, his…desire? Being with Amelia had awakened feelings he'd long ago buried deep inside himself. He wasn't entirely sure he was ready.

He arrived back at the ranch, unloaded his supplies and checked on Floyd, who was about to break for the noon meal. Ted waited and the two men headed back to the house in time for lunch. Today, with the air unseasonably warm, Amelia had made a platter of submarine sandwiches, more than enough for all three of them. She'd also put out a bowl of potato chips and a pitcher of iced tea.

Today, though, instead of pulling out a chair and eating with them, she excused herself and disappeared into the laundry room. Ted briefly thought about following her, but Floyd had already started in on one of the subs, so Ted sat down too. No doubt this was Amelia's way of trying to distance herself from him. He understood, even if he didn't like it.

She reappeared after they'd both finished stuffing themselves and picked up the platter. "Is there anything else I can get either of you?" she asked, cheerfully impersonal.

"Nope," Floyd muttered, using a toothpick to clean out his teeth. "Thank you. That was a mighty fine lunch." He checked his watch. "Looks like I have just about enough time for a twenty-minute nap. I'll be in my truck until one, boss. I'll see you back at the barn."

Ted nodded. "Sounds good."

After Floyd ambled away, Ted wasn't sure what to do with himself. Amelia stood at the counter, her back to him, fussing with the leftovers.

"Have you eaten?" he asked.

"Not yet," she replied without turning around. "I plan to, once I'm on my lunch break."

A not-so-subtle reminder that she was his employee too. Still, he was surprised how much it stung that she didn't want to spend her lunch break the way she usually did, with him and Floyd.

"I'll go," he said abruptly, pushing to his feet. "Enjoy your lunch."

He made it halfway to the door before she stopped him. "Wait."

Slowly, he turned.

She stood in the same spot, facing him now. "I'm just trying to figure out my place. Eating with you and Floyd felt too…" She waved her hand vaguely, as if she couldn't quite come up with the word.

"Too what?" he asked, his tone cool. "Floyd works for me too, and he sees nothing wrong with sharing a meal."

"But Floyd didn't kiss you," she exclaimed.

Now he thought he understood. "Is that what this is about? I thought we agreed to move past that, that we'd made a mistake which wouldn't be repeated."

She let her gaze search his face and then finally nodded. "You're right. I'm probably overthinking it." One corner of her sensuous mouth lifted in the beginnings of a smile.

Damned if he didn't want to kiss her again. Astounded at both the strength of this desire and the foolishness of it, he glanced down. "I'd just like to go back to the way we were before," he replied, meaning it.

"Me too," she replied. Grabbing a sub off the tray of sandwiches, she took a huge bite. "That's *so* good," she said, after swallowing. She continued devouring her meal with a dogged determination that he found incredibly sexy.

What the hell was wrong with him? He swallowed hard, grabbing what was left of his iced tea and draining it in one long swallow. He made a show of checking his watch, relieved to see it was nearly one, which meant time to get back to work.

"I'd better go," he told her, not having to fake his reluctance. "I'll see you later."

"Sounds good," she said, around a mouthful of food. She followed him to the door. "I'm going to stop at the grocery store when I pick the girls up from school. Is there anything you need?"

You, he wanted to say. *I need you.* But of course he couldn't and didn't. Instead, he trudged back outside, really glad to be getting back to work and his mind on track, where it belonged.

Ted had been acting strange, Amelia thought, but then, she couldn't blame him. She'd made a big deal out of distancing herself from him and Floyd at lunch. Luckily, Floyd hadn't seemed to notice. The last thing Ted needed would be to have the townspeople gossiping about him and her.

Actually, she wasn't sure what had gotten into her. Most likely some of her need for distance stemmed from the fact that she hadn't been able to stop thinking about him all morning. She'd watched him drive away, taking the girls to school, aware he planned to stop in town after. She'd really wanted to ask him to take her with him, though she'd known she couldn't.

Once he'd gone, she'd thought she'd settle into her normal routine of chores and meal planning. Usually, she found the work surprisingly fulfilling, but today she hadn't been able to focus. Instead, she couldn't stop thinking about that kiss and how good pressing up against Ted had felt.

Wrong, she knew, on so many levels. Yet she couldn't seem to make herself stop daydreaming. By the time Ted and Floyd had arrived, she'd worked herself into a tizzy of desire. Afraid Ted would notice, she'd decided to create more distance and keep herself busy.

Clearly, that plan had backfired.

Ted was right. They needed to get back to where they'd been before. She liked this job and this family. She had no reason to blow it.

She spent the rest of the day cleaning and cooking. For once, she didn't even bother to turn the television on to check for news about Simon. She'd check the internet later that night, just to make sure, but she didn't want to ruin the rest of her day.

The girls had gotten used to her picking them up from school surprisingly quickly. Or maybe they simply didn't care. Either way, she pulled up and parked. Then they came sauntering out with their separate groups of friends and made their way to her car.

She had to say, Yvonne's friends, who were all decked out in trendy, Snapchat-ready outfits, appeared to be the polar opposite of Yolanda's more bookish, studious types, some of whom carried band instruments. Interested, Amelia watched as each group walked halfway down the sidewalk before peeling off to go in their own directions.

Yolanda got in on the passenger side, smiling broadly, choosing to ride shotgun next to Amelia. Yvonne, on the other hand, slid into the back seat, her shoulders hunched, keeping her head down, almost as if she was afraid of being seen.

"How was your day?" Amelia asked, driving away from the school.

"Pretty stellar," Yolanda replied. "Jeremy Jenkins asked me to the Harvest Festival Dance."

"That's exciting." Amelia grinned at the teen. "I take it you said yes?"

"Jeremy Jenkins is a loser," Yvonne piped up from the back seat. "I wouldn't be caught dead with him."

"Well, he didn't ask you," Yolanda retorted. "So you don't have to worry about it."

Busy texting on her phone, Yvonne ignored her.

Determined to include Yvonne in the conversation, Amelia tried to catch her gaze in the rearview mirror and failed. "What about you, Yvonne?" Amelia asked, making her voice cheerful and light. "Are you going to the Harvest Festival Dance?"

Yvonne didn't bother to respond.

Unsure whether to feel hurt or angry, Amelia debated the best way to handle this. Part of her wanted to pull over to the side of the road, turn around in her seat and demand the teenager acknowledge her. However, she wasn't Yvonne's parent, so she wasn't sure if that would be the right thing to do or if it would only make matters worse. Ultimately, she decided to continue on as if she hadn't noticed anything wrong.

Though she rolled her eyes at her sister, Yolanda kept up a steady stream of chatter for the rest of the drive home, which warmed Amelia's heart. Hopefully Yvonne would eventually come around. She decided not to mention anything to Ted.

That night after dinner, the twins sat down at the kitchen table to work on their projects while Amelia was finishing up her cleanup from the meal, plus prepping for breakfast. She wasn't sure whether to stay or to leave, so she took her time working with her back to them, hoping they might say something to help her decide.

"Hey, Amelia," Yolanda said. "Want to see what I've got so far?"

Relieved, Amelia turned and smiled. "Of course." Maybe Yvonne might even follow suit. As peace offerings went, she'd take it.

Yolanda had started working on a diorama meant to show a timeline of women who'd started—and succeeded at—their own businesses. Amelia found it fascinating and knew a lot of research had gone into it.

When she said so, Yolanda grinned. "Thanks. I'm really enjoying the work, plus learning a lot."

Through all of this, Yvonne ignored them, continuing to work. Though Amelia really didn't want to know anything at all about her project, she also knew she needed to make up with Yvonne too. If Yvonne would let her, that was.

"What about you?" Amelia asked, tentatively. "How's your project going?"

"Why?" When Yvonne raised her head, anger flashed in her eyes. "You think it's stupid anyway."

"I never said that," Amelia protested. "I'm just not a fan of serial killers, that's all. That's my right, just like it's yours to do a report on one."

Yvonne eyed her warily. "Do you want to see what I've got so far?" she finally asked.

"Of course." Voice firm, her expression pleasant, Amelia looked intently at the poster board Yvonne had begun. She'd been busy, clipping newspaper and magazine articles. Amelia made sure to show none of her revulsion as she studied Simon's smug, smiling, *evil* face.

So far, Yvonne hadn't stumbled across any pictures with Amelia in them. Amelia supposed it would only be a matter of time. Surely the teenager would notice the resemblance. What then? No doubt they'd all be furious that she'd kept her true identity from them.

And once Yvonne had figured it out, news would spread. Before long, the entire town would be buzzing with the news that the witness who'd put the Coffee Shop Killer away was living in their town, at Ted Sanders's ranch.

How long before this news reached the media? How long before Simon himself heard it?

With a mounting sense of horror, Amelia realized her mere existence here would put these beautiful teenagers' lives in danger. Not to mention Ted's.

Pushing the thoughts to the back of her head, Amelia exclaimed over Yvonne's project before excusing herself to head to her room.

Once there, she took several deep breaths, trying to calm her racing heart. Paranoid? Maybe. But realistic too. She might be panicking over nothing, but she really didn't see how she could take a chance. These people, this family, knew nothing of her past. Ted had taken a chance on her and entrusted his beautiful daughters and his home to her care. She couldn't place them in danger, couldn't risk their lives.

Suddenly, she knew what she had to do. She didn't want to, the thought made her heart ache and her gut twist, but she didn't see how she had any other choice.

It took only a few moments to pack up all her belongings into her suitcase and duffel bag. Then she went to find Ted, to let him know she was quitting.

He wasn't in his room or in the den.

"Where's your father?" she asked the girls, who were

still working on their projects at the kitchen table. "I need to talk to him about something important."

"He said he was going over to the Jones farm," Yolanda put in helpfully. "That's the next one down the road. I think he got a call about a sick calf."

"Oh. Okay." Again, Amelia retreated to her bedroom, heart thumping in her chest. She eyed her packed bags sitting neatly on her bed. She'd never been an impetuous person, preferring careful planning over spontaneous actions, but right now the panic clawing at her overrode reason.

Yet how could she walk out without talking to Ted face-to-face? Of course, he'd want an explanation, which was the one thing she didn't want to give. The less this family knew, the better. In fact, it would be best if they all hated her and refused to have anything else to do with her. That way if Simon came for her, they'd be safe.

Despite the knowledge that she was right, leaving this way still wasn't easy. Hating herself, she scribbled out a quick note, folded it in half and wrote Ted's name on it. She carried it down the hall to his room and placed it in the middle of his dresser, where he'd be sure to see it.

Trudging back to retrieve her bags, she slipped out the front door and carried them to her car. Once there, she debated going back to say goodbye to the twins and decided against it. Without telling the truth, she didn't really have a good explanation.

On the way to the motel, she called Serenity and asked for her job back. Though the older woman sounded surprised, she didn't ask any questions before readily agreeing.

"Tomorrow morning?" Amelia asked, hoping she

could get right to work while she tried to figure out where to go next.

"Certainly."

At the Landshark, which of course still had vacancies, Amelia chose a different room than last time. She wanted to be on the second floor, toward the back so she had a good view of the entrance and the parking lot.

Once she had her room key, she carried her stuff inside and sat down on the bed. She'd been alone most of her adult life, but she'd never felt as lonely as she did right now.

Though it was barely eight o'clock, she didn't turn on the television, choosing instead to crawl between the sheets, curl up in a ball and try to sleep.

She must have dozed, because when her phone rang around nine, she opened her eyes and at first couldn't figure out where she was. A quick look around the small, plain room reminded her.

Caller ID showed Ted's number. Since her note would be all the explanation she could offer, she decided not to take the call. She knew if she did, she'd break down and cry.

This was all for the best.

Even so, she felt like she'd just lost far more than she had when she'd left White Plains. Then, she'd only lost belongings, easily replaceable. Now, though she'd only lived with them a couple of weeks, she felt as if she'd walked away from her own family. Much more difficult than she'd expected, but she wouldn't be able to live with herself if something happened to them.

She debated whether or not to leave town, to check out of her room, get in her car and drive until she reached another small town. Someplace like Getaway, which wasn't even a dot on a map. But she liked it here and she had a part-time job at least, so she decided to stay put for now.

Seeing Ted at Serenity's might be awkward, but she'd get through it. She'd just need to come up with a valid reason for quitting. Either that, or she'd need to tell him the truth.

Chapter 8

Reading Amelia's brief note, Ted felt like he'd been punched in the gut. She'd quit, she'd left, and hadn't bothered to say goodbye. Or even given a reason, though he suspected that kiss might have had a lot to do with it.

Still clutching the note, he wandered back into the kitchen, where the girls were still engrossed in their projects.

"Have you seen Amelia?" he asked, hoping he sounded casual.

"I think she's in her room," Yolanda responded. "She was in here earlier asking us about our projects."

"Yeah," Yvonne chimed in. "And this time she seemed okay with my subject matter. She was actually pretty cool about it."

High praise indeed, coming from Yvonne. Still, since neither girl appeared aware Amelia had left, clearly she hadn't said goodbye to them either. He might not have known Amelia for very long, but he knew she cared about the twins.

Which meant he could still fix this.

He checked his watch—10:00 p.m. He made a split-second decision. "You two need to start getting ready for bed soon," he said. "I've got to go out. I should be back in thirty minutes."

The twins exchanged looks. "New girlfriend, Dad?" Yolanda teased.

Instead of answering, he shook his head, snatched his truck keys back up off the counter and took off.

Since there was only one motel in Getaway, the Landshark, he drove directly there. He spotted her car near the back, all by itself, and parked next to it. Since he didn't want to stop by the office and ask, plus doubted they'd tell him anyway, he settled for knocking on the door directly in front of her vehicle.

No one answered. Undeterred, he tried the rooms on either side. Again, nothing. Glancing up toward the second floor, he saw one room with the light on. That had to be her.

Taking the stairs two at a time, he took a deep breath when he arrived in front of the door. Raising his fist, he rapped sharply on the door and waited. Since the door had a peephole, he stepped back a little bit so she could get a good look at him.

Amelia opened the door a few inches. "Ted? What are you doing here?"

"I think I'm the one who's supposed to be asking that question," he said. "May I come in?"

Instead of answering, she stepped aside and motioned him to pass her.

He hadn't been inside the Landshark Motel since he'd been a teenager attending someone's graduation party. The rooms still looked the same—pale green shag carpet, orange, green and yellow bedspreads, and uninspired prints hanging on the wall.

"Well?" Amelia demanded, drawing his gaze back to her. She wore her buffalo-plaid flannel pajamas, even though outside the temperature hovered around sixty degrees.

Crossing his arms, he dug the folded note from his pocket.

"I came to talk to you about this."

Slowly, she nodded. "I'm sorry. I thought it was best if I left."

"So your note said. But you didn't give a reason."

Now she looked away. "It's not working out. Clearly, neither of the girls wants me there."

"Is this about that kiss?" He took a step closer, aching to reach out and raise her chin to make her look at him. Instead, he clenched his hands into fists at his sides, aware it might be safer not to touch her.

She sighed and sat down on the end of the bed. "That kiss didn't help, but no, this isn't entirely about that."

"Then what? Don't you think I have the right to know?"

"Why does it mean so much to you?" she asked quietly. "I'm sure you can find another housekeeper."

Despite knowing better, he went and dropped down next to her. "Is that all you think you are? A housekeeper? I consider you a friend and so do the girls. We were just settling into a routine, getting comfortable. When I offered you the position, I told you the girls

Get up to 4
FREE FABULOUS BOOKS
You Love!

To thank you for being a loyal reader we'd like to send you up to 4 FREE BOOKS, absolutely free.

Just write "YES" on the Loyal Reader Voucher and we'll send you up to 4 Free Books and Free Mystery Gifts, altogether worth over $20, as a way of saying thank you for being a loyal reader.

Try **Harlequin® Romantic Suspense** books featuring heart-racing page-turners with unexpected plot twists and irresistible chemistry that will keep you guessing to the very end.

Try **Harlequin Intrigue® Larger-Print** books featuring action-packed stories that will keep you on the edge of your seat. Solve the crime and deliver justice at all costs.

Or **TRY BOTH!**

We are so glad you love the books as much as we do and can't wait to send you great new books.

So don't miss out, return your Loyal Reader Voucher Today!

Pam Powers

LOYAL READER
FREE BOOKS VOUCHER

needed someone stable, who'd stay for a while. I would never have guessed you were a quitter."

"I'm not."

"But yet you did."

Their gazes locked. Heat flickered in her eyes and down low inside his body. She made a sound, halfway between a cry and a moan, and leaned toward him.

He met her halfway. Mouth to mouth, bodies tangled together, a soft bed conveniently behind them. She tasted of mint toothpaste and smelled like peaches, an odd combo that was the most erotic scent he'd ever experienced.

This time, neither held back. The unfamiliar room, the softness of her naked skin under the flannel had him more aroused than he'd ever been in his life.

"Amelia," he began, his voice rusty. "Do you think we should—"

"Don't think," she murmured, kissing him again.

They shed their clothes, frenzied. She touched him then, long, stroking caresses that damn near put him on the edge of control.

He tried once more, needing her to be sure. "Amelia?"

"Yes," she answered, without him even voicing the question. "I want you—I want this."

Hands shaking, he located his wallet, extracting the condom he kept there. He fumbled with the wrapping, until she gave a low laugh and took it from him.

"Let me," she murmured, tearing the package open and then working it over his body, her swift and sure motions arousing him even more.

"I want you too," he choked out. "Come here."

"Nope," she told him, her husky voice cheerful. "I need to be in control this time." And then, as if to prove her point, she pushed him onto his back and climbed on top of him, lowering herself over him slowly, inch by torturous inch, until he was finally completely buried deep inside her silky warmth.

They both held still, savoring the moment, the rush of feelings, the pure explosive pleasure of intimacy.

She began to move, her body sheathing him in warm honey. He cried out, arched his back, trying to urge her to move faster. Her smile, both sensual and fierce, matched her movements. Ridiculously sexy.

His heart swelled along with his body, the heady emotions only fueling his passion. Still, he held himself back until he felt her body start to clench and shudder around him. The instant her release began, he let go and they exploded at the same time.

Honestly, he'd never experienced lovemaking like this in his entire life. Both fierce and tender, wild and protective, their bodies had fit together as if they were made for each other.

After their heart rates had settled and their breathing slowed, they simply held each other, naked and sweaty. He wasn't sure how he'd been so blessed to have this woman come into his life, but he for damn sure didn't want her to leave. They needed time to explore if this thing that had fired up between them could be something more.

"Will you come back?" he asked, pushing up on one elbow to look at her.

She gazed up at him, smiling when he tucked a few wayward strands of hair behind her ear. "I don't think so," she said.

Shocked, he wasn't sure how to respond. He'd been so sure she'd agree. Clearly, he'd been wrong. He supposed that probably meant he was wrong about what was going on between them too.

"Why not?"

With a sigh, she rolled over, pulling the sheet with her. She located her clothes, some still on the bed, some on the floor, and gathered them up. Keeping her back to him, she got dressed.

Finally, she turned to face him. "I've got something to tell you," she said, her voice heavy. "Then you'll understand why I can't go back to your ranch."

Several scenarios danced through his mind, though he certainly wasn't prepared for what she said next.

"I was the chief witness against the Coffee Shop Killer," she told him. "The only one of his victims to get away. Now that he's escaped and hunting for me, I realize my being in your house might endanger you and the girls. That's why I think it's better that I stay here by myself. No one else will be hurt if he finds me."

It took a moment or two for him to digest her words. "Now I get why you seemed so familiar," he exclaimed. "You were all over the news, though you were blonde with glasses."

Expression miserable, she nodded. "The only other person who knows is Rayna. I'll need you to keep this between us for now."

"Rayna knows?" He struggled to make sense of this.

"Yes. And now you. And I think it's time for you to go."

He frowned. "But I—"

"Please. I don't want to discuss this. You asked for my reason and I gave it. You have a family to protect. Neither of us can afford to risk them. Leave."

Because he too needed time to process and digest

everything, he nodded. Heart aching, he got dressed as quickly as he could and let himself out.

Instead of driving home, he made a split-second decision and headed toward Rayna's house. He knew it was late, and if when he pulled up, he didn't see any lights on, he wouldn't stop.

To his surprise, not only did the living room light shine bright yellow through the big bay front window, but he spied Rayna herself sitting on the top step of her front porch. When he pulled up to the curb, she recognized him and waved.

Killing the engine, he took a deep breath and got out of the truck. He walked up and took a seat beside her.

"What's up?" she asked, taking a deep drink of something from her mug. "It's kind of late for you to be paying a social call, don't you think?"

"Amelia quit," he said, not even attempting to try to hide the raw pain in his voice. "She left while I was gone, though she did put a note for me on my dresser."

Rayna eyed him. "Did she say why?"

"Not in the note. She did later, when I drove out to the Landshark to confront her. She said you're the only other person in town who knows."

Expression solemn, Rayna nodded. "She knows sooner or later, someone else will recognize her. And while it might seem she's been highly paranoid, you know how gossip spreads in this town. I don't know what kind of network this serial killer has, but I will say it must be a good one for him to be able to disappear so thoroughly despite a nationwide manhunt. If he somehow got word, you know her life would be at risk. She's very aware of that."

"She said she didn't want to endanger me or my girls." His voice sounded numb even to his own ears.

"That makes sense."

"Does it?" Ted shook his head. "Things seemed to be going so well. I'm not sure how the girls are going to take this."

Rayna grimaced. "I think you should tell them the truth. That's the only way they'll understand."

"I promised Amelia I wouldn't," he said. "And, Rayna, I know I haven't known her very long, but I understand her. Once word gets out, she's going to run."

"Again, I can't blame her." Studying him, Rayna sighed. "You have feelings for her, don't you?"

He thought about lying but didn't see the point. "I could. I'm definitely attracted to her." He cursed. "This is absurd. What would you do?"

"What can you do but wait it out? Maybe this Coffee Shop Killer will get caught. I hope so, because if anyone deserves a chance at a good life, Amelia does."

By the time Ted got home, the girls had gone to bed. He checked on them, relieved to find them sleeping in their twin beds.

After that, he went around the house and checked the locks. For the first time in his life, he considered looking into installing an alarm. One with window and door sensors that would be tripped if someone tried to enter. Or leave, such as sneaking out in the middle of the night.

Glad to find something that helped quell the niggling spark of panic inside him, he quietly got ready for bed. Since he hadn't had time to figure out anything for tomorrow's meals, they'd have cold cereal for breakfast and he'd order pizza for dinner. He'd come up with something to tell the girls too, because they'd be sure to ask where Amelia had gone.

Feeling lonelier than he had since the day the girls' mother had left, he closed his eyes and tried like hell to go to sleep.

After Ted had gone, Amelia gave in and let herself weep. She broke down and sobbed, her face pressed into her pillow, as if someone she loved had died. Simon had done a number on her back then, and she'd been so messed up after, she'd almost wished he'd gone ahead and killed her.

Would his evil essence ever stop affecting her life? She liked Ted Sanders and thought, with time, she might even have come to love him. Their lovemaking had transcended anything she'd experienced before. Even now, her body felt pleasantly sore, but her soul felt raw and exposed. Part of her had hoped he wouldn't be so easily convinced, though she understood he had his two daughters to protect. She couldn't blame him for not wanting to risk them.

Still, why had she risked her heart with a one-night stand? If she were honest with herself, she'd admit she'd been aching for this ever since she'd met him. But she'd gone and gotten her heart involved and now she had to deal with heartbreak along with everything else. Not just for Ted, but also for those precious, headstrong twin girls of his. Even in such a short time, she'd grown attached.

So she allowed herself to cry, to wallow in the overwhelming sense of loss. She hadn't truly mourned, not even when she'd abandoned her life in White Plains.

Later, eyes swollen from tears, head aching, she realized that while she had asked him to keep the information she'd given him quiet, he hadn't promised to do so. If he told the twins... Gossip would spread all around the high school and, from there, to the parents.

She couldn't take a chance of that happening, so she sent a text to Ted.

Please keep what I told you between us. I know I asked you, but you didn't agree. I'd prefer no one else find out until they have to.

A few minutes later, he texted back a simple ok.

Out of habit, she turned on the late news, hoping she'd learn that Simon had miraculously been captured. No such luck. In fact, the anchors never mentioned him, though there was a small chance she might have missed an earlier story.

Just in case, she did a quick internet search using her phone. As far as she could tell, the Coffee Shop Killer was still on the loose. With no sightings and nothing to keep the story alive, the media quickly lost interest. No doubt, she thought glumly, this was exactly what Simon had hoped for. Moving around would be much easier when there was less chance the public would recognize your face.

Again, she pushed back panic and thought of fleeing. Only by reminding herself that Simon had no idea where to find her was she able to calm herself back down enough to try to get a little sleep.

The next morning, achy and with her eyes burning for lack of sleep, she showered and dressed. She made herself a cup of bad coffee and drank half of it before deciding she had enough time to stop at the Tumbleweed Café for a hot breakfast and some decent coffee.

The café, as always, was full. She went up to the breakfast counter and sat on a stool near the far end. From there, she had a great view of not only the front door, but she could see out the window at the parking lot and sidewalk. This was a habit she'd begun after escaping from Simon. She never sat with her back to the door if she could help it.

The waitress filled her cup and offered her a menu. Amelia thanked her, sipping from her mug while perusing the offerings.

"Funny running into you here," a voice said. Yolanda, her usual smiling expression serious, stood with her hands jammed into her pockets.

Amelia froze, her heart sinking. "What are you doing here?" she asked. "Shouldn't you be getting ready for school?"

"Dad told us this morning that you'd left." Yolanda jerked her chin over toward the seating area, revealing Ted and Yvonne sitting in a booth. "Yvonne's taking it hard, blaming herself. He was going to take us over to the motel to talk to you, but we decided to stop in here and get breakfast to go." She shook her head. "We were going to bring you breakfast too, but when we saw you here, we figured we could all talk here instead."

Amelia wasn't sure how to respond. She glanced again at the booth where Ted watched them, unsmiling. Sitting across from him, Yvonne kept her head down, fixated on her phone as usual. Amelia's heart filled with such a rush of wild longing, she could hardly breathe.

"Will you come talk to us?" Yolanda asked, solemnly. "I think you owe us that much."

Amelia nodded. The waitress came back and Amelia told her she'd be moving to the booth. Carrying her mug of coffee, she followed Yolanda, who slid in next to Ted, leaving room for Amelia next to Yvonne.

"Good morning," Amelia said, trying for casual despite her racing heartbeat.

Yvonne raised her head and met Amelia's gaze. "I can't believe you went and left without even telling us. Don't we matter more to you than that?"

"Of course you do," Amelia said, her heart aching. Ted still watched her, making no move to help her out, though she could hardly blame him. "I have to admit, I panicked."

"Why?" both girls asked, in unison.

Her face heating, Amelia swallowed. She hated lying, but there wasn't any way she could tell the truth. Not right now. When and if the girls found out later, well, she'd have to deal with the fallout then. For now, she'd give the only other logical reason that would have made her leave.

"I didn't want to cause trouble between you all and your father," she finally admitted. Which also was true.

"This is my fault, isn't it?" Yvonne asked, wiping at a tear that trickled down her cheek.

"No, of course not." Amelia pulled her close. "Don't think that. I promise you, it's way more complicated than that."

"Is it?" Ted finally spoke up. "The girls need you. We need you. Won't you please reconsider and come back?"

The question hung there while Amelia's heart pounded in her ears. The girls watched her silently, neither bothering to hide their hopeful expressions.

"I'll think about it," Amelia said.

Luckily, the waitress arrived just then to take their orders.

The girls had pancakes, while Ted and Amelia both had omelets. The hot, strong coffee did wonders to help Amelia wake up. The news played on the television hung over the breakfast bar, but Amelia didn't see a story about the Coffee Shop Killer. Though she felt grateful, she'd rather they'd announced he'd been located and was now back behind bars.

Ted insisted on paying for her meal as well as theirs. Thanking him, Amelia checked her watch and told them she'd think about things and let them know by the end of the day. For now, she had to go to work for Serenity. She hugged the girls tight and, after a moment's consideration, did the same with Ted. When she walked to her car, she felt their eyes on her back. She hadn't known her heart could hurt so badly.

Driving down the block, she arrived at Serenity's ten minutes before the store was due to open. Since she spotted Serenity's Volkswagen parked out back, she went ahead and let herself in the back door.

"Good morning!" Serenity sang out. "I don't have a lot of work for you to do, but since Thanksgiving isn't too far off, I thought maybe you could set up a table of books to be thankful for."

Amelia nodded. Meeting the older woman's gaze, she decided to voice aloud something she'd suspected since her first day at work here. "You really don't need an employee here, do you?"

Serenity shrugged. "I like to offer a place when needed. Don't worry, child. You can work here as long as you must."

"Thank you." Feeling conflicted and torn, Amelia got busy. She'd make the best table display possible, as a way of thanking her employer.

It took her a bit, looking through titles on such varied subjects as the healing power of crystals, and self-regression for past-life recall, but she decided to choose books that might make people thankful to have read them. Once she'd decided this, she tried to choose varied offerings, from mindful meditation to journaling for happiness.

When she finally had the table set up, she looked up to find Serenity staring at her, her eyes blank, her mouth slack. Alarmed, Amelia froze. Was she having a stroke or about to have a seizure? "Are you all right?" she asked, keeping her voice calm and quiet.

Serenity blinked, the focus returning to her expression.

"You won't find happiness until you let go of that dark cloud," she intoned. "Even when it's nowhere near, you keep it around in your thoughts. Your reality is becoming poisoned by your fearful thoughts."

Stunned, Amelia wasn't sure how to respond. She knew Serenity considered herself a psychic, though Amelia wasn't sure she even believed in such things.

"Sorry." Serenity flashed a serene smile. "Sometimes I have no choice but to pass on a message from the spirit guides. Especially when they're this insistent." She drifted away, leaving Amelia to stare after her, still in shock.

Her stomach and head hurt. Maybe Serenity was right. She needed to let go of her fear, of her own personal dark cloud. Right now, in this moment, she was safe. If Simon somehow magically found her, she'd deal with it then. For now, though, she'd truly earned the right to live her best life.

Decision made, she called Ted. He answered on the second ring. "Amelia?"

"I've decided I'd like to come back to work," she said briskly. "Would it be all right with you if I move back into my old room this afternoon?"

"Of course." Apparently, he took his cue from her businesslike tone. "I'll let the girls know when I pick them up from school."

"About that..." She took a deep breath. "I'd like to go ahead and pick them up today."

"They'll love that," Ted said quietly. "Thank you, Amelia. We won't let you down." He ended the call.

Amelia stared at her phone for a moment, letting his words sink in. She'd do her best to make sure she did the same. Then she went to find Serenity and give her the news.

Later, parked outside the high school, her heart skipped a happy beat watching both girls' faces light up when they saw her. Yolanda actually ran to the car and jumped in, taking her usual seat in the front. And while Yvonne still took her time, even she had a broad smile on her face when she slid into the rear seat.

"Are you back?" Yvonne asked. "For real?"

"I am." Amelia sniffed, turning her head to wipe a stray tear that leaked from the corner of one eye. "What's new with you two?"

"You mean in the one day since we saw you last?" Yvonne drawled.

This made both Amelia and Yolanda laugh, which earned a pleased smile from Yvonne.

"Does Dad know?" Yolanda asked. "I mean, I'm guessing he must since you picked us up instead of him, but..."

"He does. I called him and let him know I was moving back in." She managed a watery smile. "I need to apologize. I was an idiot for panicking and running away."

"Darn right you were," Yvonne replied gruffly. "Now maybe you can help me finish my Coffee Shop Killer project."

Amelia flinched. "Sure," she said. "When is it due?"

"Tomorrow." Both girls spoke at once.

"I'm pretty much done with mine," Yolanda said. "Though I wouldn't mind you looking it over and letting me know if I'm missing anything."

"Sounds good." As she drove them home, Amelia felt a feeling of contentment settle over her like a warm blanket. She'd never really had a family, other than foster families growing up, and those changed frequently, so she'd never allowed herself to get too close.

And she really shouldn't this time either.

When she parked in front of the house, for the first time ever, the girls waited and walked in with her.

She'd taken the time to defrost some ground beef, so tonight's dinner would be simple—sloppy joes, which she figured the girls would love.

Ted came home and stood in the kitchen doorway, smiling at her while she got everything ready to make the meal. "Welcome back," he said. Neither he nor Floyd had stopped by at lunch, which she suspected was to give her time to get resettled.

"Thank you."

Everyone assembled for dinner, and even Yvonne participated in the conversation, which ranged from farmwork to school to the Harvest Festival Dance. Yvonne finally admitted that she too had a date, though she refused to say who it might be. Amelia could tell

Ted forcibly restrained himself from pressing for information. It was rare Yvonne shared even this much, and Amelia knew he didn't want to make her shut down.

The house phone rang just as Amelia had begun clearing the dishes away. The girls had just begun setting up their projects on the kitchen table. Everyone paused, almost as if they had a premonition, though most likely it was because no one in these days of cell phones ever called the landline.

Ted answered. After saying hello, he simply listened. Finally, he murmured, "Thank you for letting me know." And he hung the phone back up.

When he looked at Amelia, his dazed expression sent a frisson of worry through her.

"What is it?" she asked. "What's wrong?"

Even the girls paused in their activity to stare at their father.

"That was Rayna," he said, his voice heavy. "Donella Abernathy didn't come home after school today. Her parents are frantic."

"Oh my gosh," Yvonne declared, her eyes huge. "The Coffee Shop Killer has come to town."

Chapter 9

Ted stared at his daughter, aware how her words most likely affected Amelia. "Let's not jump to conclusions," he said. "Everyone knows that Donella has been having some problems ever since the last time she was grabbed. It's more likely she disappeared on her own."

"I hope she doesn't hurt herself," Yolanda interjected, her expression worried. "Everyone's been talking about how depressed she is."

"That's true," Yvonne seconded. "Her best friend, Heather, hangs out with us. She's really worried about Donella." She shrugged, grimacing at her father. "Sorry. This project has got me a little freaked out. Turns out this Simon guy—that's the Coffee Shop Killer's name— is really creepy."

Amelia stiffened, but that was her only reaction to hearing the name. Ted had a momentary urge to go to her and put his arm around her in support, which of course he squelched.

"Serial killers usually are creepy," Amelia said. "I sure hope they find this girl. Maybe once they do, I should talk to her."

Both Yvonne and Yolanda looked up at that. "Why? You don't even know her."

Ted could tell Amelia was regretting the slip. "No reason," she said. "I guess I just like helping people with their problems."

The twins nodded and Amelia exhaled, her relief palpable.

"Rayna is good at what she does," Ted said. "She'll find Donella."

"She didn't find her last time," Yvonne pointed out. "Not until she escaped, remember?"

How could he forget? For that matter, how could anyone? Donella had been lucky, just like Amelia had been. And if Donella hadn't escaped when she did, the killer—who'd turned out to be the son of famous syndicated advice columnist Myrna Maples—wouldn't have been caught.

"I read about that online," Amelia said. "Very freaky, especially in such a small town."

"It's what put us on the map," Ted replied. "Sadly."

"You're right," Amelia said, her expression a bit shell-shocked. "That story is what made me notice Getaway in the first place." She swallowed hard, making Ted wonder if she now worried that the Coffee Shop Killer would notice too. If he did, he'd still have nothing to make him suspect she'd come here. There were thousands of other places Amelia could have gone. Places where she maybe had family or friends. He'd assumed someone like Simon would check them first.

"I have to wonder if the Coffee Shop Killer is even still alive," he said, thinking out loud. "I mean, the guy escapes while being transported to maximum security prison and then is never seen or heard from again. It seems to me that someone like him would have to kill again, wouldn't he?"

"Maybe." Amelia's response was tempered with caution. "And he might still be killing without anyone noticing. It's possible, if he chooses his victims carefully. Drug addicts and junkies, prostitutes, women who remain in the shadowy fringes of society and aren't as likely to be missed. It's happened before with other serial killers. The police didn't even learn about all the other victims until the killer confessed to their murders."

Wide-eyed, the twins listened. "Are you saying you think this particular serial killer might be here in Getaway?" Yolanda asked.

"No." Both Ted and Amelia spoke at once.

"He was sent to Attica Correctional Facility in New York," Amelia continued. "That's thousands of miles from here. He'd have no reason to show up here in rural west Texas."

Except he did have a reason, and both Amelia and Ted knew it. Simon would travel here if he'd somehow learned Amelia was living in Getaway. And since no one except Rayna, Ted and Amelia herself knew, that scenario was highly unlikely.

But not impossible.

Shaking his head, Ted excused himself to go watch some TV and try to unwind. If he never heard of the

Coffee Shop Killer again, he'd be happy. He could only imagine how Amelia must feel.

Turning on the television, he settled in to watch a couple of sitcoms. The rest of the house had grown quiet, both the girls and Amelia having apparently gone to their rooms for the night.

By the time the evening news came on, Ted decided to shut things down and head to bed. He had his hand on the remote, about to press the off button, when a breaking-news banner flashed across the screen.

"The New Orleans Police Department believes the Coffee Shop Killer might be behind a series of killings," the pretty blonde announcer said. Heart pounding, Ted hit the pause button and went to go fetch Amelia.

Though she'd closed her door, the light was still on and he could hear the sound of her television and what appeared to be an old movie. He tapped lightly, not wanting to disturb the twins.

The door opened slowly. "Ted? What's going on?"

"There's a story on the news I think you should see," he said.

She gasped, hand to her throat. "Has he been captured?"

"No, not yet. But it appears he may have surfaced." Not thinking, he held out his hand. She took it, clasping her fingers around his.

Back in the den, he let the news story play. Still holding on to him, Amelia listened, her entire body stiff.

The story ended and Ted turned off the TV.

Amelia suddenly appeared to realize their fingers were still entwined and pulled her hand free. "They're basing it entirely on MO," she said. "That's it. No one has seen him—he hasn't left any notes or anything. It might even be a copycat."

"Maybe so. But since Louisiana is a hell of a lot closer to Texas than New York, I thought you should know."

She regarded him gravely. "Thank you. I'll talk it over with Rayna tomorrow, if she's not too busy. Thanks. And good night."

A wild urge to kiss her swept over him, though he knew better than to act on it. Instead, he nodded, remaining where he stood until he heard her door close. Then, aching, he went to his own room to try to get some sleep.

Stumbling into the kitchen after a restless night, Ted had just poured his first cup of coffee when Yvonne rushed into the kitchen, bleary-eyed, her face pale. This was so out of the ordinary—of the two girls, Yvonne had to be hounded to get out of bed—that Ted immediately went over and felt her forehead to make sure she didn't have a fever.

"Are you okay?" he asked, relieved she didn't seem hot.

"No." She met his gaze, her eyes wide. "I just got a text from Justin. He's one of my friends. Heather's parents called his. Heather has disappeared too."

"Maybe she just went looking for Donella," Ted suggested. "She can't have been gone very long. It sounds like she, what, snuck out in the middle of the night?" He didn't add *like you did*, but the implication was there.

Yvonne gave him a reproachful glare. "Heather isn't like that. She's responsible. She cares about her grades, and she's a basketball phenom. She's had perfect attendance so far all year and I can't believe she'd mess that up on purpose. If she's not at school today…"

"Don't jump ahead of yourself," he said. "Imagining the worst never works out well."

"What's going on?" Amelia walked in, looking from Ted to Yvonne. "Is everything all right?"

Yvonne filled her in. When she'd finished, Amelia went over and pulled her in for a hug. To Ted's surprise, his prickly teenage daughter held on tight.

Yolanda strolled in right in the middle of all this. She looked from Amelia and her sister to Ted. "Do I want to know?" she asked, raising one eyebrow.

"Heather's gone," Yvonne said, twisting away from Amelia to face her sister. "First Donella, now Heather. It's really freaky."

"Since they're besties, you know Heather would know the best places to look," Yolanda pointed out. "Most likely, that's where she went."

"But she's not answering her phone. She's not even responded to texts. Our entire group has been texting and calling. Nothing. That's what's got all of us so worried." Yvonne's voice broke. She appeared about to cry.

"Maybe she lost her phone." Even Yolanda appeared to realize that was a long shot. "She'll probably show up in time for first period."

"And it's *not* the Coffee Shop Killer," Amelia said. "New Orleans police seem to think he's there, starting up his killing spree again."

"What?" Yvonne gaped. "Are you serious? They've seen him?"

"Not exactly." Amelia explained what the news report had said.

"I'll need to update my report," Yvonne mused. "Which isn't going to be easy, since I have to turn it in today."

"I wouldn't. Right now, there's nothing but supposition." Amelia squeezed Yvonne's shoulder. "Or you can add a brief addendum."

Sending the girls back to their room to get ready with words of reassurance, Ted eyed Amelia, wondering if she'd had as bad of a night as he had and whether he should offer her the same. As if she knew his thoughts, she gave a slow shake of her head and got busy preparing breakfast.

The morning fell into its usual routine, for which Ted felt supremely grateful. He truly hadn't understood how much Amelia's presence added to their lives until she'd been gone. He'd never take her for granted again.

After delivering the kids to school, Ted made a point of stopping back in at the Tumbleweed. If one wanted to know what was going on in town, that was the best place to find out. And he definitely wanted to know if Donella and Heather had turned up.

He'd just sat down at the breakfast bar and gotten his coffee when two of the other ranchers came over and invited him to join them at their table. Both men had daughters about the same age as the twins. When Getaway had actually had a serial killer, they'd been instrumental in organizing a rally against the man they'd believed responsible—Parker, who was now Rayna's husband. Of course, they'd all had to apologize when they'd realized they had the wrong man. Ted hoped they'd learned from their earlier mistake. He certainly had.

Grabbing his coffee cup, Ted motioned to the waitress to let her know where he was going. She nodded and then got back to work taking orders and delivering food.

Ted slid into the booth next to a guy everyone called

Buddy. "Mornin'," he said. "Any word on the missing girls?"

"Not yet." J.R. answered, his expression worried. "Heather Peeks sometimes hangs out with my daughter. She's beside herself."

"How are the parents holding up? I imagine they must be worried sick."

"I know Rayna's been out there to talk to both families," Buddy said. "I can't even imagine. If Allena disappeared, I don't know what I'd do. Even thinking about it makes me feel sick."

Just then, the waitress arrived with Buddy's and J.R.'s food. "Do you want anything?" she asked Ted.

He shook his head. "No, thanks. I'll stick with coffee."

Once she'd left, he glanced around the crowded café. The low buzz of conversation carried undertones of anxiety and speculation. "I'm hoping Donella and Heather just took off together. I mean, what else could it be?"

"Right?" Buddy shoveled his eggs into his mouth, barely chewing before swallowing. "Getaway already had a serial killer. It'd be weird having another."

"Unless it's a copycat," J.R. put in. "I've watched shows about people who really admire someone evil, so they set out to emulate them."

"Emulate?" Buddy asked. "Mighty big word there."

"It means 'copy,'" J.R. explained. "Anyway, I'm just saying there are some sick and twisted people out there."

"There sure are," a querulous voice said. Two elderly ladies stopped by the table. "We are of the opinion that this is happening again." She leaned forward, barely lowering her voice. "Some people even think that Coffee Shop Killer feller has come to town."

"The news said he'd been spotted in New Orleans," Ted pointed out. "That's quite a distance from here."

"And why would he come to Getaway anyway?" Buddy interjected, his mouth full of food.

But the two women had already moved on, stopping at a booth near the front to gossip some more.

By the time Ted finished a second cup of coffee, the conversation had moved on to other things. But he had the uneasy feeling that unless Donella and Heather were found soon, things were about to go downhill rapidly.

Leaving money on the table for his coffee, Ted headed out. Halfway to his truck, someone called his name. Rayna. Relieved, he turned. "I'm glad to see you," he said. "You're always the voice of reason."

He could tell his comment pleased her by her smile. "Come on now, Ted," she said. "Don't tell me you're letting rumors get to you."

"I try not to—you know that. But when you have two teenage daughters, it's hard not to worry."

"Don't," she said, squeezing his shoulder. "Believe me, we're working to locate those two girls. We've pinged their phones and—" Her cell rang, interrupting them. "I need to take this. Wait just a sec. Don't run off."

Answering, she listened for a moment, her expression going grim. "Thanks." She ended the call. "Well, that didn't work out like I thought it would."

When Ted came into the kitchen before heading out to work the ranch, Amelia could tell his mood had darkened from the tight line of his jaw and the grim look in his eyes. She marveled that she already knew this man so well, and then asked him what was wrong.

He eyed her for a moment without speaking. Then,

shrugging off his jacket, he took a seat at the kitchen table. "Neither of the girls has turned up. Rayna pinged both their phones, but it turned out they'd left them at a friend's house. They weren't there, just their phones. Which kind of makes Rayna think they took off deliberately."

"I hate to point out the obvious, but what teenager goes anywhere without her phone?" she asked. "I'm not even sure they're aware that they can be traced."

"I thought the same," he agreed. "I stopped at the Tumbleweed this morning and speculation is running rampant. Half the people think the girls ran off with boys and the other half are convinced another serial killer has taken them."

Amelia nodded. "At least they're not worried the Coffee Shop Killer has come to town." She shuddered, unable to help herself.

"Oh, I heard that one too." His phone rang. Digging it out of his pocket, he blanched when he saw the screen. "It's the school. I wonder what Yvonne's done now."

After answering, he listened and ended the call without speaking. "Automated," he rasped, worry creasing his brow. "The high school has been placed on lockdown. There might be an active shooter."

Amelia's stomach twisted. "Oh no." Hand to her mouth, she tried not to picture how terrified the students and teachers must be.

Ted hesitated. "I want to text both of them to make sure they're safe, but what if they're in hiding and the sound gives their location away?" Shaking his head, he shoved the phone back into his pocket.

"My first instinct is to go out there and make sure

my girls are safe," he said. "I'm sure every other parent has had the same reaction."

"Are you?" She wanted to ask if she could go with him.

He appeared torn. "The recording specifically asked us not to. I'm sure every worried parent who received that call is heading down there. Rayna will have one of her men set up a roadblock."

Amelia eyed him.

"Let's go," he said, holding out his hand. "That is, if you don't mind coming with me for moral support."

"Of course I don't mind." She slid her fingers into his and squeezed his hand once before letting go. "I'm worried too."

As Ted had suspected, one of the Getaway Sheriff's Department squad cars had parked sideways in the drive leading to the school. Numerous other vehicles had pulled over and parked, lining the curb on both sides. A large group of people had gathered on a grassy area that afforded a good view of both the school and the parking lot.

"Let's join them." Ted pulled up behind another pickup. He gripped the steering wheel so tightly his knuckles were white. As he turned to open his door, she couldn't help but notice how his hands shook.

Aching, trying to mask her own fear, Amelia got out, hoping she wouldn't hear gunshots. She remembered watching numerous news stories of different schools and shooters, the shell-shocked expressions on the parents' faces, the weight of their terror and worry showing in their red-rimmed eyes. She thought too of seeing the awful grief, the pain of learning there had been injuries and fatalities. No, she wouldn't go there. Not now, not today. Instead, she forced herself to remember more positive outcomes. Crushing hugs and loud, grateful shouts, reunions and tears of joy.

This last would be the outcome here. It had to be.

She hung back as she and Ted reached the group of parents. A few of the women shot curious glances her way, but most were focused on the school building, the several law enforcement vehicles parked in front, lights flashing blue and red. An ambulance and a fire truck also waited, clearly at the ready. There were no other signs of movement or—thankfully—sounds of gunfire. Several people stared at their phones, making Amelia wonder if they'd tried to reach their child or were waiting for word.

"Has anyone heard from someone inside?" one of the other fathers asked.

"My daughter texted me," one of the women said. "Just that she was all right but hiding. I was afraid to reply."

A couple other people voiced similar concerns. Like Ted, no one had wanted to risk texting in case doing so gave away a hiding place.

Amelia's stomach felt twisted. She could only imagine how Ted and the other parents must feel.

A small knot of people broke away from the larger group and began advancing on the school.

"Folks, I'm going to have to ask you to stay back," the deputy ordered. "For your own safety and that of everyone inside."

"I need to make sure my daughter is safe," a tall, thin man shouted. "You can't stop me from doing that."

"J.R.," Ted said, moving toward the other man. "You know he's right. If any of us went in there, Rayna and her people would have to worry about more than catching the shooter and keeping our kids safe." He took J.R.'s arm and turned him away, back toward the other parents. "Let's let the sheriff's department do their job."

"Look!" Someone pointed. "They're coming out!"

Rayna and two of her deputies emerged, walking someone who appeared to be handcuffed between them. One of the deputies carried a long shotgun of some sort. Rayna loaded the person, who appeared to be a teenager, into the back of her car and pulled away from the front of the school.

When she reached where her deputy's vehicle blocked the drive, she motioned at him to move. While he did, she got out and walked over to the clustered group of worried parents.

"All clear," she said. "No one shot, not even any injuries or anything. We have a suspect in custody. The school will be releasing the lockdown shortly and sending both texts and emails. Y'all have a good day."

People began asking questions. Rayna ignored these, climbing back into her vehicle and driving away.

"Look!" someone else shouted. "The kids are coming out."

Students and faculty began streaming out the high school doors, some running.

All at once, most of the parents took off running for the school. Others went back to their vehicles, choosing to drive there.

"Let's go," Ted said, clearly intending to go on foot. Amelia hurried to keep up, understanding and sharing his urgency.

Once they reached the group of students, faculty and other parents, chaos ensued. Some people reunited with their child immediately, while others milled about through the crowd, calling out names. From all around them, Amelia heard weeping and laughter and sounds of every emotion in between.

Her heart leaped when she spied Yolanda moving toward them, her head turning left and right, clearly looking for someone. When she spotted her father, a huge smile lit up her face as she barreled toward him. "Dad!"

"Yolanda!" Ted gathered his daughter up in a bear hug, holding her tight. When he released her, he clearly struggled to maintain his composure. "I'm so glad you're all right. Where's your sister?"

"I'm not sure." Yolanda continued scanning the crowd. "I haven't seen her or any of her group of friends."

At Ted's expression of alarm, Amelia touched his arm. "Remember, Rayna said no one was hurt. Yvonne's around here somewhere."

As the crowd of students pouring from the school began to thin without any sign of his other daughter, Ted began to fidget. "I'm worried," he said. "I'm going in to look for her. I'll be right back."

"Wait." Yolanda grabbed his arm. "I want to go with you."

Amelia saw the flash of panic in the teenager's eyes and understood that she didn't want to be separated from her father. "I'll go also," Amelia said.

The three of them, walking against the slowing tide of people, entered the school.

"There she is." Yolanda pointed. "With all of her new friends."

Sure enough, Yvonne stood in the middle of a group of other students, all clustered together in a tight circle. One of the boys, tall, dark haired and with the look of an athlete, appeared to be talking to the others earnestly.

As Ted, Amelia and Yolanda moved toward them, Yvonne glanced up. Her instant panicked expression spoke volumes, making Amelia wonder what she and her group were up to.

"My dad," Yvonne warned, which made the circle of students break apart just before Ted reached them.

"What's going on here?" Ted demanded, his gaze touching on his daughter before he glared at the others. "Don't you have something better to do? Most of your parents are anxiously searching for you outside right now. Maybe you should go find them."

Immediately, the kids scattered. Some moved quickly, their expressions guilty. One or two, like the tall boy who'd been speaking, sauntered defiantly away, a smirk on his face.

Tears in her eyes, Yvonne faced her father. "You embarrassed me."

Amelia and Ted exchanged a look. Even Yolanda appeared stunned.

"After what just happened, this is what you're worried about?" Yolanda asked, her mouth twisted wryly. "Everyone else has been panicked. What's wrong with you?"

"What's wrong with *you*?" Yvonne sneered, mimicking her sister. "No one got hurt. Shots weren't even fired. We're all okay. No big deal."

Ted's jaw tightened. "Let's go." He pointed toward the door. "Now."

Chin up, Yvonne sauntered toward the door.

Insides twisting in shocked disbelief, Amelia followed her. Ted and Yolanda were right behind.

They rode home in silence. Yvonne, apparently unconcerned, hummed to herself as she stared out the window. Yolanda fidgeted in her seat, but also didn't talk, though she kept stealing glances at her sister. Amelia, who'd turned around in her seat, tried to catch Yvonne's eye, but the teenager wouldn't even look at her.

Driving, Ted appeared lost in thought. Judging by the tension vibrating from him, Amelia figured his girls would be getting an earful when they got home.

His cell phone rang just as he pulled into the driveway. After he killed the engine, he glanced at the screen. "It's Rayna," he said. "You girls go ahead into the house and wait for me. I'll be inside in a minute."

Both Yvonne and Yolanda took off for the house. Amelia started to get out, but Ted touched her arm, stopping her. "Wait," he said and answered the call.

Whatever Rayna had to say, she kept it brief. Ted listened for a moment and then said he'd be on his way in ten minutes.

"Rayna has called in all the parents of Yvonne's new friend group," he said, the worry in his voice reflected in his eyes. "I'll need to be down at the sheriff's department in a little bit."

"What's this about?" Amelia asked.

"No idea. She said she'd discuss it once everyone got there." He heaved a sigh. "Right now, I need to have a little chat with the girls. Maybe Yvonne might be able to shed some light on this thing."

Privately, Amelia wondered about that. "Would you like some privacy?" she asked, as she followed him into the house. "I've got laundry I can do."

He stopped and met her gaze. "Actually, if you don't mind, I could use your support. I almost don't recognize my own daughter."

Both girls were seated at the kitchen table. Yolanda

appeared jumpy, on edge. Possibly a delayed reaction to the events at school. Yvonne, on the other hand, seemed nonchalant, the only sign of any nervousness the constant motion of one leg.

Ted pulled out a chair and straddled it. "Today was terrifying," he said bluntly. "For me and I'm sure definitely for you. Did either of you see the kid with the gun?"

"Not me," Yolanda answered. "I'm not even sure who it was."

Head down, Yvonne traced invisible patterns on the tabletop. Instead of responding verbally, she shook her head.

"Yvonne?" Ted prompted. "Any idea why the sheriff's office wants to talk to the parents of your new group of friends?"

She snapped her head up at that. "That's ridiculous," she muttered. "None of us had anything to do with this."

Checking his watch, Ted sighed. "I guess I'm just going to have to go down there and find out. So help me, Yvonne, if I find out you're lying to me…"

"I'm not." Though she spoke with defiance, her mouth trembled a bit. "I'm not a bad person, Dad. You should know that."

Ted relented and gave her and then her sister a quick hug. "I know," he responded quietly. "I love you both. I'd better go find out what Rayna has to say. I'll be back."

Chapter 10

When Ted arrived at the sheriff's department, he sat in his truck for a moment and took deep breaths, trying to calm his shattered nerves. This raising teenagers wasn't for the faint of heart.

Finally, he climbed out and headed toward the door. As he walked inside, he spotted several other people who all looked like other parents. He recognized a couple of them from earlier, and some others he'd known for years, though he wasn't 100 percent sure of all their names.

Making small talk, they milled around in the reception area. Ted could tell most of them were as worried as he was. Judging from their comments, no one seemed to know exactly why they were there.

One of the deputies came up front. "If you all would follow me back to the conference room, Rayna will be in to talk with you shortly."

"Is this about what happened at the high school today?" one of the mothers asked.

"Ma'am, I'll let Rayna give you the explanation."

As they followed him back to the conference room, Ted exchanged looks with another man, who appeared familiar. Then he realized. This guy was Donella's father.

And that meant all the others were parents of Yvonne's new friends.

"Take a seat. Rayna will be in shortly."

There were enough chairs around the conference table for everyone. Ted took a seat at the end of the table, closest to the door. When Rayna walked in, he caught her eye and she dipped her chin in acknowledgment, though she didn't crack a smile.

The room quieted as she strode to the front.

"As you all are aware, we had an incident at the high school this morning. I'm sure the school will be putting out an official statement soon, but I've asked you all to come in because the boy we took into custody—whose name won't be released just yet—feels all of your children are part of a group who had something to do with Donella Abernathy and Heather Peeks's disappearance."

Everyone started talking at once. Stunned, Ted simply sat back and watched. He had no idea what Rayna meant, though he knew she'd tell them as soon as the others calmed down.

Eventually, the rest of the parents figured that out as well and got quiet.

Rayna nodded, her smile professional, her green eyes cool. "Today at 10:03 a.m., our dispatch received a call that a teenage boy had been spotted on the campus of Getaway High School with a hunting rifle. The school was immediately placed on lockdown," Rayna said, her tone brisk. "The boy had shepherded a group of children—your children—into an empty classroom and appeared to be holding them hostage."

"What?" The word escaped Ted before he had time to clamp it back down. Yvonne had claimed to know absolutely nothing about the incident. Maybe now he would also find out why.

The news shocked other people as well. A couple of the women gasped. One put her head down on the table, as if she believed she might faint.

Again, Rayna waited for them to grow silent. "Apparently, this boy knew where your children were all hanging out as a group. He'd used his weapon to threaten them and had herded them into an empty classroom. He demanded the other kids tell him where to find Donella and Heather, claiming he'd start shooting if someone didn't start talking." She held up her hand. "No shots were actually ever fired. When I entered the room with my weapon drawn, he immediately complied with my instructions and placed his rifle on the floor."

"Who was he?" someone asked. "I want his name."

"I'm not at liberty to release that right now," Rayna replied. "He's a minor and he's being charged with a federal crime."

"Then answer me this. Why are we here?" a man demanded angrily. "Surely you don't actually believe that our children had anything to do with those two girls' disappearance."

Donella's father stood. "Please, I'm begging you. Just ask your kids if they know anything. I'm worried sick about my daughter, and Heather's parents are too. They're still out searching, along with my wife, which is why they couldn't be here right now."

Ted thought of Yvonne and how secretive she'd been about her new friends. She'd actually lied to him when he'd asked her about what had happened at school. He pushed to his feet, determined to find out if any of the other parents had similar experiences. "I don't know if this group of kids recently formed, or if they've been hanging around together for a while. I do know that my daughter apparently recently became friends with them and she's been very secretive about it. None of them have been over to my home, and despite living in Getaway my entire life, I don't even know their names. Do any of you?"

Several of the other parents exchanged glances. Ted could have sworn some of their expressions were uneasy.

"What are you trying to say?" Anita Watters, a stocky brunette with frizzy long hair, stood up. Ted had gone to school with her, though they'd run in different groups. "Are you accusing our children of something? If so, spit it out."

"I'm not accusing anyone of anything," Ted replied, using as reasonable a tone as possible. "I'm worried about my daughter, just like I'm sure the rest of you are worried about your daughters and sons. Especially you." Ted nodded at Donella's father. "I'm just thinking if we get together and compare notes, we might get a better understanding of what's going on."

Joe and Marcine Turner pushed back their chairs in unison and stood. "We've heard enough. This is getting ridiculous."

"Sit. Back. Down." Rayna's voice, razor-sharp, cut through the air. "I'm not finished." She waited until they'd both taken a seat again before continuing. "I asked you all here not to accuse your children of anything, but to ask you to talk to them. Find out what they know, if anything. Any tidbit you might learn could be useful in locating the missing girls. Please call my office if anything turns up. That's all I have to say." Meeting each person's gaze individually, she smiled warmly. "Thank you for your time."

Then, head held high, Rayna left the room.

Everyone silently watched her go. A few seconds after she closed the door behind her, everyone started talking at once. Ted listened for a moment, hoping to hear something productive. Instead, accusations were slung. When the name-calling started, Ted got up and walked out the door.

On the way home, he reflected on what he wanted to ask Yvonne. Ever since the twins had been small, he'd taught them the value of honesty. As they'd grown older, he'd made it clear lies would not be tolerated. And now here they were. What all did Yvonne have to hide?

As he pulled into his driveway, he dug out his phone and called Yvonne's number. The call went straight to voice mail. Of course. Next up, he called Yolanda, who picked up immediately. "Will you please tell your sister to come outside?" he asked. "She and I are going to take a little drive."

"Sure thing, Dad."

He waited. And waited. Just when he'd started to think Yvonne would defy him and refuse to go, the front door opened and she slunk on out. As she climbed up into the front seat of his truck, she refused to look at him.

Putting the truck in Reverse, he backed out of the driveway and turned south, away from town. There were miles and miles of farm-to-market roads he could drive, with nothing but fields of crops and the occasional farmhouse to look at. Thinking roads, his father had called them. He'd taken Ted on more than a few drives just like this.

"I just got back from a meeting with the sheriff," he said a few minutes later. Yvonne continued to drum her fingers on the passenger door and acted as if she hadn't heard him.

"Why'd you lie to me?" he asked, his voice breaking. "That's not how we do things in this family."

Now he had her full attention, though she still didn't speak.

"Rayna had all the parents of your new group of friends come in. That's where I—and all the others— learned that the kid with the rifle took you all hostage."

"*Hostage* is a pretty strong word for what really happened," she protested.

"Oh really?" Amazed that his word choice was what she wanted to argue about, he continued. "Then what would you call moving a group of people into a room at gunpoint?"

At her shrug, he shook his head. "Why did you act like it was no big deal? You gave me the impression that you weren't closely involved in this at all."

"I never said that. I said no one got hurt—that's why it wasn't a big deal."

"Semantics," he snapped. "I also learned—from Rayna, not from you—why this young man targeted you and your friends, who I'm liking less by the moment."

"That's not fair. You don't even know my friends."

"Precisely," he replied. "Back to the kid with the rifle. You know, the one who caused the school to go into lockdown? The one who held you and these wonderful new friends of yours at gunpoint? According to the sheriff, this boy believes you all had something to do with Donella and Heather's disappearance. Want to tell me why he would think such a thing?"

Defiance flashed in her eyes. She tossed her head, sending her long, dark hair swinging. "I have no idea. Donella and Heather are our friends too, Dad. Why would we do something to harm them?"

"You tell me," he shot back. "And what do you mean by *harm them*?"

"That's what Keith said." Now Yvonne appeared truly miserable. "He said he thought we hurt them. It's ridiculous. I'm pretty sure Donella and Heather took off for Dallas. That's all they ever talked about. Heather would have wanted to do something to help Donella get out of her depression."

Patience, he reminded himself.

"That would be a great theory, except Donella disappeared first. If they went somewhere together, then why would they leave a full day apart?"

She opened her mouth and then closed it.

And Ted decided he'd had enough. He let the pickup coast to a stop before shifting into Park and turned in his seat to face her. "I need you to tell me the truth right now. What do you know about this? Any of it? Do you know what happened to those girls?"

"No," she replied, though she didn't sound positive.

"Kids talk," he pressed. "Surely someone in your group of friends has an idea. And Keith—the kid with the rifle—is going to be charged with a felony. He'll probably go to prison, depending on how old he is. Unless he has serious mental health issues, there's got to be a reason for his accusations."

"I don't know." Now on the verge of tears, she sniffed. "Why are you treating me like I did something wrong?"

Though his heart ached, he could only answer honestly. "Yvonne, your behavior has totally changed lately—and not for the better. You're skipping class, getting in trouble at school, and now I have to worry about your being targeted by an angry boy with a rifle." He took a deep breath, glad he'd managed to keep a reasonable, even tone. "I have to think your new choice of friends has something to do with it."

Wiping at her eyes, she shook her head. "I'm not a bad kid. Stop treating me like one."

He unclicked his seat belt and pulled her over for a hug. "I'm worried about you, Yvonne. Every single parent with a student at your school died a little bit inside while waiting to hear what had happened. You could have been shot. So could your friends."

"Yolanda could have been shot too," Yvonne protested, pulling back. "Why aren't you lecturing her?"

He shook his head. "This isn't about her and I think you know why. I want to meet these friends of yours. Not in a week or two, but in the next few days. Invite them over to the house."

Her eyes went wide. "I can't," she protested. "That would make me look like a loser. You don't understand. These are the cool kids. If I start acting like that, they'll dump me."

"Maybe that would be a good thing," he pointed out gently.

"You're trying to ruin my life." Ever the queen of mercurial moods, Yvonne started to weep. Loud crocodile tears.

Ted sighed and shifted into Drive. A few miles down

the road, he turned around in a farmhouse driveway
and headed back to the house.

Amelia had seen Ted pull up in the driveway earlier. She couldn't tell his expression from this distance,
but the fact that he didn't come in wasn't good. A minute later, she watched Yvonne march out to get into his
truck. As they drove away, Amelia exhaled. It must have
been a doozy of a meeting if he'd decided he needed to
talk to his daughter alone. Her stomach twisted, both in
worry for Yvonne and sympathy for Ted. A sudden mental image of her comforting him, late at night while the
house was dark and silent, their naked bodies twisted together under the sheets, made her go weak in the knees.

What the hell was wrong with her? Was this what
Serenity had seen when she'd made those cryptic comments the other day?

She started cleaning the house, trying to scrub away
her rising sense of panic. Earlier, when she'd heard about
the shooter at the high school, her terror over Yolanda's
and Yvonne's safety had been unbearable. She had gotten far too attached to this family and too quickly. Worse,
she'd already run once. How could she do that to them
again?

She couldn't. Honestly, unless Simon showed up, she
had to stick it out and try to make it work. If only she
could figure out a way to turn off her emotions. Not
just for the twins, but for Ted. At first, she'd chalked up
her attraction to him as merely physical. They'd kissed
and then they'd made love, but instead of slaking her
thirst, she only wanted him more. Craved him constantly,
every breath she took somehow coming back around to

him, though she tried not to allow herself to even think about it.

Being around him on a daily basis, watching the love with which he parented his girls, had made her realize she had come to care for him on an entirely different level. It both terrified and exhilarated her.

Still, she was enough of a realist to understand Ted might not feel the same way. If she wasn't careful, she'd likely end up with a broken heart. And right now, with her life still in upheaval and Simon remaining on the loose, she shouldn't even be thinking about relationships.

As always when she felt stressed, cleaning helped. She tackled the bathrooms first, scrubbing and mopping until the entire rooms gleamed. From there, she moved on to the kitchen and the den, before she vacuumed the entire house. Pleased to learn that nearly two hours had passed, she eyed the now-sparkling house with a sense of accomplishment and pride.

Yolanda, apparently afraid she'd be asked to help, had remained in her room the entire time. Once Amelia had turned the vacuum off and sat down at the kitchen table with a cup of hot tea, Yolanda cautiously emerged.

"Dad and Yvonne aren't back yet?" she asked, dropping into a chair across from Amelia. "I wonder what happened. He sounded mad when he told me to send Yvonne out."

"I'm wondering the same thing too."

"On the plus side, we don't have to go to school on Monday," Yolanda said, her eyes gleaming.

"What do you mean?"

"A bunch of kids have been talking, and almost all the parents want to keep their sons and daughters home on Monday. It got so bad that Principal Mahoney sent out an email and text to all the parents letting them know that classes are canceled for Monday." She grinned. "I'm sure Dad will see it eventually."

Amelia eyed the teenager. "How are you dealing with all this? It must have been scary, knowing someone brought a gun to school with the intent of harming people."

Yolanda's smile faded. "Honestly, it doesn't seem real. I mean, I know it's a miracle no one got hurt or killed, but most of us had no idea anything was going on until they announced the lockdown, shelter in place. Even then, we weren't sure what had happened." She shuddered. "The rumors are so out of control I had to put my phone away."

Fourteen, Amelia thought. Yolanda was just fourteen. "Come here," she said, holding out her arms.

Jumping up, Yolanda didn't hesitate. "I needed a hug," she said, her voice muffled against Amelia's shoulder. "How did you know?"

Amelia smoothed her hand over Yolanda's long, dark hair. "Because you're human, honey. Of course you'd need a hug after going through something like that."

After a moment, Yolanda moved away. "What about Yvonne?" she asked, her expression troubled. "I think she's going to need a hug too. And I really doubt Dad will think to give her one."

"I'll take care of that."

"Good." Yolanda pointed. "Because they're back. I'm not sure if I should disappear into my room or hang out here."

"That's up to you. But maybe your sister could use your support."

Yolanda nodded. Meanwhile, Amelia worked on trying to figure out if she should try to fade into the background or stay.

Neither Ted nor Yvonne were smiling when they came into the house. Amelia eyed Ted, noting the grim set of his mouth, and then purposely turned her attention to his daughter. "Yvonne, are you all right?"

Yvonne blinked. The question appeared to startle her. "I... No." And she began to cry.

Without hesitation, Amelia gathered her in her arms and simply held her. She met Ted's gaze over the teenager's head. For a moment, he appeared devastated. Then Yolanda rushed over to him and threw her arms around him, offering up her very own hug.

Heart full, right then and there, Amelia hoped she'd never have to leave. She'd never expected to find this—a sense of belonging, the bone-deep love for this family—but she had.

Ted's cell phone rang, cutting into the moment. With emotion thick in the room, he fumbled for it, no doubt intending to turn it off. But too late, the sound had Yolanda stepping back and Yvonne pushing away from Amelia.

Ted made a disgruntled sound as he managed to silence the offending phone. "How about we all go out to dinner later?" he offered. "We can do pizza, if you want."

Yolanda immediately perked up, though Yvonne didn't react. Amelia watched both of them, glad she hadn't started anything yet for the evening meal.

"I'm in," Yolanda said.

"What about you, Yvonne?" Ted asked, his voice gentle.

She sniffed, wiping at her eyes. "I guess," she finally allowed.

Ted looked at Amelia. "How about you? It's buffet style, all-you-can-eat."

"Sounds good," she said. "I'd actually welcome a distraction."

He nodded, appearing to notice the superclean house for the first time. "The house looks great," he said.

"That's what you pay me for," she quipped. "Are you going to work out on the ranch now?"

Expression solemn, he shook his head. "Not today. I feel like staying close to home. We need to stick together today."

Liking that he included her in the *we*, she smiled. "Let me know what time we're going out, so I can be ready."

They ended up leaving the house shortly after five. Both girls had changed into sweatshirts and jeans. Watching them walk into the room, Amelia felt a sense of pride. And then when Ted showed up, her mouth went dry.

He wore clean Wranglers, a pair of what had to be dress boots and a cotton button-down shirt. He carried his cowboy hat in his hand. He could have been, Amelia thought, a poster for a Western novel, or a sexy actor in a commercial for the newest pickup truck.

If he noticed her weak-kneed reaction, he didn't show it. The girls were both absorbed in their phones. Just this once, Amelia was relieved.

Evidently, most of the other parents in town had come up with the same idea—dinner out. Whether to celebrate family, the relief and joy of knowing that none of their kids had come to serious harm, or as a distraction from a terrifying event.

Every single eating establishment that they passed had full parking lots. Pizza Perfect was no exception.

Ted managed to luck into a spot another vehicle was just backing out of. They headed toward the door and got in line.

"I'll find us a table," Yolanda said, ever helpful. She dashed off, weaving through the crowded restaurant, in search of a four-top.

Ted paid and they were given plastic drink glasses. Yvonne, clearly having done this before, got two trays and two plates. "I know what she likes to eat," she told Amelia.

"That's nice of you." Amelia smiled. She couldn't remember the last time she'd gone to a pizza buffet. She decided to try a slice of just about everything.

Once they were all seated at the table, everyone started eating. Around them, the buzz of conversation hummed. Amelia heard the words *school* and *shooter*, but tried to block out the other conversations. She only hoped the girls were able to do the same.

"Hush." The word rippled through the restaurant, and the diners began to quiet.

"Turn up the television," someone said, pointing to the large flat-screen that hung on the back wall. "It looks like Rayna is giving a news conference."

Indeed, Rayna stood in front of a room crowded with reporters. It looked like all the major media outlets were represented. She spoke with the clipped, confident tones of someone who had done this sort of thing before. And she had, when Getaway had actually had their own serial killer.

A fact many of the reporters appeared determined to remind her of. After numerous attempts to interrupt her, Rayna finally held up her hand. "Once again, I will attempt to answer questions when I am finished giving my statement. I ask that you give me a chance to do that."

The entire pizza parlor listened as she outlined the events at the high school earlier that day. "We have the suspect in custody," she concluded. "There were no injuries or deaths. Now I will answer questions."

"What about the disappearance of two female students?" a tall woman with short, dark hair asked. "Is it true that Getaway might actually have yet another serial killer?"

"We have no evidence that would suggest such a thing," Rayna responded. "And we are actively searching for the students. There is a possibility that they might have taken off on their own. Next question."

"What about the Coffee Shop Killer? We've spoken to several residents who believe he is behind this."

Amelia stiffened, her attention riveted on the TV.

"Again, we have no evidence to suggest that the Coffee Shop Killer has come to west Texas," Rayna said. "In fact, last I heard, he was believed to be in New Orleans."

After that, there were a few more questions about the incident at the high school, and then Rayna ended the news conference.

Instantly, the buzz of voices all talking at once resumed.

Though they continued eating, both Yvonne and Yolanda appeared rattled by what they'd heard. Amelia met Ted's gaze across the table. He shrugged and got up to go back for seconds, clearly not picking up the nuance of his daughters' moods.

"Are you okay?" Amelia asked them. They both nodded, though Yvonne wouldn't meet her gaze.

"I wish I'd never heard of that Coffee Shop Killer

guy," Yvonne said angrily. "I should have done a report on someone else."

"Why?" Amelia put down her last slice of pizza. "Did you not get a good grade on it?"

"We haven't gotten our grades yet. But all my friends have gotten totally obsessed by him. I tried to tell them what you told me—how he is an evil person—but they don't want to hear it." Again, she appeared on the verge of tears, picking up a paper napkin to blot her eyes.

"A lot of the kids in school are really into him," Yolanda agreed. "It's really sick and weird."

The thought of anyone being into Simon and his depraved deeds made Amelia feel ill.

Ted reappeared, his plate loaded up with dessert pizzas. "Your turn," he told his daughters, including Amelia in his smile. Instantly, both girls pushed to their feet and took off.

"They both love the caramel-apple pizza," he said. "You should try it."

"I've lost my appetite," Amelia told him, relaying the conversation he'd missed. "Why would kids find a serial killer cool?"

"No idea." He shook his head. "Maybe once Donella and Heather show up, they'll all settle down back to normal."

Normal. A word Amelia wished with all her heart to be again.

Except what would she consider normal these days? She couldn't imagine going back to her old life as a therapist living in her trendy condo in White Plains, New York. As far as she could tell, Getaway had no one offering counseling or therapy, except for the churches. People like Donella who were sorely in need of help would have to travel to Abilene or maybe even Midland–Odessa. Maybe once Simon was recaptured, she could stay here and set up shop.

Lost in thought, she blinked as she realized Ted was eyeing her across the table.

"Are you all right?" he asked. "You looked a thousand miles away."

"I'm fine," she replied, managing a smile. "In fact, I've changed my mind. A slice of dessert pizza sounds wonderful."

As everyone returned to the table, their plates once again piled high, Amelia looked around at the little family and her heart squeezed. When they'd finished, they drove home, the Coffee Shop Killer once again forgotten by everyone but Amelia. As long as the specter of Simon hung over her head, she knew he'd never be far from her thoughts.

As soon as they arrived back at the house, the girls immediately disappeared to their room. Instead of heading into the den to watch TV like he usually did, Ted said he needed to go to the barn to check on one of the horses. "Floyd called me earlier and said she had a bad case of thrush, so he put her in a stall in the big barn. I've got medicine for that and I need to go put some more on her feet." He hesitated. "Would you like to join me?"

"I'd love to." Stretching, she smiled. "I feel like I need to move around after eating all that pizza."

Out the back door, gravel crunching underfoot, they walked side by side in companionable silence toward the barn. He didn't try to hold her hand and she told herself she was grateful. The full moon provided enough illumination, and they didn't need a flashlight. Once at the barn, Ted flipped a switch and turned on an outside light high up on a pole.

Amelia breathed in the night scents of fields and hay and horses, feeling better than she had all day. Looking up at Ted, she opened her mouth to tell him so. Instead, he pulled her close and covered her lips with his.

Chapter 11

Ted hadn't meant to kiss her, but something about the way the light hit Amelia's upturned face had touched him in ways he didn't want to examine too closely.

The instant his mouth covered hers, heat roared between them, so fierce he instinctively tightened his hold on her.

She kissed him back, with so much intensity he knew she'd been wanting him too. They clung to each other, and he took his time, kissing her slowly and thoroughly, until they were both breathing hard. When they broke apart, she still held on to him, almost as if she was too dizzy to stand on her own.

"I want you," she murmured, the husky thrum of desire in her voice nearly undoing him. "I know we agreed we wouldn't—"

"Shh." One more kiss, to keep her from saying the

words. He craved her so badly he shook. The barn, the hay… He had a flash of a mental image of them naked in the hayloft, like teenagers.

As if she knew his thoughts, she shook her head. "Not here, not now." Pointing to the house with yellow light shining from the windows, she sighed. "I know they most likely won't come looking for you, but it's been a rough day. I don't want to take a chance of them seeing us like that."

"Though I hate to admit it, you're right." Tugging her to come with him, he found her a seat on a bale of hay. He needed distance and time to tame his fully aroused body. "Wait here while I take care of my horse."

Though she nodded, she got up and followed him anyway, remaining outside the stall and watching while he doctored each of the mare's feet. The routine task and the pungent smell of the medicine went a long way toward helping him get himself under control.

When he'd finished, he eyed her. "Do you want to go back to the house or would you rather sit out here and talk?"

Instead of answering, she hopped back on the hay bale and grinned, patting the spot next to her. "Just to talk," she clarified, still smiling.

Damned if she wasn't the most beautiful woman he'd ever seen. In that instant, his need for her made him ache. Somehow, he managed to act normally and sit down beside her, hoping she wouldn't notice her effect on him.

"You know what? I'm worried about those two girls," she mused. "It's not a good sign when more than forty-eight hours has gone by without any sign of them."

As changes of subject went, this was a doozy. It actually took him a moment to drag his mind away from carnal thoughts to focus on her statement.

"I agree," he said. "Especially knowing Donella. These days, she's inclined to run toward trouble rather than away from it. I wish her parents would have gotten her the help she needs."

"Me too. Sadly, so many teenagers cry out for help and their parents either ignore them or are too ashamed to get them counseling. I've seen it happen time and time again in my practice. By the time they made it to me, sometimes I wondered if I could even help or if it was too late."

"Is that what you specialized in, before? I know you said you were a therapist. Did you also counsel teenagers?"

Eyes wide, she slowly nodded. "Yes. That was my specialty, actually. I only took on Simon because he knew one of my patients' parents. I'm a licensed therapist in the state of New York. It's called the LMHC—Licensed Mental Health Counselor."

New York. So far away. He wondered if she'd return there once Simon was recaptured and locked away. The thought brought him an aching pain, strong enough that for a moment he couldn't catch his breath. "Do you miss it?" he asked, not sure if he meant New York or her profession.

"Sometimes." She glanced sideways at him, her gaze assessing. "I'm a damn good therapist. I actually feel it's what I was born to do." Hesitating, she paused. "This might seem strange to you, but I've even been thinking maybe once all of this with Simon is over, getting my license for Texas and setting up shop here in Getaway."

She'd thought about staying? A rush of happiness

swept through him. "Getaway could really use some-one," he told her honestly. "There's nowhere in town people can get counseling other than one of the churches. Which would be awkward if you didn't belong."

Silent, she nodded. He couldn't tell her thoughts from her expression, so he decided to change the sub-ject. "What do you think of all this talk about the Cof-fee Shop Killer?" he asked, tucking a wayward strand of hair behind her ear.

She shuddered. "It's like I can't escape him. Every-where I go, people still talk about him. Honestly, I'm surprised no one else has recognized me yet."

"Maybe because the news hasn't been replaying his trial anymore," he pointed out. "They've mostly been focusing on the New Orleans killings and the fact that there still haven't been any sightings of him."

"At least I'm ninety-nine percent sure he hasn't come to town." Leaning her head on his shoulder, she slipped her fingers in between his. "Otherwise, people would have been talking about a stranger asking around about me."

"About you?" He eyed her. "Didn't you change your name?"

"I...I did, but only my last. I figured 'Amelia' wasn't uncommon enough to worry about."

"Well, it's not that common either," he said. "Actu-ally, you're the first Amelia I've ever met."

Head down, she swore softly under her breath. "Still," she said, "no one has come to town asking around about an Amelia. Someone would have told you, right?"

"I'm thinking so. Since most everyone knows you're staying at my place." He could sit with her like this all night, he thought, though he ached to bury himself inside of her and make love long and slow until neither could take any more. His body hardened at the thought.

Oblivious, Amelia sighed. "I just wish the authorities would hurry up and catch him. I'm tired of feeling as if my life is on hold."

On hold. For the first time, he realized that he and his family might just be a place marker for her. Even if she decided to stay in Getaway, that didn't guarantee that she'd still want him and his girls in her life. And now, with so much going on, definitely wasn't the time to press her.

Pushing to his feet, he held out his hand. When she took it, he pulled her up as well. "Let's walk," he said. "Even though it's pretty dark by now, that moon has got everything well lit."

They left the barn. On the way out, he turned off the pole light.

"You were right," she mused, slightly breathless. "The moonlight is amazing."

Holding her hand, he led her up a different path, one that went on the far side of the barn and into one of his larger fields.

"Too much open space," she said. "And not enough cover."

Startled, he stopped moving. "I'm sorry—what?"

She smiled sheepishly. "Old habit. Ever since I've been hiding out from Simon, I automatically scope out available escape routes. That's what I was doing the first time you took me out here."

He remembered her insisting they see what lay over the ridge. Now he knew why. "Damn, that's tough."

At his comment, she lifted her chin. "True, it is. But I'd much rather be prepared. If he ever finds me and comes for me, I'm going to need every advantage I can find."

"Come here." Pulling her close, he tucked her into his body and held her tight. "You know I'll always have your back, right?"

At first, she didn't respond. Finally, she nodded her head. "Thank you for that."

"I mean it. So will others here in town. Rayna and Serenity and some of your customers who came in the store, to name a few. You've got friends, and here being a friend is the same as family."

This time, when she looked up at him, a sheen of tears glimmered in her eyes. "That means a lot to me," she whispered, her voice breaking.

Ah damn. Unable to help himself, he kissed her again. Slow and deep, the drugging sort of wet, openmouthed kisses that eventually led to the shedding of clothes.

Reluctantly, he pulled away.

"Tease," she said, with a half smile, which made him laugh despite his aching arousal.

"I wish I didn't have to be," he admitted. "Come on. Let's go back to the house. It's getting chilly and I bet a nice hot drink would hit the spot."

"Rum toddy?" she guessed. "Or hot cocoa with Irish Cream?" All the way back to the house, she kept up with a running list of hot drinks, some of which he'd never heard of. But by the time they reached the front porch, he was grinning as big as she.

"That was fun," he told her, holding open the door for her to pass. Laughing, she agreed.

"Dad?" Yvonne waited for them in the kitchen, her expression worried.

Instantly, Ted went to her. "What is it? What's wrong?"

"I heard from Donella," she answered, her voice quavering. "At least I think it was her, even though she didn't text from her regular phone number."

Alarm bells sounding inside his head, he held out his hand for her phone. "Let me see, please."

For the first time since she'd become a teenager, she willingly relinquished her phone, handing it over without another word.

Don't worry, I'm safe. Just a lot going on and my head is messed up. Tell the others I'm fine. Donella.

After reading the text out loud, Ted frowned. "We need to call Rayna."

Eyes wide, Yvonne nodded. "I haven't told anyone else yet," she said. "But can I? Donella wanted me to tell our friends."

"Let's wait and see what Rayna says."

Rayna arrived ten minutes after Ted called. After reading the text message on Yvonne's phone, she eyed the teenager. "Did you try calling the number back?" she asked.

"Calling?" Yvonne spoke the word as if it was foreign. "You mean like *talking* to her?"

"Yes, like talking to her. Don't tell me you kids don't speak on the phone."

Yvonne shrugged. "We'd rather text. Or Kik or Holla. Some of the kids use Lipsi."

"What do you mean by all that?" Ted asked, scratching his head.

"Those are apps," Rayna told him. "Like Snapchat and Instagram."

Yvonne nodded. "Sort of," she said. "That's why I

was surprised that she texted me. Especially since she and I aren't really close and she's been gone a couple of weeks."

"I'm going to call the number back and see what happens," Rayna explained. "I'd feel a lot better if Donella herself actually answered."

She punched the icon to call the number. "It went straight to voice mail. Whoever set up the voice mail didn't make it a personal account. It was the standard 'The person you are trying to reach is not available. Please leave your name and number at the tone.'"

"I don't think Donella would do something like that." Yvonne appeared worried again, her eyes huge. "Do you think whoever texted me might be the person who has her?"

About to reassure his daughter, Ted stopped when Rayna nodded in agreement. "That's good thinking and a very realistic possibility," she said. "Right now, I'm going to take this phone to the FBI and let their analysts work on it. And, Yvonne, we're going to be careful."

"Careful how?" Ted asked, fear for his girls settling in his gut.

Rayna met his gaze. "I'm worried someone might be targeting your daughter," she said. "It's highly unlikely that person who sent the text was actually Donella. For that reason, I'm going to have to ask you all to keep quiet about this."

"I can't even tell my friends?" Yvonne asked, her expression incredulous.

"No. Not right now," Rayna responded. "I'm sorry."

Eyeing her phone, Yvonne sighed. "How long until I get my phone back?"

"I don't know." Rayna made a noncommittal face. "But I'll tell them to put a rush on it, okay?"

"No, it's not okay." Yvonne turned to Ted. "Dad, you know how much I depend on my phone. School assignments, school news, and it's how all my friends and I stay connected."

She sounded, Ted thought, very adult right now. "I'll see what I can do about getting another phone and adding it to our plan. You can use that until you get yours back, though you'll have to give everyone the new number. Will that work?"

"Can I have the newest iPhone?" Yvonne asked, her expression hopeful. "Yolanda will be so jealous."

Amelia laughed. Even Rayna cracked a smile.

"We'll see," Ted replied. "But probably not, since it's a temporary phone."

"Humph," Yvonne snorted. "I'll be in my room if you need me." And she flounced out of the room.

"Teenagers," Ted and Amelia said at the same time, which made Amelia laugh. Ted couldn't help but smile back at her, an interaction that Rayna watched with interest.

"Listen," Rayna said, "I'm not sure what exactly is going on, but I seriously doubt whoever sent that text message to Yvonne was Donella." She sighed. "Though who knows—it might have been. It's entirely possible Donella could be reaching out to let folks know she's okay."

"Is she okay?" Ted asked. "I mean, with her being gone so long, do you think she's all right?"

Rayna eyed him, her grave expression answer enough. "I really can't speculate," she said. "We still don't know if she ran away of her own free will or not. Her parents have actually stopped cooperating with us, which starts an entirely different sort of narrative."

This was news to Ted. Horrified, he tried to process Rayna's words. "You don't think they had something to do with her disappearance, do you? They seemed really worried when all this happened."

"I have no clue. Anything is possible in a scenario like this." Rayna turned to go. "If you hear anything new, please keep me posted. I'll let you know when you can pick up Yvonne's phone."

Ted followed her out. "Are you sure we shouldn't let some of the other parents know about this?" he asked.

"Not until we have an idea what we're dealing with." Rayna got into her car. "Ted, I know you've had a little bit of trouble with Yvonne. If I were you, I'd keep a close eye on her. She's vulnerable right now, torn between loyalty to friends and to family."

With those chilling words, Rayna started her engine and drove away.

The text came through just as Amelia finished turning down her bed. The evening with Ted had been magical, right up until the moment they'd returned home and learned someone had apparently targeted Yvonne. Worse, the teenager was too young to realize the possible implications of this. Luckily, she had a father like Ted to take care of her.

Hearing that Donella's parents had stopped cooperating with the police had hit her like a punch to the stomach. In the past, when parents stopped cooperating in missing child cases, that tended to indicate that they'd done something to the child. Every single time.

Which really made her worry for Donella.

Still trying to figure out who had texted Yvonne and why, she'd been about to change into her pajamas and wash up when the text alert chimed. Heart skipping a beat, she snatched up her phone, wondering if Ted had changed his mind and wanted to come to her room.

But no, her screen showed a number she didn't have stored.

I need your help. My name is Donella Abernathy. I recognized you from TV and know you're a therapist. Would you talk to me, please? Could you meet me at the end of your driveway? Now?

Which sent warning alarms shrieking. Donella. Right. Her heartbeat stuttered. Real or, like the text Yvonne had received, a suspected impostor? What if both times it really had been her? Where'd you get my number? she texted back, curious to learn the answer.

I saw it on Yvonne's phone a while back.

Strange, but not out of the realm of possibility. Still, she hesitated. Because even though she couldn't think of a single reason why whoever might be impersonating Donella would target her, it still could be possible.

Please.

Another text.

I'm desperate. I texted Yvonne to let her know I'm all right, but I'm not. I don't know what to do. I can't go home.

This tugged at her emotions, exactly as anyone who knew her true profession would realize. Especially Simon. Her blood turned to ice. It was entirely possible that Simon would operate this way, using one of his other victims to lure Amelia in. Damn, she hoped not, but on the other hand, if Simon had tracked her down, even though every instinct screamed she needed to run, she was more than ready to end it with him. One way or another.

Reaching under her bed, she retrieved a locked metal box. She put in the combination and, once it clicked open, retrieved her .38 Special. One of the first things she'd done when she'd arrived in Texas had been to purchase a pistol and take lessons, though she hadn't gone so far as to obtain her concealed-handgun permit. She'd been afraid that the legalities would draw unwanted attention.

After checking to make sure she had it loaded with the Winchester PDX1 Defender hollow-point bullets she'd purchased, she strapped on her shoulder holster. Suitably armed, she slipped on a light jacket and took a deep breath.

Should she go get Ted, just as an extra precaution? At first, she rejected the idea. If this truly turned out to be Donella, she knew that sometimes people in need wouldn't talk in front of someone they knew. The fact that Donella had been desperate enough to reach out to a total stranger spoke volumes. This was the kind of crisis Amelia had been trained for. What else could she do but go out and talk to the girl? Alone.

If, in fact, this truly was Donella. Again, she couldn't think of a single reason other than Simon why she would be targeted, just as she couldn't see why Yvonne would be either. It seemed entirely possible that a scared and confused teenager had reached out to two people she felt she could trust.

Or she was being royally played.

Never one to let misgivings paralyze her, she pulled out her phone.

On my way, she sent back.

Stealthy as a wraith, she slipped through the house. As she reached the front door, she once again hesitated, her suspicion getting the best of her. Though she wanted to help, the fact that Yvonne had gotten a text the same day from someone purporting to be Donella could be good or bad. Truthfully, she leaned toward thinking the young girl had finally decided to reach out, but then that begged the question of what had happened to her friend Heather.

Amelia reconsidered. She needed to actually alert Ted but ask him to remain inside the house, so she'd have backup in case she needed it.

Back down the dark hallway she went. Though his door was closed, she thought she could see a sliver of light coming from underneath.

She tapped lightly, hoping the sound wasn't enough to disturb anyone else. It took a moment, but finally his door creaked open.

Hair tousled, blinking back sleep, Ted peered out at her. "Amelia? What's wrong?"

Pushing her way past him, she motioned at him to close the door before she rapidly explained. Just as she finished, another text came through.

Where are you?

Give me a minute.

Wide-awake now, Ted shook his head. "I'm not buying this. You heard Rayna earlier. I don't think you should go out there at all."

"I'm very suspicious," she admitted. "But, assuming this is Donella reaching out for help, this kind of thing is exactly what I do."

"What if it's Simon?" he asked, cutting right to the heart of the matter. "What if he really does have those girls and is using them to draw you out? What then?"

She pulled aside her jacket to give him a clear view of her pistol. "I know how to use it," she said.

"Do you want me to go with you?" Without waiting for an answer, he went to his closet, opened the door and began keying in the code for his gun safe.

"What are you doing?" she asked, even though it was obvious. The sight of his pistol had her feeling both alarmed and relieved. Backup.

"More protection," he told her. "Are you ready?"

"Yes." She took a deep breath. "But you can't walk out there with me. If it is Donella and she sees you, it will likely spook her and she'll bolt. Either you stay just inside the door or go around the back."

"You've got to be kidding," he groused, clearly aware she wasn't. Then, when she shook her head, he cursed under his breath. "All right. Here's what we'll do. I'll slip out the back door, open the gate and go up one side of the house. I'll stay hidden right there. You go out front, meet Donella and talk. But whatever you do, don't leave the property, understand? I can't protect you if you do."

"I got it." With her heart pounding like a jackhammer, she took a steadying breath. "Let's do this."

Ted nodded. "If it isn't Donella or if you see something wrong—anything at all—get back inside and bolt the door."

"I will."

He pulled her close, pressing a quick kiss on her mouth. "Remember to give me a minute to get out the backyard gate."

Her phone pinged again as she reached the front entryway.

If you're not coming, I'll just leave.

I'm almost there. At the front door now.

Then, taking a deep breath, she opened the door and stepped outside.

A young girl stood between the house and the driveway, taking care to remain in the shelter of the large oak tree.

"Donella?" Amelia called softly, crossing the distance between them, glad of the full moon.

As she drew closer, keeping a careful eye on her surroundings, she saw both indecision and regret on the teenager's face. "Yes," the girl answered.

Relief flooded Amelia. "Honey, why don't you come inside, where it's warm, and we'll talk there?" She reached out to take Donella's arm.

That was when she saw the absolute misery in Donella's eyes. "I'm so, so sorry," Donella whispered. "But I didn't know what else to do."

A tall teenage boy whipped around from the other side of the tree. He had a gun, pointed right at Donella's head. "You come with me, or she dies," he ordered. "Right now."

Amelia froze. "What is going on here?" Was it Simon after all? Did he have this boy working with him?

"No one move." Ted stepped out from the side of the house, his own weapon drawn, aimed directly at the boy. "What's going on here?"

Donella began to cry. "They're making me do this. Heather is sick and she needs to see a doctor. But they're—"

"Shut up, Donella," the kid snarled. "Or I'll blow your stupid brains out right here."

"What is it you want?" Amelia asked, keeping her voice calm and level.

"You," he said. "You need to come with us."

"Why? Are you working with Simon?"

Gun still pressed against Donella's temple, he glowered at her. "Who?"

"The Coffee Shop Killer. Are you working with him?"

"They want to," Donella interjected, her voice quavering. "They—"

"Shut up!" the boy yelled. "Or I will pull this trigger. Is that what you want?" he asked Amelia. "To be responsible for her death? Not to mention her friend Heather, who really is sick. She might even die."

Amelia exchanged a glance with Ted. "It seems we're at an impasse," she said, still maintaining her cool tone. "Ted here will shoot you if you so much as harm a single hair on this girl's head. I'm not going to go with you. Your move. What are you going to do?"

From the kid's incredulous expression, he hadn't anticipated her refusing to go. He looked as if he was about to be sick.

The front door opened and Yvonne stepped outside.

She took in the entire scene and her eyes widened. "Jacob? What are you doing?"

"Yvonne, get back inside right now," Ted ordered, keeping his pistol trained on the boy. "Call 911 and get Rayna out here. Immediately."

Yvonne froze. "But I know Jacob," she said. "He's one of my friends." Her gaze drifted past him to the girl he had his pistol on. "Donella?" Incredulous, Yvonne took a step toward them. "It *was* you who texted me, wasn't it?"

Though Ted didn't take his gaze off the boy or lower his gun, the kid didn't seem worried. A second later, another boy emerged and grabbed Yvonne, holding a pistol against her head. "Now," the other boy said, "what's it going to be? We can take Yvonne or we can take you, Amelia."

Ted froze. "Take your hands off my daughter."

"I'll go," Amelia said quietly. "Where is your vehicle?"

Jacob began backing away, still holding Donella. "The black cargo van," he said. "Get in."

Amelia did, noticing they'd left the engine running.

Then, with mounting horror, she watched as the other boy began dragging Yvonne toward the van. "You said you'd let her go," she protested.

Jacob pushed Donella in, knocking Amelia aside. He climbed into the driver's seat and put the shifter in Drive. "Hurry up," he yelled to his friend.

As the other boy reached the van, he jumped in and shoved Yvonne away. She fell hard to the ground just as Jacob floored the accelerator. As they peeled off, Amelia tried to look to make sure Yvonne was okay, but since the cargo van had no windows in back, she only got glimpses. She saw Ted running toward his fallen daughter, but then the van made a sharp right, pitching Amelia into a softly weeping Donella, and she saw nothing else.

Chapter 12

After quickly checking Yvonne to make sure she was okay, Ted ran for his pickup. He realized he didn't have his key and dashed back into the house, Yvonne limping along behind him. By the time he reemerged outside, the van was long gone.

He didn't care. He'd still go after them.

"Dad." Yvonne grabbed his arm, her voice urgent. "Look. They've slashed all four of your tires."

He wanted to curse. He wanted to scream. He did none of those things because Yvonne started to wail, on the verge of hysterics.

"This is all my fault," she cried. "I thought those kids were my friends."

Hugging his sobbing daughter close, Ted called Rayna's personal cell instead of 911. He was still in shock, his fingers shaking. He couldn't believe what had just happened.

With Yvonne still crying in the background, he relayed tersely what had happened.

"Sit tight," Rayna said. "I'm on my way."

Ted sat down on the front porch step, one arm around Yvonne, and waited.

Less than five minutes later, he spotted headlights as the sheriff's vehicle made its way up his long gravel drive.

Stepping out of her squad car, Rayna strode toward them. "Inside," she ordered, looking around them as if she expected more people to jump out from behind trees and start converging on them.

Still in shock, Ted shepherded Yvonne into the house. Rayna followed close behind.

Once they were inside the kitchen, Rayna glanced back at the door. "Someone has already alerted the media," she said, her grim voice matching her expression. "Probably that Jacob kid. He's trying to spin it as tied to the Coffee Shop Killer."

"Why?" Ted crossed his arms. "What is he trying to pull?"

"I don't know, but my office has started fielding calls from various news outlets. They're coming in fast, which means Jacob or whoever sent out multiple anonymous tips. First, the calls were local, then state, and now the national news has jumped on the story. I'll need to work on putting together a statement. In the meantime, I don't need to tell you how bad this is for Amelia."

"Because they might hurt her?" Yvonne asked, her eyes welling up again.

"No. I doubt they'll do anything to her," Rayna replied. "They grabbed her for another reason entirely. They want to get someone else's attention."

At first, Ted didn't understand what she meant. He'd been solely focused on Amelia being in danger from a young punk with a gun. But Rayna was right. When he realized the other implications, he swore. "If Simon wasn't actually behind this, once they start plastering Amelia's face all over the news coverage, he'll know exactly where to look for her."

"Bingo," Rayna said.

"I don't understand," Yolanda said. She stood just inside the doorway, eyeing them all with a look of confusion. "What's going on?"

Yvonne drew herself up, wiped her streaming eyes, grabbed a tissue and blew her nose before explaining. Yolanda listened with mounting concern. "Let me make sure I understand. You're telling me Donella is all right, Heather is really sick and Jacob had something to do with their disappearance. And now he's kidnapped Amelia as well?" Yolanda looked from one adult to the other, her incredulous expression practically begging them to tell her otherwise.

"Exactly," Ted said.

"Why would Jacob want to hurt Amelia?" Yvonne asked, still sniffling. "I mean, I don't get why he'd want to hurt anyone, but what's the deal with Amelia? And who's Simon?" A second after she spoke the name, a look of horror crossed her face. "Not Simon the Coffee Shop Killer?"

Slowly, Ted nodded. "Amelia was the only one of his victims that got away. She testified against him."

"And Simon swore to make her pay," Rayna finished. "So far, Amelia has been successful in keeping her whereabouts hidden from him. That will no longer be the case once the news picks up this story."

"Oh my gosh!" Eyes huge, Yolanda gaped at him. "That's why she looked so familiar."

"Yep." Rayna gave her a tight little smile. "I'm surprised more people didn't recognize her. She worries about that all the time. Now, once those idiot kids get her face plastered all over the media, Simon will know exactly where to locate her."

"Making her pay is the entire reason Simon has remained in hiding," Ted said. "Amelia lived in fear of him figuring out she was here."

"We can't let that happen. We've got to find Jacob," Yvonne said. "He's one of the kids who was really obsessed with the entire Coffee Shop Killer case, but I don't know why he went this far. I think at one time, he and Donella were together."

Though Ted wanted to ask what *together* meant— boyfriend and girlfriend or something more—now wasn't the time.

"I sent one of my deputies out to pick up his parents." Rayna eyed the teenager. "Hopefully they can shed some light on where he might be keeping the other girls hidden."

Yolanda spoke up again, her gaze locked on her sister. "Isn't Jacob one of your new besties?"

"He's in our group." For once, Yvonne didn't sound defensive. "He seemed like an okay kid. I can't believe he'd do something like this."

"Who was the other boy with him?" Ted asked.

"Lincoln Frazier," Yvonne answered. "He's Jacob's best friend. The two of them were really mad that I got the Coffee Shop Killer case for my project. They tried to pay me to give it to them." She shook her head. "I didn't believe they were serious, but they were."

Rayna's phone chimed. After glancing at it, she looked at Ted. "I've got to go. Keep your doors locked and stay inside. If I learn anything, I promise I will call you immediately."

Once she'd left, Ted checked the dead bolts on both doors. He made a quick call to Floyd, wincing at the late hour. Floyd was most likely sound asleep. When the call went to voice mail, Ted left a message, asking Floyd to pick him up in the morning and run him to the budget tire store in town.

Once he'd finished, he began to pace. He hated sitting around and doing nothing while Amelia was in danger. Both girls watched him, wide-eyed, making him realize they needed him to be calm and reassuring, strong in the way he'd always been for them. He took a deep breath and squared his shoulders before moving to the couch. Once he'd taken a seat, he motioned both girls to join him.

Exchanging quick glances, they rushed over and sat, one sitting close on each side. He put his arms around them and hugged them close. They sat that way together for a few minutes before he spoke. "Yvonne, it's time to start telling me whatever you know about those boys. I want to find Amelia before something really awful happens."

Eyes huge, she nodded. "I don't think either of them actually understand what a monster this Coffee Shop Killer guy is. I didn't either, until Amelia pointed that out. Once I started thinking about what his victims must have gone through, and how much he enjoyed torturing them, I felt sick. The report started out like a video game—not real, lots of action and kind of fun."

"Fun?" Ted asked, unable to keep the disbelief from his voice.

"It didn't seem real." Yvonne shrugged. "To Jacob and Lincoln, it's still not. I'm wondering if they've considered what they'll do if Simon wants to kill them too."

Yolanda gasped. "I didn't even think of that. Seriously, this guy isn't known for leaving any witnesses alive. Amelia was the only one."

Amelia. He wanted to help her, find her, save her. Right now, the knowledge that she was armed was the only thing keeping him sane.

"You're worried about her, aren't you?" Yolanda asked softly.

"I am," he acknowledged. "I just wish we had some idea where they might have taken her."

"I don't think they'll actually hurt her," Yolanda offered.

"I don't either," Yvonne seconded. "It's what will happen if they do succeed in getting the Coffee Shop Killer's attention that I'm worried about."

Ted thought about Amelia, sweet, generous Amelia, with her premapped escape routes and her passionate kisses. He couldn't stand the thought of something happening to her.

"You care about her." Ever astute, Yolanda stated this as fact rather than a question.

Considering, he slowly nodded. "Don't you?"

Again, the twins exchanged glances.

"We do," Yolanda answered, snuggling back into his side.

"Oh my gosh." Yvonne bolted up to her feet. "I just remembered something! I think I might know where they've taken her! Lincoln and Jacob were always wanting to set up a clubhouse at Lincoln's family's deer lease. They have a cabin there and it sits empty all year except for deer season."

"Which is right around the corner," Ted pointed out.

"Right. But it's not here yet. I'm betting that's where they're holed up."

"It's worth checking out," he agreed. "Do you know where it is?"

Her expression fell. "No. But it's not too far from here. If the sheriff's department talks to Lincoln's parents, they can find out."

Nodding, he called Rayna and told her what Yvonne had said.

"We just picked up the parents." Rayna sounded tired. "I'm headed down to the station to talk to them now. The FBI is in town, so I'll have to brief them and get them up to speed."

"The FBI?"

"Yep. As soon as word got out about the kidnapping, an FBI agent I've worked with before contacted me. They're here to assist. Once they find out that Amelia Ferguson is here, I'm sure they'll have lots of questions."

Ted swore. "She'd better be all right."

"I'm sure she will be. Those boys need her alive to act as a lure for Simon Barron. Anyway, once I have the location of this hunting cabin, I'll swing by and pick you up."

"I'll be ready," he replied. "Let me know when you're on your way."

"Will do." Rayna ended the call.

For the first time, Ted thought he'd better learn everything he could about Simon. "Yvonne?" he asked. "Do you mind if I read over your report on the Coffee Shop Killer?"

"Let me get my rough draft." She slid off the couch and hurried down the hall to her room. When she returned, she handed him a spiral notebook filled with paper. "Here you go. It's all in here."

"Thanks." Opening the notebook, Ted settled back to read.

What he learned chilled his blood. Yvonne had been thorough, which would no doubt get her an excellent grade. She'd clearly done her research, citing multiple sources from various types of media—print, television and online. From all accounts, Simon Barron had been a charming yet unremarkable man, the kind who could easily blend into a crowd. Nothing in his bland, ordinary features made him stand out in a crowd, and Ted suspected most people forgot his face five minutes after meeting him.

In true serial killer fashion, Simon had started out hurting small animals. From there, he'd progressed to torturing and killing them, which had appeared to keep him happy for a while. Until he'd been caught torturing a smaller classmate in middle school.

In the years between middle school and college, Simon had perfected his technique. He'd learned to choose a certain type of woman, the intellectual introvert who tended to hide behind her laptop and her books. He'd set out to become their best friend and even wingman if necessary. With his unassuming appearance and agreeable nature, they'd all quickly come to trust him. He met most of them in a local coffee shop—thus his nickname of the Coffee Shop Killer. He'd taken the time—weeks often—to befriend them, working side by side in the coffee shop with them. Always ready to make small talk, careful never to hit on them, so by the time they were willing to go somewhere alone with him, they'd never suspected what kind of monster lurked inside.

The torture these poor women had endured turned Ted's stomach. Even though Yvonne hadn't gone into graphic detail in her report, she'd included enough details to get the point across.

His last victim had been the one exception to his meet-in-the-coffee-shop rule. Amelia Ferguson had been his therapist, and while also educated and intelligent, she'd been hired for the sole purpose of hearing his deepest, darkest secrets. Ted noted that Yvonne hadn't made the connection between the Amelia in her report and *their* Amelia.

Interesting to note that, as far as anyone knew, he'd lied to her just as he had to all his other victims, spinning tales designed to garner sympathy and the natural desire to help.

Right there, Ted paused. He wasn't sure he could stand to read about what Simon had done to Amelia, though he knew he had to try.

"It's okay, Dad," Yvonne said, patting his shoulder clumsily. He looked up, realizing she'd been reading along with him. "She got away before he did anything really awful."

"Good." Clearing his throat, he got back to the final few pages. Basically, it finished with what he already knew. Amelia had testified, Simon had been convicted and sent away to life in prison without parole, but had escaped. During the trial, he'd sworn that Amelia would pay for what she'd done, and Yvonne had ended with her suspicion that he'd meant exactly what he'd said.

His phone rang. Rayna.

"We've got a location and we're on our way now," Rayna said. "I can swing by and pick you up, if you can be waiting outside."

"I'd like that," he replied.

"I should be there in five." Rayna ended the call.

Both Yolanda and Yvonne stared at him, wide-eyed.

"I'm going to go with Rayna and see if we can find Amelia," he told them. "I want you both to stay inside this house and lock the doors. Do you understand?"

Slowly, the twins each nodded.

"I want to go too," Yvonne said. "I thought those kids were my friends. I feel like this is my fault."

Gently, Ted reached out and smoothed her hair away from her face. "None of this is your fault, sweetheart. You couldn't possibly have known those boys would do something like this. I can't let you come—Rayna's bending the rules even to take me along—but I promise I'll call you as soon as I know something. Okay?"

Her sullen expression told him it was anything but.

"It's okay," Yolanda said, bumping her sister with her shoulder. "Just find Amelia and bring her back. That's what matters."

Riding in the dark, Amelia tried to keep an eye out for something that would tell her where they were going, but all she could see from the back were headlights on a highway and tall streetlights with flashes of white that cut through the darkness before disappearing again.

Donella's sobs had subsided and she sat curled into a ball on the opposite side of the cargo area from Amelia.

"Why are you doing this?" Amelia asked, keeping her voice as calm and reasonable as she could manage under the circumstances.

Instead of answering her, Jacob turned up the radio. Death metal music blared from the speakers, making Donella curl up even tighter.

Glad they hadn't noticed her holstered pistol, Amelia moved as close to the front as she could get, the better to see out the front window.

Finally, they turned off the highway and eventually onto a rutted dirt or gravel road. Jacob drove fast, considering the condition of the road. Each pit and pothole jolted them, bouncing both Amelia and Donella from their unsecured spots on the cargo bed. Due to the absence of streetlights out here, the darkness seemed absolute. All she could see ahead of their headlights was the thin sliver of road.

"Slow down," the other boy demanded, turning down the music. "The turnoff is right ahead."

Jacob slowed, the van bouncing and rattling as they hit yet another pothole.

Taking advantage of the reduced bouncing, Amelia scooted over to get closer to Donella. "Where are they taking us?" she asked, sotto voce.

Donella raised her head. "This is Lincoln's family's deer lease," she replied, jerking her chin toward the boy in the passenger seat. "They have an old hunting cabin up here. Since deer season doesn't start until November 3, they have the place to themselves."

November 3 wasn't far away. Which meant that they planned to wrap this up, whatever *this* might be, before then.

"You and Heather have been staying here?"

"Yeah." Donella nodded. "At first, it seemed like fun. Jacob and Lincoln have always talked about us using this place for a clubhouse. But then Heather got sick. She's really sick and they won't take her to a doctor. She can hardly breathe. She needs to go to the ER now, I think."

Amelia took a deep breath, wondering about one other thing. "Are the boys staying with you?"

"Not at night."

"What are you two talking about back there?" Lincoln demanded, turning in his seat.

"Nothing," Donella muttered.

The van coasted to a stop, the headlights revealing a small, rustic cabin with a metal roof. Clearly, it had electricity, since there appeared to be a light on inside.

"Welcome to your new home, Amelia. At least for now." Jacob's mocking smile had her gritting her teeth. "Let's go inside. Maybe you'll know what to do to help Heather. She seems kind of sick."

"Kind of?" Donella retorted. "She needs to see a doctor."

"I already told you," Jacob interjected. "No hospitals, no doctors. Everyone knows the two of you are missing. If she turns up, people are going to start asking questions."

"Maybe so." Donella stood her ground. "But now that you kidnapped an adult right in front of Yvonne's father, I think people are already asking questions."

Ignoring her, Lincoln opened the door and motioned everyone past him.

Inside, the two-room cabin appeared remarkably tidy, considering teenagers were using it. There were wood floors, wood walls and worn but comfortable furniture. A metal wood-burning stove sat in one corner. A small kitchen sat off to one side, with bags and boxes and paper plates piled high on the counter.

"Where's Heather?" Amelia asked.

"In the bedroom." Donella took her arm and led her into the second room. A lump under the blankets on a full-size bed had to be the other girl, though she didn't move or make a sound when Donella flicked on the light.

For one horrified moment, Amelia feared she'd died. Then a bout of hoarse, hacking coughing shook her, and Heather sat up in the bed, rasping and wheezing, clearly struggling to breathe.

Touching her forehead, Amelia winced. "She's burning up."

"What do you think is wrong with her?" Donella asked, her expression worried.

"I'm thinking pneumonia," Amelia murmured. "You're right—she does need immediate medical care."

"They're not going to let us take her."

Clearly exhausted, once the coughing subsided, Heather closed her eyes and curled back up under the covers.

"I gave her some antibiotics," Lincoln said, having followed them into the room. "I stole some leftover ones from my mother."

Amelia winced. "What kind and how many did she take?"

"I don't know." Defensive again, he shrugged. "But they didn't help. Actually, she got worse after that."

"Hey, Lincoln," Jacob called from the other room. "Bring Amelia out here really quick. It's picture time."

"Come on." Grabbing her arm, Lincoln steered her into the main room. He tried to hand her a newspaper. "Hold this and stand against the wall over there."

She eyed him and Jacob, who stood with his phone

ready, with horror. "You don't really understand what you're about to do," she said. "Simon is a monster."

"He's a legend." The fervor in Jacob's voice sent a chill through her. "We can't wait for him to reward us for finding you for him."

"Reward you?" Incredulous, she shook her head. "Most likely he'll torture and kill you both too, just for the fun of it. Did you even read what kind of awful things he did to his victims?"

For a brief second, Jacob appeared uncertain. But then he glanced at his watch and shook his head. "You're wrong."

Desperate, Amelia tried to figure out a way to stall. "What time is it? I'm guessing it's after two in the morning. If you're going to send this out to the media, isn't this the wrong time to do it?"

Jacob grinned, the smug expression back on his face. "This is the perfect time. Once I get the story out there, it'll be on time for the early-morning news cycle."

Horrified, she shook her head. "Please don't do this," she begged. "Please."

"Take the paper," Lincoln ordered. "And stand where I said."

Amelia didn't move, conscious of her holstered pistol and careful to keep it out of sight. "What if I don't?"

Lincoln tossed the paper to the floor and grabbed Donella hard, making her squeal. "Then she gets hurt."

While Amelia stood staring, he smirked and then twisted Donella's arm so hard she screamed.

"I'll break it," Lincoln threatened, waving his pistol in his other hand. "And then I'll shoot her."

Briefly, Amelia considered pulling her own gun. But judging from the crazed gleam in Lincoln's eyes, he might actually *welcome* a shoot-out. She realized Lincoln might actually be a sociopath like Simon, which would explain the admiration.

"Take it." Jacob picked up the paper and waved it at her. "And stand against that wall."

Seething, she did as he asked. She hated feeling helpless, but she couldn't see a way out of this without someone getting hurt. "You know," she said, speaking through clenched teeth, "if that girl in the bedroom dies because you refused to get her medical help, you'll be charged with manslaughter."

"She won't die." As he was busy snapping pics with his phone, Jacob's voice oozed confidence. "I've known Heather since the second grade. She always gets this crud at this time of the year."

"Yeah, but her parents always take her to the doctor and she gets medicine," Donella put in. "That's why she gets better. Instead, she's getting worse. Seriously, she can hardly breathe."

Apparently finished taking photographs, Jacob scrolled on his phone. "Perfect," he crowed. "It'll just take me a minute to send these out to all the news places. So far, they're eating this up."

Amelia's heart skipped a beat. "What are you saying my picture is for?"

Her question made him laugh. "Ever since you disappeared, people have been wondering what happened to you. Now they'll know. I can see the headlines now. Missing Serial Killer Witness Reappears."

"Or we can try to make it look like the Coffee Shop Killer got her," Lincoln said. "I think that would be more fun. If the media thinks he has her, the story will get more coverage."

"Good point." Considering, Jacob scratched his head. "I've already sent a couple, but I can amend them."

Twisting away from Lincoln, who let her go, Donella eyed Jacob as if she thought he'd lost his mind. "You do know they can trace that phone," she said.

"No, they can't. It's a burner." He grinned, clearly tickled by the term. "I bought it at Walmart. It's one of those temporary phones, not registered to anyone."

"Oh." Deflated, Donella edged toward the bedroom. "I'm going to go check on Heather again."

Amelia didn't move. She wondered exactly how many guns these boys had. Not that it mattered, because clearly they weren't averse to hurting one of the girls to keep her in line. Still, the fact that they hadn't noticed she was armed could still work to her advantage. Maybe.

Then she remembered that Donella had said the boys went home at night. That would be her chance to escape. As long as she could figure out a way to take the girls with her. Donella wouldn't be a problem, but moving a seriously ill Heather would be.

"If you're finished with me, I'm going to go check on Heather too," Amelia said.

Jacob barely looked up from his phone. "Go."

In the bedroom, Donella sat on the side of the bed, gazing down at her friend.

"It's late," Amelia said, sitting gently on the edge close to Donella. "I thought you said these boys don't sleep here."

Bleary-eyed, Donella yawned. She'd gone to lie down next to her sick friend, though Heather didn't appear to notice. "They usually don't."

"Why haven't you tried to leave?" Amelia asked. "Why stay here?"

Donella looked down. "Because we thought it would be fun and we wanted them to like us. Now it's not and I really want to go home. Heather needs to see a doctor."

"I agree." Relieved, Amelia patted Donella's shoulder. "I'm hoping we get a chance to escape soon. If they ever go."

Donella nodded. "What time is it?"

Amelia checked her Fitbit. "Nearly 1:00 a.m."

This made the teenager frown. "That's past their curfew. They should have left by now." She eyed Amelia. "I bet they're scared to leave you here alone with us."

Which would be smart. But none of this made sense. They were going to get caught eventually. Which would be way better than what would happen to them if Simon got here first.

She could only hope Rayna found them before that happened.

Moving quietly, Amelia went to check the other room. Both boys had fallen asleep on the couch, though Lincoln had kept his pistol on his lap.

Briefly, she considered whether or not she could take it from him. Weighing the possibilities, she decided she couldn't take the risk of getting shot. However, she could go up behind him and hold her own gun to his head. But if Jacob was armed, he could then threaten one of the girls, which would completely negate her efforts to get Lincoln to do what she asked.

No way out. Not yet.

The sound of tires crunching on gravel made her freeze. Headlights briefly illuminated the front of the cabin before they were switched off. Rayna? Amelia could only hope so.

Meanwhile, both boys stirred.

"What was that—" Jacob started to ask. Before he could complete the sentence, the front door slammed open.

"FBI and sheriff's office. Hands in the air." Rayna and another woman burst through the door. The other woman wore a vest with FBI in white letters on it. Both were armed.

Acting out of reflex, Lincoln grabbed his own gun.

"Put it down," Amelia ordered. "You don't want to get into a shoot-out with the sheriff."

"Lincoln?" a woman's voice called from outside. "What on earth are you doing? Get out here right this instant."

The boy blanched, looking afraid for the first time. "That's my mother," he said. "What is she doing here?"

"Both your parents are outside, son." Rayna kept her tone gentle, even though she didn't lower her pistol. "Now drop your weapon."

Frozen, he didn't move.

"Drop. Your. Weapon," Rayna barked. "If you don't, you will be shot."

Finally, Lincoln complied. Rayna cuffed him and one of her deputies took care of Jacob. As they led them from the building and the EMTs came in to take care of Heather, Amelia ran to Ted and let him wrap her up in his arms.

"I've got you," he murmured. "You're safe."

She only wished she could believe him.

Chapter 13

Since Rayna and the EMTs insisted she go get checked out, Ted went with Amelia to the hospital. During the ride there, she sat huddled with Donella in the back seat, comforting the visibly shaken teenager.

Figuring the twins would still be sleeping since it was shortly before 4:00 a.m., Ted sent a text message to both their phones, letting them know Amelia was safe. Neither responded, which told him they were in bed as they should be.

"I've called your parents, honey," Rayna told Donella, glancing over her shoulder. "They're going to meet you at the hospital."

"I don't want to see them." Donella enunciated each word clearly, as if afraid they wouldn't hear her. "They don't understand what I'm going through. They seriously want to have their preacher perform an exorcism on me."

Ted and Rayna exchanged glances. "Is that so?" Rayna asked, her tone deliberately casual. "How old are you?"

"Seventeen," Donella replied. "Five months shy of eighteen."

"You're old enough to have a say in your own medical treatment." Rayna crossed her arms. "I'll make sure and inform your parents of that fact."

"She needs to see a doctor," Amelia interjected. "A genuine medical professional. After all she's been through, and now this..."

Expression grateful, Donella nodded. "I tried to talk to them about it, but they don't want to help that way. They don't believe there's anything wrong with me."

"Come with me." Rayna held out her hand. "Let's get you looked over and then we'll talk about this more." She glanced back at Amelia pointedly. "You too."

"I'm fine," Amelia protested. "I'm just going to wait right here with Ted."

Though Rayna shook her head, she didn't argue.

Ted watched as the sheriff walked the girl up to the triage desk. "We might as well sit," he said, indicating one of the chairs.

With a nod, Amelia dropped into one so quickly he wondered if her legs had given out. "Are you sure you're all right?" he asked, concerned.

"A little shook-up," she admitted. "Nothing that any doctor can help me with." She met his gaze. "You do understand what this means, right? I've got to go. As soon as possible."

Something twisted inside him at her words. "Let's talk to Rayna first. Maybe she was able to contain all this."

Though she crossed her arms, Amelia didn't respond. Ted reached over and took her hand. She linked her fingers through his and put her head on his shoulder, which made him feel as if he'd won the lottery.

A few minutes later, Rayna returned alone.

"I have some good news and some bad," Rayna told them, grimacing at the overused phrase but using it anyway. "Which do you want first?"

"The good," Amelia answered, sitting up straight, though she still held tight to Ted's hand.

"Donella seems to be fine. A bit dehydrated and malnourished, but she's otherwise physically healthy. Heather has been admitted to the hospital and started on IV antibiotics. She has a severe case of pneumonia, but since she's young and otherwise healthy, the doctors feel confident that she'll make a full recovery."

"What a relief." Amelia glanced up at Ted. "That poor girl could hardly breathe. I was really worried."

Ted squeezed her fingers, wishing he had the right to pull her close for a hug.

"Now for the bad news," Rayna said, looking from one to the other, taking in their joined hands. "We were too late to stop the story from getting out. We were able to correct it, letting the media know that two minor boys staged the entire thing to try to get the Coffee Shop Killer's attention. Jacob had already sent the photos he took with his phone, so your face is going to be plastered all over the news, along with the story."

"Which means Simon will know where to find me." Amelia looked as if all the blood had drained from her body. Ted knew this was her worst nightmare coming to life.

"We'll protect you," Rayna promised. "The FBI is

already in town, and now that they know you are here, they're assigning a couple of agents specifically to keep you safe."

Though Amelia nodded, her faraway expression told him she'd already started planning her escape.

Someone called Rayna's name, drawing her attention. "I'll be back shortly," she said, moving away.

"Running won't solve anything," Ted said, wishing he knew for certain he was right. He'd never been in a situation like this, and he didn't know what he'd do if one of his daughters was. Every instinct told him he'd fight like hell to protect them, but the urge to gather them up and disappear would be strong too.

"Won't it?" Her fierce tone told him the depth of her emotion. "Do you want to know what I'm thinking right now? This time, since the news has already gotten out there, I won't even have time to go inside your house to collect my belongings. Nope," she continued, "I'll have to settle for just my money, my purse and my car. This will have to be enough, though I'll need to switch the car for something else once I've gotten far enough away."

Worried, he went ahead and pulled her close. She allowed him to hug her for a few seconds, before pulling away from his embrace and meeting his gaze.

"No one," she said, "not the local sheriff's department nor the FBI, can protect me from Simon once he knows where to find me. Running is my only option. I can't take the chance of endangering anyone else—you know that."

Ted started to protest, but then he remembered Yvonne's report and nodded instead. "I hope they kill the bastard this time," he said.

"Me too." The pain in her voice broke his heart. "If you won't mind driving me to my car, I'll be taking off."

"It's still at the house. You might as well go in and grab your things."

"You don't get it. Simon is most likely already on his way. Since he can't hop on a plane, I'm sure he's coming by vehicle. I imagine he'll be here before you know it."

The bleak resignation in her eyes broke his heart. "What about if we hide you somewhere?" he said. "It doesn't have to be far away, especially if we make it look like you took off. We could send Simon in the wrong direction."

For the first time, Amelia appeared interested. "I'm listening. Because I'm getting damn tired of trying to outrun that monster."

Rayna returned. Looking from one to the other, her gaze sharpened. "What's going on?"

"Ted has a plan," Amelia said. "And I'm going to take it one step further. I want to set a trap for Simon. It's time to take him down."

Horrified, Ted started to protest, to say that wasn't what he'd meant at all. But the gleam in Amelia's eyes told him she meant what she'd said.

Rayna, however, didn't appear convinced. "I'm not sure that's wise. You're an unarmed citizen. I can't allow you to become a sacrificial victim."

Pushing to her feet, Amelia tucked a wayward strand of hair behind her ear. "I have my license to carry and I know how to shoot. I'm pretty good at it too." Turning slightly, she let Rayna see her still-holstered pistol. "Don't get me wrong. I'm terrified. Everything about this man chills me to the bone. But he won't let up until he catches me. And while I've gotten really good at running and hiding, clearly so has he. Would you want to spend the rest of your life on the run?"

Slowly, Rayna shook her head. "Let me talk to the FBI and get their thoughts."

"Wait." Amelia touched the sheriff lightly on the arm. "The less people who know about this, the better. If you want, I can keep you out of the loop. That way, if something happens, you and your department won't be involved."

"You've got to be kidding me." Expression incredulous, Rayna looked from one to the other. "No way am I abandoning you like that. Not only are you one of the townspeople I'm sworn to protect, but you're my friend."

Ted could have sworn Amelia's eyes got a little teary at that.

"However," Rayna continued, "this will be a joint effort, working with both my department and the FBI. We will coordinate with them. Once we come up with a plan, we'll all step back and stay behind the scenes, but you won't ever be alone."

"Damn right," Ted added, pushing to his feet. Deciding to follow Amelia's brave example and realize the time had come to stop hesitating, he crossed to her and put his arm around her shoulders. Then, when she looked up at him with a question in her eyes, he kissed her. The deep, lingering kind of kiss that he hoped left no doubt about his feelings for her.

When they finally broke apart, they were both breathless. And Rayna was laughing. "Best thing I've seen all day," she said. "You two wait here. Two FBI agents are waiting outside and I want to see if they can help come up with a plan."

Once Rayna had walked away, Amelia looked up at him. "Why'd you do that?"

"I—"

"Wait." She put her finger up to his lips, effectively silencing him. "Never mind. I don't want to know. I can't afford to allow myself to be distracted right now."

"I don't want you to be either," he replied. "All I want is you to give me your word that you'll stay safe."

Gaze locked on his, she gave a slow nod.

Rayna returned with two serious-looking men wearing dark windbreakers with FBI emblazoned on the back. "These are Agents Smalley and Figeroa. I have to tell you that they are not on board with your plan."

"That's good." Amelia's flippant tone matched her closed-off expression. "Because I'm not on board with them being involved."

"It's not really up to you," the agent named Figeroa said. "If we're going to do this at all, I'm going to need you to promise to do exactly as we say. We have a much better—and safer—plan."

When Amelia opened her mouth, no doubt to protest, Rayna forestalled her with a light squeeze of her shoulder. "Please, Mel. These are trained professionals. They—and me—are your best chance of getting through this alive."

"Exactly," Agent Smalley said, stern-faced. "If you're set on making yourself bait, we've got to put a protocol in place so you aren't an easy target."

"Simon will see through any kind of setup," Amelia said.

"That's why we're going to make this as natural as possible. You will go back to Mr. Sanders's ranch—"

"No." Ted cut him off. "I have two fourteen-year-old daughters. I won't allow you to put them at risk."

The two FBI agents exchanged glances. "Where are

your children right now, Mr. Sanders? Since it's Saturday, I'm assuming they're not in school."

Suddenly uneasy, he glanced from one to the other. "At home. Why?"

Instead of answering, Agent Figeroa consulted his watch. "We need to head out there right now and pick them up. I'm going to take a wild guess and speculate that Simon Barron has already learned where Ms. Ferguson has been staying."

Ted froze, staring hard at the agent. "How?"

"Social media. Those damn kids posted a picture of your house with the caption 'Letting the entire world know where Amelia's been living.'"

Feeling sick, Ted swallowed hard.

"He's right," Amelia rasped. "Damn it, he's right. Simon is probably on his way there right now."

Heart pounding, Ted didn't hesitate. He spun around and sprinted for the exit, before realizing he didn't have his truck. "Rayna," he barked, a desperate order. "Help me get home."

Grim-faced, Rayna nodded. "Let's go." She ran too, with Amelia right on her heels.

As Rayna drove, lights flashing and siren on, Amelia worked hard to calm her racing heart. This was her worst nightmare. She couldn't bear it if Simon hurt the twins because of her.

Nails digging into the palm of her hand, she swallowed back the nausea that rose into her throat. Judging by the speed Rayna drove and the way she blazed through lights, the sheriff wanted to make damn sure they got to Ted's before Simon.

"How long?" Amelia asked, her voice a rasp of nerves.

"How long does it take to drive from New Orleans to here?"

Rayna's steady gaze met hers in the rearview mirror. "It's over eight hours from there to Fort Worth and another three or four here, depending on traffic, so eleven or twelve hours, give or take. There's no way he's here yet, even if we go with the earliest possible time the news broke."

The earliest possible time. Taking deep breaths, Amelia tried to think. What time had it been when Lincoln had forced her to pose with the newspaper so Jacob could take her photo?

Around 2:00 a.m. Because Jacob had wanted to make sure and catch the morning news cycle. She did the calculations in her head. Say the early-morning news came on in New Orleans at four or five. Even going with the earlier time, that meant Simon could arrive in Getaway by four this afternoon.

Since it wasn't even sunrise yet, this gave her a little bit of wiggle room.

Unless he'd seen something on social media. The thought chilled her blood. She wouldn't put it past kids to post there. Which meant they would have even less time. Still, 2:00 p.m. would be the earliest. They were still safe. They had to be.

"Are you still up for doing the news conference in an hour?" Rayna asked. They'd decided to put Amelia in the public eye just briefly enough so that her location could be established. After the conference, which would be held in front of the sheriff's department, they planned to make a big deal out of escorting Amelia to an anonymous vehicle to "drive her out of town." Except Rayna had planned an elaborate switch and the vehicle would actually contain a female FBI agent wearing the same clothes. Two other male FBI agents would be riding along as they drove out of town, into the flat west Texas plains.

Their hope was that this would draw Simon to what he thought was her there, away from any innocent bystanders. When he made his move, they'd be ready for him.

Meanwhile, Amelia would be safe inside the sheriff's office, surrounded by armed law enforcement personnel. It seemed like a solid plan, a good plan. But Amelia wanted to prepare for any and every possibility.

"When we get to Ted's, I want you to have someone get the girls out of there," she told Rayna. "Have the FBI protect them or lock them up in a cell in your office. Make sure someone is with them 24/7. They need to be kept safe."

Ted nodded his agreement.

"Will do," Rayna promised, all her attention on navigating the streets. "The FBI is right behind us."

When they turned onto the gravel road leading to Ted's ranch, the squad car fishtailed. Rayna easily regained control and kept them on track. They pulled up in front of the house in a flurry of dust.

"Come on." Amelia jumped out of the car at the same time as Ted. Running, she was one step behind him when he opened the door.

The house felt middle-of-the-night silent. Which made sense, since the girls loved to sleep and never, even on a school morning, got up before six. On Saturdays, like today, Amelia had seen them stay in bed until eleven.

"Yolanda! Yvonne!" Ted shouted, racing down the dark hallway toward their room, turning lights on as he went. He stopped in front of their closed door, breathing hard, clearly trying to calm himself before knocking. He'd have to wake them up and no doubt didn't want their first reaction to be screaming panic.

Behind him, Amelia did the same. Rayna and the FBI agents had waited in the living room to give them some privacy while they explained to the girls what was going on.

"Girls." Ted rapped on the door, three sharp beats of his knuckles. "I'm coming in." Slowly, he pushed his way inside and flicked on the switch.

The room was empty. The beds, still neatly made, didn't appear to have been slept in at all.

Staring, Amelia felt her heart stop a moment before thudding heavily inside her chest.

"Damn it." Ted dug out his cell phone, his hands shaking. "The last thing I said to them before going out front to wait for Rayna was to lock the house up and stay inside. It was the middle of the night. They know they're not supposed to go anywhere without letting me know, especially at that hour."

Watching while he waited for one of the girls to pick up, Amelia replayed the words *He hasn't had time to get here... He hasn't had time to get here...* over and over inside her head.

Ted tried again. After a moment, he ended the call and eyed Amelia grimly. "Neither one of them is picking up."

"Rayna." Though Amelia called her name softly, the sheriff immediately appeared. "We've got a problem."

Rayna took in the empty bedroom and nodded. "Do you have any idea where they might have gone?" she asked Ted.

"None whatsoever. Especially at this hour of the morning. Even though I'm going to be waking people up, I'm going to make a few calls and see what I can find out."

While Ted tried frantically to phone all the girls' friends, Rayna conferred with the two FBI agents. Watching Ted valiantly trying not to panic, Amelia knew he didn't have the names or the phone numbers for any of the kids in Yvonne's new circle. The group that had included both Jacob and Lincoln. She couldn't help but wonder if the others had the same mindset as the two boys and if they too wanted to draw Simon to them.

Expression bleak, Ted shoved his phone back into his pocket.

"No luck."

Though Amelia's stomach was churning, she quietly took Ted's hand. "Come on," she said. "Let's go look and see if they left us a note."

A thorough search of every room turned up nothing.

"Think," Rayna said, her voice soft yet commanding. "What might have made them do the exact opposite of what you asked?"

"Somehow," Ted said slowly, "I think Yvonne is behind this. I can imagine a scenario where one of her friends calls and she decides she's going to go and meet them. Either Yolanda tried to stop her or followed her."

"But why?" Rayna asked. "We have the two boys in custody."

"Maybe the rest of the group has a backup plan. After all, from what Donella said, they started out all in this together," Amelia replied. "Though, honestly, I can't imagine Yvonne or Yolanda wanting anything to do with that group after what they did."

"That's it!" Ted almost shouted. "Yvonne told me earlier tonight that she feels all of this is her fault. If she hadn't gotten involved with that group, she believed they'd never have noticed Amelia. She's gone to the others to try to make this right."

Amelia felt as if all the color had drained from her face. "But if they're trying to draw Simon to them, the twins could be in terrible danger."

"Damn it." Jaw tight, Ted looked like he wanted to punch something. He tried calling them again, his expression growing more and more furious. "Why won't they pick up their phones?"

"Ted." Rayna's voice rang with authority. "Take a deep breath. We need you to be calm and rational. What we don't know is where Simon will go first. Either he'll head to wherever those foolish kids invited him or he'll come here. If he comes here, the girls being gone is a good thing."

"But if he goes there," Ted finished for her, "my daughters are in real trouble."

Just then, they heard a sound out back. Rayna drew her weapon and motioned at them to remain quiet. The back door opened, apparently unlocked, and both girls walked in. When they caught sight of their father, Amelia and Rayna, they stopped short and froze. Rayna lowered her pistol and shoved it back into her holster.

"Girls?" Amelia asked, confused and relieved and on the verge of tears.

"Amelia!" Yolanda cried. With loud sounds of relief, the twins ran to Amelia, wrapping their arms around her and holding on tight.

"You're safe!" Yvonne said, over and over, her voice breaking. "I can't believe you're safe."

After her first initial shout, Yolanda held on to Amelia more quietly. Of the two girls, she appeared much quicker to realize they might be in trouble with their father. She kept cutting her gaze to Ted and then back to Amelia.

For his part, Ted simply waited, his arms crossed, his face expressionless, though his jaw remained tight.

Rayna checked her watch and then motioned to Amelia. "You need to start packing."

"Right." With an apologetic look at Ted, Amelia hurried to her room and began grabbing her clothes and stuffing them into her duffel. This didn't take long, partially because she didn't own much, but mostly because she was überconscious of the passing time.

When she returned to the kitchen, Ted and the girls appeared locked in a stalemate.

"There you are." Rayna appeared relieved to see her. "I'm going to have my deputy take the twins and Ted away. Amelia, you're coming with me. One FBI agent will wait here for Larry, my deputy. Per my dispatcher, the media people are already assembling in my parking lot."

"I still want an explanation," Ted said.

"That's going to have to come later." Rayna's voice was firm. "My deputy will be here in five minutes. I want you three to go with him. I'm taking Amelia now. She's got a news conference to do."

Both of the girls started talking at once, demanding to know what was going on. Rayna grabbed Amelia's arm and led her out of the house, shaking her head. "I wish Ted luck with that."

"Me too." As they climbed into Rayna's squad car, Amelia couldn't resist looking back at the homey ranch house. "Will they be okay until your deputy shows up?"

"I believe so. The FBI agents have promised to stay

in their vehicle and keep watch until the girls and Ted have been taken safely away."

As they turned onto Main Street, Amelia could see the cluster of media vans ahead. Once the sheriff's department parking lot had filled, the overflow had spread out into the street.

"Wow." Amelia felt her stomach somersault. "You weren't kidding."

"I wasn't." Rayna shrugged. "The Coffee Shop Killer is big news. We've been fielding calls from national media as well. CNN, MSNBC and Fox have all sent reporters."

"Great. I don't even know what I'm going to say."

Reaching over, Rayna gave Amelia's shoulder a quick squeeze. "You'll be fine. Just talk about what happened to you, how you went on the run once you learned Simon had escaped and how you ended up here. Then you can touch on how Jacob and Lincoln grabbed you—only don't use their names. It'll be fine. We're going to do ten minutes, then allow a few questions, before we do that whole spirit-you-away thing."

"Okay." Amelia pushed away her misery and replaced it with determination. "I can do this."

"You can." Rayna parked the cruiser in a spot marked For Official Sheriff's Department Vehicles Only and killed the engine. "You've got this."

As they got out of the car, the instant the reporters spotted them, they rushed over and surrounded them. Shouted questions, microphones shoved in Amelia's face, and jostling by men balancing huge video cameras.

"No comment," Rayna said, at least twenty times. "There will be questions allowed after the news conference. Save them until then." Hand in the middle of Amelia's back, she ushered her inside.

The instant the doors closed, Amelia exhaled. The relative quiet, in sharp contrast to the mob scene outside, felt surreal. "Who knew almost being a serial killer's victim guaranteed instant celebrity?" Amelia quipped. With the slight quaver to her voice, she couldn't quite disguise her nervousness, but she tried.

"It's all going to be fine," Rayna promised. "Stick to the truth and you won't have any problems."

Though Amelia nodded, the thought of facing Simon again made her feel sick.

One of Rayna's deputies poked his head around the corner. "Five minutes until showtime," he said.

"You got this." Rayna patted her shoulder. "This is a piece of cake compared to testifying in court."

That truth made Amelia stand a little bit taller. "I'm ready," she said, meaning it. "Let's get this show on the road."

"Let me check in with my deputy." Rayna held up a finger. But before she could, the mayor strode into the reception area, in full public relations mode.

"I'm going up there with you," he boomed, grabbing Amelia's hand and pumping it. "Just to show everyone that you and the sheriff's department have Getaway's full support."

Amelia glanced at Rayna, who discreetly rolled her eyes.

One of the mayor's employees pushed the door open, stepping aside so that Rayna, Amelia and the mayor could go through. Outside, the roar of conversation quieted as Amelia walked up to the podium and stood before the microphone.

She let herself look around the assembled crowd, studying all their faces, bracing herself in case she caught a glimpse of the one person she never wanted to see again.

Chapter 14

The sense of urgency didn't dissipate once Amelia left with Rayna. Instead, Ted fought the urge to do something, though he didn't know what. With four flat tires, he couldn't load the girls up in his truck and take off. Only the knowledge that he had a trained FBI agent guarding the outside allowed him to remain calm enough to wait for Larry Newsome to show up.

Plus, he figured as soon as Simon learned of the news conference, he'd head downtown. He wanted Amelia, not Ted or his daughters. They should be fine.

But he still couldn't relax.

Both of the girls were staring at him as if he'd been hiding some dark secret.

"Tell us everything," Yvonne demanded. "How did you find Amelia and where are she and Rayna going?"

The kid had nerve; Ted had to give her that. "First,

I need you to fill me in on where you and your sister were just now. I gave you strict instructions to lock up and stay put." He took a deep breath, trying like hell to keep his tone level and even. "I'd also like to know why neither of you answered your phone." That alone had taken ten years off his life.

"Oh." Yvonne looked sheepish as she dug her phone from her pocket. "We turned the ringer off so there wouldn't be anything to give away our location."

"Which was?" he asked pointedly.

The girls exchanged glances. "We were setting something up in the barn," Yolanda finally answered. "We can show you, if you'd like."

"Just tell me." He let a bit of his exasperation come through in his voice. "The deputy is going to be here at any moment. We don't have time for games."

"Speaking of games…" Unbelievably, Yvonne lifted her chin, her gaze challenging him. "Would you mind telling us what the heck is going on? Why did Rayna rush Amelia away?"

"Because she's in danger." Ted checked his watch. "Thanks to those two boys, her face and name have been plastered all over the internet and the news. Now the Coffee Shop Killer knows exactly where to find her." He made a gesture, attempting to convey his frustration. "Anyway, we'll talk about all this in the car. You heard Rayna. Larry Newsome is on his way to pick us up. Right now, go and throw a couple of days' worth of clothes into an overnight bag. Grab shampoo, and whatever else you can't live without, and do it quickly."

Instead of moving, they both stood staring at him, maybe even a little bit past him, as if frozen in place with shock. "Go," he barked. "Now."

Still nothing. In fact, he finally registered the identical horrified looks of terror on their faces at the same time as he felt a particular tingle of warning on the back of his neck.

Slowly, he turned. And found himself facing Simon Barron, the Coffee Shop Killer, holding a gun trained on the twins. He looked smaller than he had in the photos Ted had seen. But he had the same pale skin, large, heavy-lidded eyes and a shock of thinning hair flopping over onto his forehead.

"Hello there," Simon said.

"Amelia's not here," Ted rasped, terror for his children sending his heart rate into overdrive. Luckily, he still wore his own weapon in a holster under his jacket. Armed, which at least gave him a fighting chance, as long as Simon didn't notice and take the gun away. He had a couple more in the gun safe, though the girls didn't know how to shoot. He'd intended to retrieve them anyway before they left with Rayna's deputy. Speaking of which, where was that guy? And what had happened to the FBI agent standing guard outside?

All these panicked thoughts ran through his head, tumbling over one another while he faced a monster. "Amelia isn't here," he repeated.

"Really?" Simon's thin brows rose. He glanced from Ted to the twins, his gaze lingering too long on the girls. "I'm willing to wait. Well, maybe I'll just amuse myself with these two until she gets back."

Like hell he would. Teeth clenched, Ted struggled to speak normally. He'd already calculated his chances if he simply rushed the man. Not good. For now, he'd have to pretend to go along and watch for his chance to shoot. Though if this monster even so much as laid a finger on one of his girls, he'd take the risk as long as they weren't in the way. That would be the hard part—keeping them out of the line of fire.

Maybe if he could keep Simon talking…

"How'd you get here so quickly?" Ted asked. "It's a long drive here from New Orleans."

"Who says I drove? I have a friend with a small plane." Smirking, clearly enjoying terrifying his captives, Simon laughed. "New Orleans was a lot of fun. I did some of my finest work there."

"And yet somehow they never managed to capture you." Ted let a note of admiration slip into his voice.

"I know, right?" Simon said, preening. "They're a bunch of inept fools. They never seem to realize how many fans I have around the country willing to help me."

Fans. Like those foolish teenage boys. Still, that explained a lot.

"There was an FBI agent outside," Ted said, hoping the guy was still alive. "What happened to him?"

"He's unconscious. I think. Maybe dead. I don't know." Still smirking, Simon shrugged and eyed the twins again. "Clearly, he didn't expect trouble. He never saw it coming. He was texting on his phone when I took him down. Handy crowbar you keep out in the barn. I used it to bash in his skull."

The thought made Ted feel queasy.

"I always prefer the element of surprise," Simon continued. "People really are foolish to let down their guard." He glanced around the room. "You three were quite surprised, I think. The expression on all of your faces was priceless. Though I wish I could have caught Amelia before she left. Where exactly is she?"

Ted checked his watch, deliberately casual though

his insides were buzzing. "In about five minutes, she's giving a news conference at the local sheriff's office."

"A news conference?" For a moment, this appeared to take Simon aback.

"Yes. Don't you want to see it?" Ted taunted. "I'm sure the only thing Amelia is going to talk about will be you."

Perfect bait for a narcissist.

Simon swung his gaze back around to Ted and then nodded toward the TV. He kept his pistol pointed at the twins. "Turn it on," he ordered. "I think I would like to hear what my Amelia has to say."

His Amelia. Chest tight, Ted moved slowly to get his remote and turn on the television. He'd thought maybe only the local channel would carry the news conference, but there Rayna and Amelia were, on the national news.

Amelia had just stepped up to the microphone and appeared to be preparing to speak. She looked nervous.

"There's my girl," Simon crooned. He alternated between watching the screen and keeping his eyes on his hostages. The twins now huddled together, arms around each other, their eyes huge, reflecting utter terror. Ted ached to go to them, to promise everything was going to be all right. Instead, he stayed where he was, watching and waiting. If the opportunity presented itself, he didn't want Simon to be anywhere near the girls when he took this monster down. One clean shot was all he needed.

"Dad?" Yvonne asked, drawing Simon's attention. "When you asked where we were earlier? We were out in the barn, just messing around. There's a lot to do out there."

She'd already told him that. Ted's mouth went dry.

Was she trying to get Simon to take them out to the barn? If so, why?

Eyes gleaming with interest, Simon focused on her. "A lot to do?" he asked. "Tell me more."

Yvonne swallowed. "I—"

"That's enough," Ted ordered, pushing back the panic clawing at his chest. "You don't need to tell this man anything."

Narrowing his eyes, Simon laughed. "Maybe I should just kill you now so you can't interfere with me having fun with your twins." He cocked his head, considering. "But no, making you suffer while you watch seems even more fun. A new twist. Who says you can't teach an old serial killer new tricks?"

On the television screen, Amelia had started to speak. Ted jacked up the volume, hoping to draw Simon's attention away from his daughters.

It worked. At the sound of Amelia's voice, calm and smooth and remarkably composed, Simon turned. Transfixed, he stared at the screen, though he still managed to keep his pistol pointed at the girls.

Because of this, Ted still hesitated. He couldn't take a chance that Simon might squeeze off a shot and injure one of his children. Not yet. He needed to be patient. There'd be only one chance. He'd know his opportunity when it came.

Headlights swept the front window, letting him know Rayna's deputy had arrived. Ted wished he had a way to warn the guy that he was about to walk into a huge mess. Of course, once he caught sight of the downed FBI agent, he'd realize it himself.

The headlights cut off. Ted braced himself for a knock

on the front door any minute now. Instead, he heard a muffled cry and then a thud.

"Deputy down." Watching him closely, Simon grinned. "You didn't think I came alone, did you?"

Ted mentally cursed. An accomplice changed everything. Even if he succeeded in taking out Simon, there would still be one other person to deal with while keeping his daughters safe.

On the TV, Amelia continued to speak, detailing the ordeal with two misguided teenage boys. Listening, Yvonne and Yolanda exchanged nervous looks. Ted got the idea that they were hiding something, though he had no idea what.

Catching him looking, Yvonne mouthed something. The only word Ted could catch was *barn*. For some reason, it appeared the girls wanted Simon to go to the barn.

Simon alternated between watching the press conference and Ted. "Go ahead," Simon drawled. "Try me. See which one of your daughters I can shoot first."

Ted raised his hands up. "I'm not doing anything. Please, I'm begging you. Let my girls go."

"She's leaving," Simon muttered, almost to himself. "The FBI is taking her to a safe house or something. Which means the time has come for me to take drastic measures." He spun back to face Ted, then slowly took the few steps necessary to bring him near the twins. "I'm going to shoot one of them," he announced. "Not a kill shot, but enough to seriously wound. Which one do you want it to be?"

Yolanda gasped, clutching her sister. Yvonne glared at Simon, her eyes full of rage.

"Choose," Simon ordered, putting the pistol against Yolanda's temple. "Or I'll decide for you."

"Why?" Ted found his voice, managing to take a step closer. "What's the endgame here? Amelia's safe. Hurting any of us won't bring her back."

"Won't it?" With a smile full of malice, Simon considered him. "Call your sheriff right now. Tell her to have Amelia brought here or your children will both die. And not quickly and easily either. A long, slow, painful end to lives not yet fully lived. Is that what you want?"

"Don't, Dad," Yvonne said, her fierce tone matching her expression. "Don't give him what he wants."

Simon squeezed off a shot, hitting Yolanda in the upper arm. She screamed, a bloodcurdling sound of pain and shock. Ted rushed over to her, grabbing a dish towel and trying frantically to stop the bleeding.

Yvonne stepped away from them, moving closer to Simon. "You coward," she said, her voice seething with hatred. "Hiding behind your gun and shooting a defenseless little girl."

"Yvonne…" Ted warned. "Get back over here right now." Continuing to press the towel against Yolanda's gunshot wound, he could tell the bullet was still in there. Yolanda had slid to the floor, back against the wall, and whimpered over and over, clearly in pain.

More than anything, Ted wanted to pull out his pistol and shoot Simon Barron right in the heart. But as long as Simon had his own gun trained on Yvonne, Ted couldn't take a chance.

"You've become less," Yvonne declared, clearly taunting a madman.

Eyes glittering, Simon cocked his head and studied her. "I take it you want me to shoot you next?"

She ignored him. "I did a report on you," she said. "I bet I get an A. All the research I found must have lied.

Because according to that, every killing you did was hands-on. Not once did you ever use a gun."

Simon smiled, a thing of gleeful malice. "I think I like you," he said. "I'll make sure you die an especially painful death."

Terrified for his other daughter, Ted moved Yolanda's hand, showing her how to apply pressure to her own wound. He couldn't speak, afraid he'd draw Simon's attention. But he wanted to have both hands free when the time came to take the killer down.

"Will you, now?" Yvonne asked softly, clearly enjoying herself. "I don't believe you. But you can prove it. I set up the perfect place for you in the barn. I re-created—as best I could with what I had—your garage laboratory."

The place where Simon had for years kept, tortured and killed his victims. Horrified, Ted eyed his daughter, a different kind of fear knifing through him.

"Why would you do that?" Simon asked, preening. "Don't tell me you're another member of the fan club those two boys started."

Yvonne laughed, the coldness of the sound at odds with her youthful face. "They didn't start it," she corrected. "I did."

Was she telling the truth? Ted had no idea what to think, but he had to stop this before Simon did anything worse than he already had. As he opened his mouth to speak up, Yolanda touched his arm with her other hand. Despite her obvious pain, she managed to mouth a word of caution. *Wait.*

"No," Simon decided, swinging his gaze back to Ted. "Call your sheriff and do as I asked, or I'll shoot her again in the leg. Lots of painful bullet holes, bleeding. Is that what you want for her?"

"Of course not," Ted snapped. "But you saw the television. Amelia is with the FBI. I doubt the sheriff can do anything."

"Call. Her."

Damned if Ted wanted Amelia's life at risk too. "You do understand once the FBI learns of your location, they're going to surround this place. There's no way they'll let you get out of here alive."

"I don't care." A twist to Simon's upper lip revealed his inner turmoil. "I'm not going to let them take me back to prison. I'll gladly die first. As long as I can take Amelia down with me, I'm good."

Could this get any worse? A serial killer with a death wish?

Simon took a step closer to Yolanda. She gasped, shrinking back, though with the wall behind her, she had nowhere to go. Blood had soaked the dish towel, turning the white terry cloth red. "Call your sheriff or I'll shoot her again. And put her on speaker. I want to speak with her myself."

The instant Amelia finished talking, the reporters began shouting questions. They were so aggressive that Amelia took a step back. Rayna shook her head and moved up to the microphone. "You know better," she chided. "If you want Ms. Ferguson to answer anything, we need to approach this in an orderly fashion. Raise your hand if you have a question, and when I call on you, then you may ask it."

This worked. Most of the questions were about Simon, as Amelia had anticipated. Asking her what she'd do if he showed up, as if she'd reveal that. Asking for her feelings about all this, her future plans and her relationship with local rancher Ted Sanders. Since she didn't feel comfortable answering most of these, she did as Rayna had instructed her and stated, "No comment."

Finally, Rayna grabbed her arm and told the reporters there would be no more questions. She then marched Amelia over to a pair of waiting windowless vans while the cameras rolled. One belonged to the FBI and the other to the Getaway Sheriff's Department.

Now would be the tricky part. A female FBI agent with the same coloring as Amelia and wearing the exact same clothing waited just inside the sheriff's department van, which was parked nearest the reporters. She handed Amelia an FBI cap and jacket and waited while Amelia put them on. Amelia shoved her hair up under the cap and put on a pair of dark aviator sunglasses. "I'm ready," Amelia said, settling into the back seat to wait for Rayna.

With a quick nod, the agent got out and, head down, walked quickly over to the second van and climbed in the passenger side. A male FBI agent sat at the wheel and there were two more in the back seat. All cameras followed that van as it drove away.

Meanwhile, Amelia ducked down in the back seat of the other van, while Rayna climbed into the front to drive. They pulled out after the FBI van but turned in the opposite direction when they reached Main Street.

"Stay down a few more minutes," Rayna said. "I wish them luck. Capturing Simon has become an FBI operation now. Keeping you safe is my responsibility too."

"How'd you manage to get them to agree to that?" Amelia asked, still crouching on the floorboard in back.

"I told them that was the only way you'd go along with them being involved."

Amelia felt sadder than she'd felt since leaving White

Plains. She missed Ted and the twins and missed the easy routine of their life on the ranch. She turned on the brand-new cell phone Rayna had handed her, wishing she could call or at least text Ted. But Rayna had strictly instructed her not to make contact with anyone until they had Simon in custody. She couldn't risk messing up the operation, no matter how badly she wanted to hear Ted's voice.

Toying with her phone, she couldn't shake the feeling that something was wrong. But nothing could be. So far, everything had gone according to plan.

"That's weird." Rayna sounded worried. "I can't reach Larry. Larry Newsome, the deputy I assigned to pick up Ted and the girls."

Just then, Rayna's phone rang. "It's Ted," she told Amelia, sounding relieved.

"Ted, what's—" Rayna's relaxed expression completely changed, becoming tense and focused. "I understand. Yes, put me on speaker. I'll do the same." Glancing at Amelia, she held up her finger, warning her not to speak. Amelia nodded.

When Rayna pressed the speaker button, Amelia waited to hear Ted explain why he'd called. Instead, she heard a voice that she'd never wanted to hear again as long as she lived.

"Hello, Sheriff," Simon drawled. "Both the FBI agent and your deputy are out of commission. In addition to that, I've already put a bullet in the arm of one of these children. I'm about to put another, unless you do as I ask."

"Ted? Can you ask the girls to speak up for me?" Rayna asked, in full law enforcement mode. "I need proof of life."

Silence. Then Simon laughed, magnanimous. "Go ahead, girls. You first."

"It's me, Yvonne." The teenager came through as remarkably steady, though Amelia detected a slight quaver in her voice.

"Yolanda's been shot."

"As I said," Simon agreed. "Not fatally, not yet."

Not yet. Amelia felt sick. Of course, he meant to kill the girls. That was what he did.

"Yolanda, are you able to speak to me?" Rayna asked, ignoring Simon. Knowing how much that would infuriate him, Amelia winced. But she couldn't blame Rayna. They needed to know that both girls were still okay.

"I'm here." The quavering pain in Yolanda's voice hit Amelia like a knife to the heart. Amelia opened her mouth to offer reassurance, but once again, Rayna shook her head to let Amelia know she still needed to remain silent.

"All right," Rayna conceded. "Now that I know they are alive, what do you want, Simon?"

"Amelia."

Hearing him say her name sent a chill down her spine.

"She's with the FBI, on her way to a safe house," Rayna replied, her tone all business. "There's nothing I can do to change that."

"Then I'll shoot." They heard the sound of a gunshot and then the most horrible screaming. One of the twins. Amelia couldn't tell which one.

"Damn you," Ted shouted. "I'll kill you."

Tears stung Amelia's eyes. She felt as if she might be sick. Having Simon capture and torture her had been one thing. Hearing him do something to people she cared about, *children* she cared about, was another.

"I only scraped her," Simon said, gloating. "Go and check it out. She's not really hurt. Not like her sister. Though that can change."

Ted cursed. A moment later, when he spoke, relief sounded clear in his voice. "He's right. She's okay. It's just a scratch. Nothing serious." A brief pause, then Ted spoke again. "I'd still like to kill you."

Simon laughed. "Go ahead," he taunted. "Take one more step. I'll shoot her again."

Amelia had heard enough. This was all her fault. Ted and his family were in danger because of her. "It's me, Amelia. I'm here, Simon," she said. "With the sheriff. Let the girls go and you can have me."

Though Rayna shook her head in warning, Amelia ignored her.

"My Amelia," Simon purred. "So good to hear your voice, my dear. How far away are you?"

Revulsion made her shudder at the sound of *him* saying her name. To think that she'd once thought she could help him, oblivious to the danger he posed to anyone with whom he came in contact. Even after he'd been convicted and she'd believed him to be safely locked up where he could not hurt anyone else, she'd been wrong. She'd never underestimate him again.

Before Amelia could respond, Rayna touched her arm, her green eyes flashing a warning. "It's not going to be that easy, Simon. I don't trust you," Rayna began. "We're going to need more than just your assurances."

"I don't really care what you think," Simon responded smoothly. "No one does, actually. This is between Amelia and me."

Amelia swallowed. "I don't trust you either, Simon,"

she said. "Let the entire family go, and then we'll talk about me meeting you."

"And give up my only advantage? I don't think so. If I no longer have these people, you have no reason to come take their place. You know better than to treat me like a fool." Simon laughed, the harsh sound grating on Amelia's nerves. "Since I'm the one holding all the cards, let me tell you what's going to happen. I'm going to take this little family to the barn and have some fun with them. I'll stop whenever you get here or they die—whichever comes first. So chop-chop, Amelia baby. What happens next is on you."

And he ended the call.

Shaking now, Amelia swallowed back wave after wave of nausea. "We've got to go there," she told Rayna, her voice rising in panic. "There's no other choice. I can't live with the thought of that monster touching either of those girls or Ted."

"I need you to try really hard to remain calm," Rayna ordered, her soothing, compassionate voice helping Amelia move back from the metaphoric ledge. "Allowing yourself to panic won't do anyone any good. We need to stay alert and think rationally. Now, first up, I'm calling the FBI. They've got that whole decoy thing that they can abort now. They need to know what's going on. We've got a hostage situation and they've got master negotiators."

"Negotiations will be a waste of time," Amelia responded, twisting her hands together in her lap. "I know Simon. He will want to go out in a blaze of glory, as long as he can take me along with him. He won't care who else he hurts in the process. Actually, he'll enjoy it. He'll call it his last hurrah. Because there's no way he's going to let himself be taken back to prison. He'd rather die first."

"Good to know. Give me a minute and I'll fill the FBI in."

Amelia nodded, working diligently on taking deep breaths and trying to slow her racing heart. She listened while Rayna relayed information to her contact with the FBI.

"We're about to head that way now," Rayna said. "Yes, we'll wait until you get there before going in. What's your ETA?" She listened for a moment before ending the call.

"They're calling in a special team and heading that way," Rayna said. "They couldn't give me a time estimate, though the decoy van is turning around, so they should be at Ted's place shortly."

Shortly. Meanwhile, the lives of innocents hung in the balance.

Something in her expression must have relayed her thoughts to Rayna.

"I'm driving as fast as I can," Rayna said.

"Good," Amelia replied. "And fair warning. I have no intention of sitting around waiting for the FBI."

"Me neither," Rayna answered, surprising her. "These are our people. We'll do whatever we can to get them out safely."

Chapter 15

The instant Simon said *barn*, Yvonne looked up at Ted and smiled. Seeing this, Ted wondered what exactly the girls had set up in the barn. There was no way they possibly could have known Simon would come here. Unless... Again, Ted thought about his daughter looking a monster in the eye and stating that she was the head of his fan club. The thought made him feel ill all over again.

"You three." Simon gestured with his pistol. "Lead the way."

Gazing up with teary eyes, Yolanda shook her head. "I can't. It hurts too much."

"Do you want me to shoot your sister?" Simon asked, his tone as reasonable as a man asking for directions or discussing the weather. "Or how about your father? Maybe you'd enjoy watching him take a bullet in the gut, huh?"

Tears streaming down her cheeks, Yolanda struggled to get to her feet. Ted rushed over and helped her. "Take it slow, honey. We don't want to get that arm bleeding again."

Once she finally stood, she swayed. Ted let her lean on him as they moved slowly toward the back door, with Simon right behind them. Once again, Ted calculated his chances, thinking maybe he could spin around and knock the pistol out of Simon's hand.

"Don't try it," Simon cautioned. "I know what you're thinking, and believe me, I will manage to shoot and injure one of your precious children first. Or you. And this time, I won't be too picky about where I hit. It could be a fatal mistake."

Ted glared at the other man over his shoulder and kept moving. Yvonne led the way, her back straight and her head held high. Again, Ted found himself wondering about his daughter's part in all this.

Outside, the wind came from the northwest, which meant the cold front had arrived. Thunderstorms were expected along the back edge of the front. Luckily, he'd already had Floyd bring the cattle in to closer pastures, where there were places the animals could shelter to get out of the rain.

As they neared the barn, the motion sensor light came on. Ted had a vivid memory of walking out here with Amelia, and her explaining her need to always have an escape route. He hadn't truly understood until now.

Glancing back at them, Yvonne pulled open the barn door and switched on the interior light. As Ted and Yolanda shuffled in after her, Ted looked around. Everything appeared the same. Hay bales stacked in one corner, horses still in their stalls. If the twins had done anything different out here, it wasn't apparent to the naked eye.

Once they were all inside, Simon gestured with his pistol. "Someone close that door."

Moving quickly, Yvonne complied.

"Well?" Simon said. "Show me my spot. You claimed it was a replica of a place near and dear to me. So far, I see nothing but livestock and hay."

Yvonne held out her hand. "I converted one of the empty stalls. Let me show you."

Staring at her, Simon hesitated. Ted figured his hesitation was because he didn't want to tie up one of his hands. While that made sense, there was no way Ted could do anything with Simon that close to his daughter.

Finally, Simon shook his head. "You lead the way. I want all of you in front of me. Anyone moves the slightest bit wrong, and I'll shoot you in the back. Understand?"

Yvonne motioned for Ted and Yolanda to go ahead of her. Ted didn't like her putting herself in between Simon and him, but in case she had some sort of a plan, he allowed it. Yolanda, clearly in pain, stumbled along, tears streaming down her face. Blood had started seeping through the dish towel again.

Several of the horses eyed them curiously as they passed. One or two came to the stall door and poked their large heads out, probably hoping for a treat or a pat. Bringing up the rear, Simon ignored them, his focus and his pistol on the small group ahead.

"Ta-da." Gesturing like the grand master at a circus,

Yvonne opened the last stall's door. She stepped aside, clearly expecting Simon to precede her.

"You first." He motioned with the gun. "All of you."

One by one, they moved into the stall. Once inside, Ted stared. Yvonne had set up a metal laboratory table on one side of the stall. On the other, she'd used several hay bales as a table and assembled the kind of tools from a horror movie's prop list.

"Where did you get all this?" Ted demanded, his voice sharp.

"They were part of my presentation on the Coffee Shop Killer," Yvonne replied. "I borrowed all of them from both the science department and the handyman's closet. I had to make it all look real."

Simon ran one hand over the shining metal table. "Good job," he said. Though he still held his pistol, right now it wasn't pointed directly at anyone. Ted figured now would be as good of a chance as any.

But then, as Simon inspected the tools, Yvonne pulled on a heavy rope she must have strung up over the rafters into the large area where Ted stored his winter hay. Two large bales of hay tumbled down, knocking Simon off his feet.

Quickly, Ted grabbed for the gun. Yvonne jumped on top of one of the heavy bales, evidently hoping to use her weight to keep Simon down.

But Simon managed to roll out from under both her and the hay. Snarling, he reached for Yvonne, clearly intending to choke her.

Ted yelled at her to move away. As she leaped sideways, he used Simon's own gun to shoot him, praying his aim would be true.

The loud sound spooked the horses. Yvonne screamed,

and Yolanda whimpered. Heart in his throat, Ted watched the blood bloom on Simon's chest as he fell back, unmoving. Ted had gotten off a clean shot, right through the heart. The Coffee Shop Killer wouldn't be terrorizing anyone else ever again. Ted had killed a man, but his girls were safe.

Shaking, Ted called Rayna.

"We're less than five minutes out," she said upon answering the phone. "The FBI is en route also."

Talking quickly, Ted explained what he'd done. "We're out back in the barn. I'll need an ambulance for Yolanda. She's lost quite a bit of blood and I'm pretty sure the bullet is still in her arm."

"I'll get it called in."

"Thanks." Ted ended the call. He crossed over to his daughters, gathering them close, careful not to jostle Yolanda's arm. "Rayna and an ambulance are on the way."

"What about Amelia?" Yvonne asked. "Is she all right? You know that's why he came here, right?"

"I figured." He eyed her. "Did you have anything to do with him knowing where to go?"

"No, I promise." Eyes huge, Yvonne tried to avoid looking at Simon's body. "But after I saw what Lincoln and Jacob posted, I knew Simon would head here. So Yolanda and I spent hours setting up this trap." She shrugged, looking at her sister with concern. "I'm just glad you store all that hay up there. All we had to do was cut away the plywood floor and then drag it over the top of the stall and tie a rope around that."

"Pretty good thinking," he said, hugging her.

"Thanks, but it was Yolanda's idea." She cut her eyes sideways toward Simon. "Is he…?"

Ted knew he'd taken a clean shot, but just to be sure, he went over and checked the other man for a pulse. He found none. "He's dead," he said. "You're both safe. Amelia's safe."

"Okay." She met his gaze, her own filling with tears. "I really did start a Coffee Shop Killer fan club, before I knew the truth about all the awful things he'd done. That's what put me together with that new group of friends." She swallowed, her mouth working. "Honestly, I tried to disband it after I realized, but Jacob and Lincoln were really into it, so they kept it going. This is all my fault and I'm really, really sorry."

Crossing back to her, he hugged her again. "It's not your fault. I'm just glad you had sense enough to understand the truth."

She turned into him and cried, her body shaking with silent sobs. He held her, his precious little girl, and hoped with every fiber of his being that this incident hadn't caused deep scars in both his daughters. He knew they'd never forget this and he didn't want them to either. The lessons learned from all of this would help them become strong women later in life.

Until then, he knew they'd all be haunted by what had happened.

Looking up, he met Yolanda's pain-filled gaze. She'd let herself sink down onto a bale of hay on the other side of Simon's body.

Suddenly, the stall felt claustrophobic. He didn't want to look at Simon anymore. "Let's all go outside and wait."

Yvonne nodded, wiping at her eyes with the back of her hand. "Yes, let's."

He took her arm and together they reached to help

Yolanda up. Even with their help, she struggled to get to her feet and failed. "I can't," she muttered. "It hurts too much. I'll have to wait right here. You two go on without me."

"As if," Yvonne responded, taking a seat next to her.

A siren sounded in the distance.

Ted also sat down on the other side, next to his wounded daughter. "That will be the ambulance. We're going to get you some help so you can be feeling better soon."

She nodded, wincing at the slight movement. "Good," she managed. "Because this really hurts."

Rayna and Amelia rushed in, arriving before the ambulance. Amelia ran immediately over to the girls, dropping down to her knees in front of Yolanda and asking them all if they were okay. To Ted's surprise, Yvonne got down next to her and wrapped her arms around Amelia's waist. "I'm glad you're safe," she said, crying again.

Yolanda lifted her head, her bleary gaze struggling to focus. "Amelia," she rasped. "He's dead. Daddy killed him. We're all safe now."

Amelia's eyes filled with tears. "Hang in there, honey. Medical help will be here at any moment."

The siren grew louder, cutting off just as the ambulance parked in the driveway. EMTs rushed in, and Amelia, Ted and Yvonne moved out of their way while they checked Yolanda over.

One arm around Yvonne, Ted watched the medics with his other daughter. When Amelia walked up to his other side and slipped her arm around his waist, Ted fought the urge to pull her in for a kiss. Not the time nor the place, but he needed something tangible to ground him.

He accidentally bumped Yvonne, making her wince. "We should have them check out your arm too," he told her.

She shook her head. "Let them take care of Yolanda. I'll get it looked at later. It's really just a scratch."

The FBI pulled up a few minutes later. Standing together in their little group of three, they stayed away from everyone, having moved out of the stall and into the hallway of the barn.

The next several minutes became a blur of people and lights. The EMTs got Yolanda up on a stretcher. Ted wanted to go in the ambulance with her, but was told he couldn't leave yet. Neither could Yvonne. Slipping out from under Ted's arm, Amelia took one look at Yolanda's pale face and volunteered to go with her. Grateful, Yolanda started to cry.

"It's okay," Amelia told her, gently wiping away her tears. "You're safe. Once they fix you up, you'll feel so much better, I promise." She turned to Ted. "I'll take good care of her until you can get there," she promised, taking his hand and squeezing it before letting go.

Again, Ted wanted to kiss her, but settled for thanking her instead. Following the EMTs outside, he watched as she climbed up in the back of the ambulance with his little girl. He didn't move until the ambulance had driven out of sight.

"We're going to need you back inside," Rayna said, her voice apologetic as she came up behind him. "Sorry."

"Do I have to go?" Yvonne wanted to know. "I'd like to head back to the house and see about cleaning up my arm."

"Let me take a look at it," Rayna asked. Then, without waiting for Yvonne to agree, she pushed aside Yvonne's sleeve to examine the cut there. "It needs cleaning and an antibiotic cream," she said. "Then a bandage. You should have let the EMTs take care of it."

Yvonne shrugged. "I wanted them to focus on my sister."

"Rayna," someone called. "We need you back here."

"Come on, y'all," she said. "The sooner we can get this done, the better."

Back inside, the FBI swarmed around, taking photographs and marking off areas inside the stall for their investigation. They had people and equipment clogging the barn aisle, and the horses were all restless still. Ted knew they wouldn't calm down until everyone left.

Someone had summoned the medical examiner, and the body couldn't be moved until it was pronounced dead. Ted and Yvonne both had to answer questions separately. As the one who'd shot Simon, Ted also had to give a lengthy statement describing what had happened to an unsmiling FBI agent, with Rayna looking on.

By the time he'd finished, Ted wasn't sure if they were going to arrest him or not. When the FBI agent completed his notes, Ted wondered if he could finally leave.

"Come on." Rayna took his arm and led him a short distance away. "They're still talking to Yvonne."

He frowned. "Why are they treating me like the bad guy here?" he asked.

"They're not. They're just being professional and thorough. You did good, Ted Sanders." Rayna punched him lightly in the arm. "You not only protected yourself and your daughters, but Amelia as well."

Though he nodded, Ted didn't feel jubilant or proud. Maybe a bit relieved, but mostly just numb. Rayna moved away to speak with several agents.

"Dad?" Yvonne's voice, quavering a bit. He looked up to find her watching him, her eyes huge and dark in her pale face. "They're done with me. Can we go now?"

Suddenly and thoroughly exhausted, Ted went to Yvonne and put his arm around her, moving them both to a seat on their hay bale. "What a mess."

They sat silently for a moment, Ted trying to summon up enough strength to somehow pass on to her. It had been a long day for them all. "We made it. We survived," he said. "That's all that matters."

"True, but are you all right?" Yvonne asked, eyeing him with a concern far more mature than her fourteen years. "I mean, it's got to be tough, knowing you just killed someone, even if it was self-defense."

Humbled by her compassion, he hugged her tight. "I did what had to be done. There was no other choice."

"I know." She hugged him back. "But it's still got to bother you."

"I imagine it will set in later." He knew it would. Monster or not, he'd taken another life. Though when he considered all the things that Simon would have done to those he loved, he knew what he'd done had saved a lot of pain and anguish. The world would be a much better place without the Coffee Shop Killer in it.

After conferring with one of the FBI agents on the other side of the room, Rayna walked up to them. "If you two are ready, I can run you both up to the hospital to check on Yolanda."

Relieved, he stood. Yvonne pushed to her feet a bit more slowly. "Are you all right?" Ted asked, concerned.

"My arm just still hurts." She smiled bravely. "I know it's just a scratch and nothing like what he did to Yolanda, but I think I'm going to ask them to fix it while we're there."

"Good idea," Rayna agreed. "Let's go."

Amelia had to lie to get the medical personnel to allow her to remain with Yolanda. "I'm her aunt," she said, not daring enough to claim to be the young girl's mother. "Her father and sister will be here as soon as they can."

Even so, they made her go sit in a waiting area while they took Yolanda into the operating room to remove the bullet from her arm. Only once they'd finished up and had a bandage in place did they allow Amelia to return to the room.

"She's on IV painkillers and antibiotics," the nurse told Amelia. "There's a huge risk of infection from any sort of traumatic wound like that."

Amelia nodded. "How long will she have to stay in the hospital?"

"It's up to the doctor, but most likely a day or two. We'll keep her on the IV and watch her. If all goes well, then she'll be discharged with pain medication and antibiotics that she'll take by mouth." The nurse checked her watch. "Do you have any idea when her parents will be here?"

"I'm sure her father will arrive as soon as he can," Amelia responded.

"Good. We'll need him to sign some papers." The nurse smiled. "I'll be back soon." She hurried away.

Amelia went to sit in the chair next to Yolanda's bed. "How are you feeling, sweetie?"

"Pretty good." Yolanda gave a slow smile. "You were right. I do feel a lot better." Her smile faded a bit. "Where are Dad and Yvonne? Is she all right? You know Simon shot her too."

"They're just finishing up with the FBI. Your dad said she barely had a scratch, but I'm sure she'll get checked out once she gets here."

Yolanda's eyes drifted closed. "Wake me up when they get here," she mumbled.

Amelia watched her sleep, her heart full. Though she hadn't known them very long at all, she adored these girls and their father. In fact, she was in love with Ted.

Rather than a lightning bolt, a sense of calm, quiet certainty settled over her. Getaway, Texas, with its strange, keep-at-arm's-length name, had become her home. The Sanders family had welcomed her as if she were one of their own. Rayna and Serenity were the kind of friends she knew she could always count on. This was where she belonged.

It dawned on her then that she'd finally been freed. No more would she have to stick to shadows and keep her head down. No longer would she have to use a last name that wasn't hers, and never again would she feel the need to make certain she always had an escape route planned.

She could be…normal.

The thought made her want to weep. Her eyes welled up, happy tears only, just happy tears. She let them roll down her face unchecked while she struggled with the nearly overwhelming sense of relief.

The door opened, and Ted, Yvonne and Rayna walked in. Luckily, all their attention was focused on Yolanda, asleep in the bed. Except Rayna, who immediately crossed over to stand in front of Amelia, blocking her from the others' view.

"Are you all right?" she asked, low voiced, as she pulled Amelia in for a hug.

Amelia nodded, wiping furtively at her eyes. "Sorry," she murmured. "I just can't believe it's finally over and we made it out alive."

"What's wrong?" Ted asked. "Is Yolanda going to be okay?"

"She is," the nurse answered from the doorway. "We've removed the bullet and given her both pain-killers and antibiotics. She has a few stitches. I take it you must be her parents?"

"I'm her father," Ted replied.

"Perfect." The nurse smiled at him. "Someone will be in here shortly with some paperwork for you to fill out."

Suddenly, for whatever reason, Amelia felt the need to get some fresh air. She excused herself and hurried out of the room and down the hall, past the small waiting room and into the main triage area, before finding the automatic doors that led outside.

"Amelia." Ted's voice, right behind her. "Are you okay?"

"You need to be with your daughter," she replied, her posture stiff, keeping her back to him. She didn't want to break down in front of him. Not now, not yet.

"She's still asleep." Moving carefully, he gathered her close. At first, she didn't respond, feeling as if she might shatter. But then, as his body's warmth got through to hers, she let herself relax and leaned into his familiar embrace.

"It's over," he told her, pressing a light kiss to her temple. "You're finally free."

Struggling to swallow past the lump in her throat, she nodded. Now what? She'd spent so long being defined by her need to escape, she wasn't sure what to do with herself now. She loved him, she loved his girls and his ranch, but part of her knew she needed more. Except how could she abandon them when they all depended on her so much? Conversely, how could she abandon her own dreams? The idea of setting up her own therapist office in downtown Getaway could easily become a reality. She'd noted several suitable spaces for rent at prices far less exorbitant than anything she'd ever been able to find in White Plains, New York.

She wanted it all. Ted and the girls and the life they shared on the ranch, plus her career as a therapist so she could once again devote her life to helping others. She knew she'd have to make a choice soon, but right now, even thinking about it exhausted her.

So she clung to Ted, inhaling his familiar scent of outdoors and pine, and wished life could be simple.

"Come on back inside," he told her, his dark eyes kind. He released her and took her hand. "You're shivering."

She nodded. He had no idea her shivering wasn't entirely from the cold.

Once back inside the ER, the nurse buzzed them through to the back. When they got to Yolanda's room, she was sitting up in her bed, talking with her sister and Rayna. When she saw her father and Amelia, her eyes lit up.

"Dad!" She held out her arms for a hug. Crossing to her, Ted gently gathered her close, careful of her bandaged wound. "When can I go home?"

"Good question." He looked at Amelia. "Do you know?"

She relayed what the nurse had told her earlier.

Yolanda's face fell. "I don't want to stay here a couple of days."

"You've got to stay on the IV," Amelia pointed out gently. "They need to make sure your wound doesn't get infected."

Just then, a woman arrived with a computer and paperwork. Hearing the end of Amelia's comment, she smiled. "We're getting your room ready for you upstairs," she said. "I just have some forms for you to sign. The doctor will be back to talk to y'all soon."

From Amelia's experience with hospitals, *soon* could mean anything from one hour to four. Rayna sidled up next to her. "Should we have them look you over?"

"No. I'm fine." Amelia eyed Yvonne. "But Yvonne got clipped by a bullet. We need to have someone look at her arm."

Hearing that, Ted looked up from the paperwork and nodded. "My other daughter needs to be checked out too," he said.

"I'll send in the nurse when we're finished," the woman replied.

"Amelia?" Rayna asked. "Walk with me?"

"Sure." Still, Amelia glanced at Ted. He caught her gaze and nodded.

They made their way to the small waiting area. "Do you want some coffee?" Rayna asked, pointing to a coffeepot. "It's not the greatest, but it's strong and free."

Suddenly, coffee sounded like ambrosia. "I'd love some."

Rayna fixed them both a cup, adding cream and sugar to Amelia's without asking. "Here you go." After handing it over, Rayna made her way to a seat. "Sit. You look like you're about to topple over at any moment."

"That bad, huh?" Amelia sat. She exhaled, glancing at her friend. "Thanks for everything you did today. I don't know what I'd do without you on my side."

Rayna grinned. "That's my job. I'm damn good at what I do."

Her words brought another wave of melancholy. Once, Amelia would have said the same thing. She'd been a good therapist, caring, educated and comfortable with putting ideas into practice. She'd loved her work, enjoyed it so much that waking up every day filled her with anticipation.

Until Simon. He'd tricked her, fooled her with a completely false persona, and made her question her competence. She'd once considered herself an extremely astute judge of character. Simon had proved she was wrong about that too. Who was she now to think she had any right to counsel others when she couldn't even heal herself? Had Simon managed to completely take her self-confidence away from her? Wouldn't that mean he'd won?

"Earth to Amelia." Rayna nudged her with a gentle shoulder bump. "What are you worrying about?"

"How do you know I'm worrying?" Amelia countered, genuinely curious.

"You have a very expressive face. So spill. That's what friends are for."

Talking to someone else, someone who cared, was half of therapy. Amelia took a deep breath. Then, speaking haltingly at first, she told Rayna everything she'd been thinking. Everything, that was, except her feelings for Ted.

When she finally finished, Rayna sat and sipped her coffee for a moment, considering. "That's a lot to deal with alone," she finally said. "I know you're a therapist and all, but have you considered that you might want to talk to someone about all this?"

Amelia shrugged. "I've considered it. Except I know what they would say and do, so I can't really see the point. In the end, it's a decision I have to make on my own."

"True, but I'm talking about the loss of your self-confidence," Rayna gently pointed out. "Simon is dead. He's no longer a threat."

"Yet his dark cloud still hangs over me," Amelia finished. "I get it, believe me. But all of this just happened. I'm still processing everything."

"Maybe so." Tossing back the rest of her coffee, Rayna set the empty cup on the table. "Does Ted know?"

Taken aback, Amelia wasn't sure how to respond. "About what?" she asked, deflecting a bit. "I mentioned to him that I might want to open my own therapist office downtown, but if you're asking if he's aware of all my self-doubt, no."

Rayna's gaze softened. "I wasn't talking about that. I'm asking if Ted knows how you feel about him."

"Is it that obvious?" Amelia gave up on her lukewarm coffee, placing her cup on the table next to Rayna's.

"Only because I know both of you. The sparks you two give off when you're together light up the room."

Stunned, Amelia stared at her friend. "Are you serious?" she whispered, her heart pounding.

"Anyone with eyes can see that you two have feelings for each other." Rayna grinned. "Especially those of us who've recently fallen in love. Parker and I danced around the truth for a bit too."

Amelia sat silently for a moment, trying to process this. "I do love him. I also love his girls. And, quite frankly, that terrifies me."

"That's when you know it's real." Rayna pushed to her feet. "We'd better go back in. They're going to wonder where we got off to." She touched Amelia's arm, giving her a sideways glance. "We redheads need to stick together, you know."

"About that..." Amelia began.

"You're not really a redhead," Rayna finished for her. "I know. But the color suits you."

"Thanks." Amused, Amelia touched her hair. "But it will honestly be a relief not to have to dye it anymore."

When they got back to Yolanda's room, the ER doctor was there, finishing one last check. Catching Amelia's eye, Yvonne held up her arm and showed off her new bandage. Amelia smiled and gave her a thumbs-up.

"The doctor says you have to stay here until tomorrow," Ted told a clearly disappointed Yolanda. "But we'll be back first thing in the morning and hopefully they'll discharge you then."

Slowly, Yolanda nodded.

"Do you want me to stay with you tonight?" Ted offered. "I can sleep in the chair."

"No." Yolanda lifted her chin. "I'll be fine. Go get some rest and I'll see you tomorrow."

Though Ted nodded, he appeared torn.

"Is everyone ready to go?" Rayna asked cheerfully, taking Ted's arm as if she planned to drag him from the room if necessary. "I just happen to be driving a van that's big enough to hold everyone."

"We're ready," Ted replied, catching Amelia's eye. "More than ready to go home."

Home. Heaven help her. Amelia loved the sound of that word.

Chapter 16

Ted had hoped that everything would return to normal once the FBI investigation had been completed and the media tired of running reports on the Coffee Shop Killer's death. For a few days, news vans had camped down at the end of his driveway, which made taking the girls to school problematic. After numerous refusals to speak to them, they finally gave up and went away. He'd had to disconnect his landline because they wouldn't stop calling, but since everyone had cell phones, no one seemed to miss it.

Everyone appeared to settle back into their old, familiar routines. The girls went back to school, Amelia continued to cook and clean and nurture, and Ted returned to working with Floyd around the ranch. One problem. He couldn't stand to go inside his own barn. His skin would crawl, and he'd swallow back nausea and force himself to power through it.

Several times, he wished he could simply burn the barn down and build a new one. He'd never be able to walk into it again without remembering what had happened there. He made plans to convert the last stall into a closed-off storage room for grain and tack. He knew he wouldn't be able to stable a horse in there ever again. Even the usually unruffled Floyd, once he'd heard the entire story, offered to work overtime to help Ted work on it. Relieved, Ted took him up on his offer, happy for the extra work, aware the physical exertion might help him sleep.

A few times a week, Ted had nightmares. He'd wake, heart pounding, drenched in a cold sweat. If he worried more about the twins than normal, he chalked that up to what had happened. He hoped that, with time, he'd push past this.

Amelia worried him the most. Though he'd done his best to restore everyday life to normal, for everyone's sake, Amelia had changed. Though she smiled and cooked and helped the girls with their homework, she wasn't entirely present. She seemed to have withdrawn into herself. Ted debated whether or not to confront her, but he didn't want to press her too soon. He couldn't help but wonder if she might be getting ready to tell him and his little family goodbye.

Even the girls noticed. They took him aside one evening while Amelia was taking a shower.

"What's wrong with her?" Yvonne demanded. "She's here, but not, if you know what I mean. She's like a ghost."

"It's probably shock," Yolanda countered. "But we're her family now. She must know she can talk to us."

"Does she?" Yvonne crossed her arms, her expression

a combination of worried and hurt. "Maybe we should do an intervention."

"A what?" Ted had to ask. "It's not like she has an addiction problem or anything. Maybe we should just try talking to her."

"Same thing." Yvonne shrugged, rolling her eyes dismissively. She'd bounced right back after the incident with Simon, as had Yolanda, courtesy of youth. In fact, Yolanda had confided that she'd become a sort of minor celebrity at school now. She and Donella, Heather and Yvonne had bonded. And while Donella's parents hadn't yet gotten her any help, Yolanda said talking things through with their group seemed to help her a lot.

"Maybe we just need to give her time," Ted suggested. "She's been through a lot, between what had happened before when Simon had held her prisoner and after."

"Time doesn't always heal all wounds," Yvonne said, wiser than her fourteen years.

"How about a family meeting?" Yolanda suggested. Ted wasn't sure whether to be relieved or worried that it hadn't occurred to either of his daughters that Amelia might not want to be part of their family any longer.

"How about I talk to her first?" he asked. Both girls immediately vetoed that idea.

"We want her to know we love her and we're there for her," Yvonne said, her tone fierce and determined.

Looking from one girl to the other, Ted finally nodded. While Amelia still worked for them, he remembered her talking of setting up her own therapist office in town. He had a feeling she wouldn't be working at the ranch too much longer.

But how to tell the girls? He suspected it might never have occurred to either of them that Amelia could have other dreams and plans that didn't revolve around being the Sanders family housekeeper. For that matter, he had other dreams too. He wanted Amelia to become much, much more.

But first, he knew he—they—had to find out what *Amelia* wanted.

"When?" he asked his girls, loving them both so much it hurt.

"How about tonight?" Yvonne said.

"There's no time like the present," Yolanda agreed. "As soon as she comes out of the shower."

Nodding, he turned on the television with the volume on low. He heard the shower cut off and, a few minutes later, the sound of her blow-drying her hair.

While they waited, Ted's unease grew. He knew his daughters meant well, but he didn't think it would be right to blindside Amelia like that. He decided he'd let the girls have their say, but he'd wait for another time when he and Amelia were alone to let her know how he felt.

After what seemed like infinity but was probably only ten minutes, Amelia wandered into the living room.

"Hey, guys." She looked from one to the other, her gaze lingering on Ted. "What's going on? You all seem so solemn."

"We're worried about you," Yolanda began. "You haven't been yourself ever since… You know."

Amelia sat down slowly. "I'm still trying to process everything. It's a lot, and honestly, it's really hard sometimes. But I promise you girls, this has nothing to do with you."

Ted took a deep breath. "I'll be honest. I'm having

some problems dealing with everything that happened too." He braced himself.

But when Amelia and his daughters looked at him, instead of censure, he saw nothing but compassion in their eyes. "You too?" Amelia asked softly. "Nightmares?"

He nodded. "Yes. And I fight the urge to be overly protective of all you. Plus, I can barely stand to get within twenty feet of the barn."

"Me too," Yolanda cried. "I've been avoiding going outside so I won't have to look at it."

Even Yvonne echoed the sentiment.

Then they all looked at Amelia. "What about you?"

"The same." Amelia sighed. "I think we could all benefit from counseling."

"Together?" the twins asked, in unison. "Like group therapy or something?"

Amelia hesitated just the tiniest bit. "That's really up to your father." She held his gaze.

"I'm game if you are," Ted finally said. "Though we're going to have to drive to either Abilene or Midland–Odessa to find a therapist."

"I'll start looking around," Amelia offered. "As soon as I find someone, I'll let you know."

"The sooner, the better," Yolanda said. "The nightmares are awful."

Yvonne nodded. "She cries a lot, into her pillow. I do too."

Ted's heart broke. He hadn't known. "We'll get something set up as soon as possible, I promise."

Amelia seconded that. "Thank you for asking me to join you in therapy," she said.

Both girls appeared relieved. "We're here for you if

you need to talk or anything before then, okay?" Yvonne asked. "We care about you."

Obviously touched, Amelia smiled. "That's so sweet of you to say. Thank you. And right back atcha, if you need to talk. I care about you too."

Both girls jumped up and ran to give her a hug. She hugged them back, her gaze meeting Ted's over their heads. Just then, he loved her so much he ached with it.

Hug complete, the girls said they had homework and took off for their room. A moment later, he heard the sound of their bedroom door closing.

Ted swallowed. Still standing, Amelia looked down at her hands. The silence stretched out between them, as heavy as lead. She'd agreed to attend group therapy. Surely that meant she wasn't leaving anytime soon.

Still, he knew they had to talk about their future. Now or never. Ted patted the sofa cushion next to him. "Come sit?"

She shook her head. "I've been meaning to talk to you, and I think it's better if I stay standing. I'm checking into the process of obtaining my license to practice therapy in Texas. I have the education and the experience. I just need to pass the licensing exam."

Surprised, he blinked. "That's great," he said, genuinely happy for her. "I'm sure you'll ace the test."

"Hopefully." She watched him closely. "But if I do open my own practice, I won't be able to work here anymore."

"I figured," he replied. "Is that what's been bothering you?"

"Maybe. Okay, yes. I don't want to let you or the girls down, but this is something I really want to do."

Both relieved and surprised, he kept his expression

neutral. "Amelia, I knew you wouldn't want to work here as a housekeeper forever. To ask you to would not only be a colossal waste of your talent, but your education as well."

"Wow. Thank you for that."

"I mean it. You're special." He took a deep breath, wondering how it could be that she couldn't see his heart pounding. "Actually, I was hoping we could explore a more personal relationship."

She blinked. "You sound so formal," she offered, appearing more relaxed than she had in what seemed like forever. "Are you saying you want to start dating and see where this goes?"

Slowly, he nodded, unable to tear his gaze away from her.

She stared at him for so long he began to worry she was about to say no. "I'd like that," she said, her smile so sexy he couldn't catch his breath. "I can either rent my room from you or move out and stay at the motel until I can afford my own place. Whichever you prefer."

"I'd like you to stay." He didn't even have to think about his answer. "And no need to pay rent. The pleasure of your company is more than enough repayment."

This made her smile. "Sounds perfect, but I think we should ask the girls first. I want to make sure they're on board. I can't help but remember how they reacted when Yvonne caught us kissing."

"They love you now," he replied, the glow in her beautiful eyes still knocking him to his knees. "As do I." The words escaped him, unplanned. But once said, he didn't even want to recall them.

"You what?" She blinked again, her beautiful blue eyes filling.

Now it was his turn to push through his fear. "I love you, Amelia. More than words can express."

"I love you too." Expression fierce, Amelia grabbed him and pulled him to her. "I know we haven't known each other very long, but sometimes you just know."

He kissed her then, a long and lingering expression of his emotions. "You're right. Sometimes you just know. Which means I should tell you that I want so much more than just dating. I want a future."

"Me too. Let's see how it goes," she murmured, right before she pulled him in for another kiss.

When they finally broke apart, both breathing hard, he took her hand. "We need to tell the girls."

"I agree."

"When?" he asked.

Linking her fingers in his, she smiled. "There's no time like the present."

Hand in hand, they walked down the hall to the girls' room.

Hand raised to knock, Ted glanced down at Amelia. "Are you as nervous as I am?"

"Probably more," she replied with a wry smile.

Three sharp raps and Yolanda finally opened the door a crack. She took in Ted and Amelia's linked fingers and raised a brow. "What's up?" she asked.

"Will you and your sister please come out to the living room?" Ted asked. "We need to talk to you."

"Are we in trouble?" Yvonne asked from inside the room.

"Not at all." Ted tugged Amelia back, down the hall. He felt the most absurd urge to laugh out loud. "Life is good."

He and Amelia had just taken a seat on the couch when his girls rushed into the room.

They caught sight of his and Amelia's locked hands and exchanged glances.

"Aha," Yvonne exclaimed. "I knew it. Pay up, Yolanda."

"Pay up?" Ted asked. "You were betting?"

"Yes. I said you two were together and she thought you were just friends."

"Maybe we're both," Amelia put in softly. "Are you two okay with that?"

"I will be, once she gives me my five dollars," Yvonne replied, holding out her hand.

In response, Yolanda stuck out her tongue.

"There's more," Amelia began. Ted squeezed her hand, hearing the slight quaver in her voice and sending her strength. "I'm not going to be working here much longer."

"What do you mean?" Yolanda asked, her expression worried. "Where are you going?"

"Nowhere. I'm going to keep my room here, but I'm going to be working on getting my Texas certification to practice therapy. You know that's what I do, right? I'm a therapist."

At both their hesitant nods, she continued.

"I'm still going to be around a lot, but your dad is going to need you to help out some too. I can still cook some, and I bet if we all pitch in, we can get this place clean once a week. Same thing with laundry."

Yvonne crossed her arms. "What are you going to be doing? Studying?"

"At first, yes. But I'm also going to be looking for a place in town I can rent for an office, and then I'll need to furnish and staff it. All of that is going to be a bit time-consuming, and that's before I can even start holding counseling sessions there."

"Wow." Yolanda moved closer, appearing impressed. "Maybe you can help Donella."

"Maybe I can," Amelia answered. "I really hope so."

"Let me see if I've got this straight," Yvonne said, her arms still crossed. "You and my dad are dating now, you're not going to be our housekeeper, but you're not going anywhere, and you're going to open your own business in downtown Getaway."

Amelia nodded. "That about sums it up."

To Ted's surprise, Yvonne didn't get upset or run away to her room and slam the door. Instead, she studied them, her gaze traveling from Ted to Amelia and back again. "I'm glad," she finally said. "You both deserve to be happy more than anyone else I know."

Smiling through her tears, Amelia tugged her hand out of his and held out her arms. "Come here," she ordered. "It's time for a hug."

"Group hug," Yolanda corrected, rushing over with her sister, including Ted in the hug.

He hadn't known his heart could be so full.

The next few weeks, Amelia found herself humming as she worked around the house. Life finally felt…right. She'd started the application process to get licensed in Texas, and while awaiting approval to take the test, she saw no reason why she shouldn't keep her job. After school and on weekends, she'd started teaching the girls to cook. Surprisingly, Yvonne loved it, while Yolanda appeared mostly indifferent.

Though Amelia ached to start looking at real estate

for lease, she knew there wasn't any reason to start paying rent long before she was able to use the place. Still, she couldn't resist heading into town one bright, sunny day. Though she and Ted had plans to meet up for lunch, she wanted to stop and visit Serenity. It had been far too long since she'd seen her friend.

When she walked into the shop, a wave of nostalgia hit her. She stood just inside the doorway, breathing in the sickly sweet scent of incense, eyeing the display of books next to the jumbled pile of rocks and crystals, and felt a sense of peace steal over her.

"Amelia!" Serenity exclaimed, hurrying over and taking her hands, her bracelets jangling. "It's so good to see you." Cocking her head, she looked Amelia over. "You're glowing."

Amelia grinned. "Being happy will do that to you," she said.

"Come, sit down and have some herbal tea, and you can tell me all about it."

Taking a seat at the small round table Serenity kept in the back of the shop, Amelia looked around. It felt like old times. "You know, when I first arrived in Getaway, I didn't know anyone. You befriended me, gave me a job and made me feel welcome. I can never thank you enough for that."

Serenity carried over a teapot and two teacups on a tray. "When I saw you, I knew," she said.

Intrigued, Amelia waited to hear the rest. But Serenity, busy arranging everything and pouring out tea, didn't seem inclined to elaborate.

"Knew what?" Amelia finally prompted.

When Serenity looked up, she smiled. "I just knew that you belonged here, in Getaway. Here you are." She handed Amelia her tea. "Now tell me what's been going on with you."

They chatted for over an hour. Once Amelia finished everything, she sat back in her chair, trying to analyze why she felt as if a huge weight had lifted off her shoulders.

Serenity simply watched her, a gleam in her eyes. "You've begun to heal," she said, appearing pleased.

"Maybe I have." Amazed, Amelia impulsively jumped up and hugged her former boss.

"Love will do that to you," Serenity added.

Since her feelings for Ted and vice versa were the only information Amelia had omitted from her story, she wasn't sure how to respond. "How did you know?" she finally asked.

"I really am psychic, you know." Serenity patted Amelia's arm. "You and Ted will be very happy together."

Amelia smiled. "You know, I believe you're right."

"I know I am." Serenity leaned closer. "And one more thing. I see the two of you growing that little family."

At first, this shocked Amelia. She'd been so focused on her career, then staying alive, that she'd never stopped to consider the possibility of having children, or if she even wanted them.

But now the idea of having a child—or two—with Ted made her heart sing. "Maybe someday," she murmured. "After I get my business up and running."

"You know you can do both, don't you?" Serenity asked. "A fulfilled mom is a happier mom."

Since this sounded exactly like something Amelia would have told a client, she had to laugh.

The little bell over the door chimed as Ted walked

into the store, his black cowboy hat shadowing his craggy face. Just the sight of him made Amelia's heart skip a beat.

"Hey there." His slow smile was just for her. Then he noticed Serenity. "Hi, Serenity. How are you?"

"I'm good, but not as good as you two." She chuckled. "Love looks good on you, Ted Sanders."

"Not as good as it does on Amelia." He grinned as he replied, holding out his hand. Taking it, she allowed him to haul her up against him. He kissed her, one quick kiss, and then released her. "Are you ready to go?" he asked.

She nodded. At that moment, she'd go anywhere with him. The thought of having babies with him made her dizzy. Someday, she told herself, glancing back at Serenity. The older woman smiled, nodded and waved.

Arm in arm, Amelia and Ted walked out into the sunshine, together.

"What were you two talking about back there?" Ted asked. "You looked pretty pleased about it, whatever it was."

"New beginnings," she answered. "I'm still trying to process everything she told me."

He glanced down at her, his gaze warm. "She did her psychic thing with you?"

"She did."

"I hope it was good," he said. "Serenity has an uncanny ability of being right with her predictions."

"Really?" she asked. "If that's the case, I guess I'd better ask you how you feel about someday having more children."

About to open the passenger-side door for her, Ted froze. She watched the emotions chase themselves across his face—uncertainty, then disbelief, and finally joy. Outright, unabashed joy.

"She said *that*?"

Slowly, Amelia nodded. "She not only said we'll be happy together, but that we'll be growing our little family."

With a loud whoop, Ted swung around and lifted her up in front of him. "Best news I heard all day!"

Delighted, she grinned at him. When he lowered her back to the ground, they kissed.

When they broke apart, Ted eyed her, his eyes dark and full of love. "You know what? Maybe it's not too soon to talk about forever."

Her heart skipped a beat. "Maybe it's not," she agreed.

"Are you saying yes?"

She laughed. "You haven't asked me yet."

"But if I did, would you say yes?"

Still laughing, she brushed past him and opened the truck door, climbing up into the passenger seat. "What fun would it be if I told you? I don't want to ruin the surprise."

When he got in on the driver's side, he shook his head before starting the engine. "Let's go eat," he said. "We can talk about this later."

At the Tumbleweed Café, despite the usual mid-afternoon crowd, they were shown to a booth near the middle of the restaurant. As soon as they were seated, the waitress brought over menus and two glasses of water. Amelia glanced around, telling herself it had to be her imagination, but it felt as if everyone was watching her. Of course, she had recently been on the news and her true identity had apparently been a shock to some. Shrugging, she opened the menu and began to study it.

"Amelia?" Ted asked. Then the entire café went silent as he pushed out of the booth and got to one knee. From his jeans pocket, he pulled out a black velvet ring box. "I've been carrying this around, waiting for the right time. This seems just as good as any. Amelia Ferguson, will you marry me?"

Stunned, she gazed at his beloved, craggy face and slowly nodded. Her eyes filled and her throat clogged, but she managed to choke out a single word. "Yes."

The place broke out in cheers. As Ted placed the beautiful diamond ring on her finger, someone else brought over a bottle of champagne and two glasses. Two waitresses wheeled out a huge cake and began slicing it, taking it around to patrons.

"What the…?" Amelia asked. "How'd they know?"

Ted grinned again, his eyes sparkling. "Maybe Serenity told them. Of course, there's a distinct possibility I did."

He popped the champagne, pouring them each a glass. When she took hers, he raised his in a toast. "To our happily-ever-after," he said.

Clinking her glass to his, she echoed his words and added some of her own. "To love."

* * * * *

"Sawyer?" Her voice sounded hoarse. She sat back on
her heels and looked behind her. He was a fair distance
away, moving more slowly than she'd have thought.
Ashley shoved to her feet, her knees wobbling as she
stepped back into the water and shouted for him. "You're
almost there! Come on!" But he was gasping for air, and
for a horrifying moment, he sank out of sight.

Panic seized her. It was pitch-black. Not even the moon
cast light on this side of the shore. No homes nearby, no
lights or guideposts. How would she ever find him?

But she would. He would not leave her like this. She
would not lose him. Not now. She waded into the water,
stumbled, nearly fell face-first, just as he surfaced. He
took a moment to wretch, his hand clutching his side as
he slowly moved toward her, water cascading from the
bag on his hip.

"What is it?" She'd seen enough injuries to know something was seriously wrong. She wedged herself under his arm and helped him walk the rest of the way to dry land. "Where are you hurt?"

"Doesn't matter," he wheezed as he dropped to the ground. He leaned back, still pressing a hand to his side. Blood soaked through his shirt and onto his fingers. "I'll be fine in a minute. We need to get moving."

She dragged his shirt up, tried to examine the wound. "I can't see anything other than blood."

"I know." He covered her hand with his, squeezed her fingers. "Ashley, listen to me. Valeri left with Mouse and Olena, but he ordered Taras and Javi to stay behind. They're coming after me, Ashley."

"Us. They're coming after us. Let me—"

"No. It's me they want. Which means you're in even more danger than you were before. You need to go on alone. Now. While it's still dark."

"I'm not leaving you." She slung his arm over her shoulders and, with enough effort that her feet sank into the dirt, helped him up. He let out a sound that told her he was trying not to show how hurt he really was.

"You have to."

"Hey." She gave him a hard squeeze. "You aren't in any condition to argue with me. I am not leaving you, Sawyer Paxton. So be quiet and let's move."

Don't miss
Prison Break Hostage *by Anna J. Stewart,*
available February 2022 wherever
Harlequin Romantic Suspense
books and ebooks are sold.

Harlequin.com

Get 4 FREE REWARDS!

We'll send you 2 FREE Books plus 2 FREE Mystery Gifts.

Harlequin Romantic Suspense books are heart-racing page-turners with unexpected plot twists and irresistible chemistry that will keep you guessing to the very end.

FREE Value Over $20

SPECIAL EXCERPT FROM

⬡ HARLEQUIN

DESIRE

*Eve Martin has one goal—find her nephew's father—
and her unlikely ally is hotelier Rafael Wentworth, who's
just returned to Texas and the family who abandoned
him. Soon, she's falling hard for the playboy despite
their differences...and their secrets.*

Read on for a sneak peek at
The Rebel's Return, *by Nadine Gonzalez.*

"I'm opening a guesthouse in town, similar to this, but better."

"You're here to check out the competition, aren't you?"

Rafael raised a finger to his lips. "Shh."

"That's sneaky," Eve said with a little smile. "I knew you had a motive for coming here."

He winked. "Just not the motive you thought."

She responded with a roll of the eyes. He noticed her long lashes fanned the high slopes of her cheeks. In the intimate light of the inn's lobby, her skin was smoother than he could have ever imagined.

Rafael was glad the tension that had built up in the car was subsiding. He wanted to make her laugh again, the way she'd laughed when they were alone in the garden. Her laughter had leaped out as if springing from a sealed cave. He'd wanted to take her in his arms and hold her close until she settled down.

"Incoming!"

Lost in the fantasy of holding her, he didn't quite understand what she was saying. "What's that?"

"Just...shut up."

She stepped up to him and brushed her lips to his in a whisper of a kiss. Rafael tensed, the muscles of his abdomen tightening. "Act like you're into it," she murmured through clenched teeth. With every nerve ending in his body setting off sparks, he didn't have to rely on dormant acting skills. He gripped her waist, pulled her close and kissed her hard, deep and slow. She gripped the lapel of his suit jacket and opened to his kiss. He heard her groan just before she tore herself away.

"I think we're good," she said, her voice shaky.

He was shaken, too. "How the hell do you figure?"

"I kissed you to create a distraction," she said. "P&J just walked in."

Paul and Jennifer Carlton were the most annoying couple in Texas, but at this moment he was making plans to send them a fruit basket and a bottle of wine.

"Here I thought you wanted to test that 'sex in an inn' theory."

"Stop thinking that," she scolded. "They're right over there. Don't look now, though."

He wouldn't dream of it. Her swollen lips had his undivided attention.

"Okay… They've entered the dining hall. You can look now."

"Nah. I'll take your word for it."

The manager returned with the keys to their suite, the one with the two distinct and separate bedrooms. The man was a little red in the face from what he'd undoubtedly witnessed.

Rafael plucked the key cards from his hand. "I'll take those. Thanks."

"Anything else, sir?"

"Send up laundry services, will you?" Rafael said. "And your best bottle of tequila."

The manager cleared his throat. "Certainly, sir. Enjoy your evening."

Don't miss what happens next in
The Rebel's Return *by Nadine Gonzalez,*
the next book in the Texas Cattleman's Club:
Fathers and Sons series!

Available February 2022 wherever
Harlequin Desire books and ebooks are sold.

Harlequin.com